Big Bad Bully

Werewolves of Wall Street
Book 5

Renee Rose

Lee Savino

Midnight
ROMANCE

Want FREE books?

To our real life bestie, Aubrey Cara. Thank you for all the time and care you've spent helping us make the Bad Boy Alpha books the best they can be. Thank you for all the ridiculous memes and lifting us up when we need a boost. Thank you for being you.

Content warning: The hero of this book suffered childhood abuse. While it's not depicted in the book, it is mentioned several times. We're including this note to provide context for Billy's behavior. Please safeguard your own mental health.

Chapter One

Aubrey

    I hate billionaires.

    No, I shouldn't say that. My best friend is going to be one soon–either through inheritance or marriage. Probably both.

That's a weirdness I still haven't adjusted to.

But Madi aside, the entitled stench is everywhere on Wall Street. Especially here, in Sentience Labs, the AI company that has blatantly stolen the creative works of artists, musicians, and authors from around the world.

Which is why I'm going to do something about it. *Tonight.*

This is my third week camped out on the twenty-eighth floor of the Sentience building. Normally, my murals depict images of social justice and a call for change. Resistance. Freedom. I'm Brooklyn's Diego Rivera. My *Occupy Wall Street* mural outside La Résistance, the Bohemian cafe where I work, has been photographed more than any other street art in the city.

I'm the last person anyone would expect to sell out to a

1

corporation like Sentience. Especially one that disenfranchises artists everywhere.

But I threw my name in the hat with a cheesy flower landscape for a good reason.

An exceptional one.

The song "Karma Chameleon" pops up on the 80's dance playlist piping through my earbuds, and I smirk to myself.

That's right, Sentience. Karma is a fucking bitch.

"You staying late again?" The security guy stops behind my ladder to observe. He's taken an unfortunate interest in me and my work. Maybe because he likes my art. Or maybe because he can sense I'm different from the soulless sharks that circle these waters. I'm life and color to the rest of the building's hollow monotone.

Under ordinary circumstances, I might flirt. He's six feet tall and gorgeous, with medium brown skin and a sexy Jamaican accent. Totally my type. But I'm trying to be forgettable. Especially tonight.

Move along, buddy. These aren't the droids you're looking for.

"Yeah. Just a few final touches," I lie, flicking my wrist in quick, deft brushstrokes along one poppy. The truth is, I finished the mural two hours ago, and now I'm biding my time. I purposely don't turn around or give him my attention, so he'll move on.

He stays a few minutes longer then finally strolls away. I wait until I hear the elevator ding and move away before I turn off my music and pop an earbud out to listen.

All quiet.

To be sure, I take a trip to the bathroom to wash up, checking the lights under every door.

It's eight at night. These execs usually leave by six, but I need to be sure.

I palm the keycard Jamie, our informant, gave me. She got fired two months ago after printing a copy of an email sent by an exec telling her that her concerns about the legitimacy of the data they were mining were unfounded.

Turns out, the creepers here are so Big Brother, they tracked that one "send to print," and she had security guards at her office removing her–minus the printed email–before the end of the day. She showed up at the legal aid clinic, and Jan–my activist lawyer friend and the wife of the owner of La Résistance–took her case.

Since I was already plotting with Jan and her wife, Caroline, about how to bring Sentience down, she connected me with Jamie.

Now I just need to get my hands on those same kinds of emails and, hopefully, find the cache of pirated artists' works, so Jan can file a lawsuit against them. Or maybe, we'll bring the information to the *New York Times* and expose the hell out of these fuckers.

I use the stairs of the fire escape to get down to the tenth floor, where much of the data mining takes place. Jamie's key card still works on that door, as she told me it would. My heart pounds as I slip through the door.

The lights are off, and it's dark. Jamie told me there are no cameras on this floor because they don't want any recordings of what they actually do here. I follow the map I memorized to get to Jamie's old office. They've hired someone new to take her place, but Jamie had a spare key from when she lost her keys and then found them again. A very happy accident in this case.

I slide the key into the lock and turn it. I may be bold when it comes to civil protests, sit-ins, and the exercise of my free speech rights, but this is breaking the law. Tonight, I'm turning the corner into breaking and entering and outright stealing corporate documents. Jan would not approve, but if I don't do this, Sentience will continue to steal from me and all the other artists, authors, and creatives they are putting out of business. Jamie tried to do something about it and was fired.

I can take this risk.

I slip inside the office without turning on a light. From the front pocket of my paint-splattered overalls, I pull the external drive I brought.

The computer is still on—it comes out of sleep mode when I move the mouse—so I quickly scroll and follow the instructions I memorized on how to clone the entire hard drive. Once I get that copying, I also download the entire mailbox, not that I think there will be anything of use in there, but you never know.

I hope this gives us something to go on!

It says the cloning will take another thirty minutes, so I slip back out of the office and head upstairs to my mural in case the security guy comes around again. I use the time to clean up my area, rinse my brushes, and fold up the drop cloth for tomorrow.

My phone rings, and I check the screen. "Madi," I answer the call. She's probably just leaving work now. Her job as head of Torrent Cosmetics fully occupies her now. More than the Moon Co job, even, because at least Brick had boundaries. He didn't work weekends or too late at night.

"Aubrey!"

"Hey you."

"Hi! How are you? I'm sorry, it feels like forever since we've hung out."

4

The familiar ache in my chest at losing my BFF to her fiancé throbs. "I know. I'm good. Can we do something together? Just you and I?"

"Yes. I'd love that. How about..." I picture my bestie flipping open the calendar app on her phone and scrolling through it. "How about next Thursday evening?"

"Does that mean a week from this Thursday?" I clarify.

"Yes. I'm sorry, I'm slammed this week, and Brick and I are going to the Adirondacks over the weekend."

It doesn't go unnoticed that she never invites me there, other than for their engagement party.

"Yeah, okay. Next Thursday it is," I say hollowly. I really need to get a life. A boyfriend. Someone to fill the gaping hole left when Madi moved out.

"What are you up to right now?"

"I'm actually painting a mural at the Sentient building this week."

"*What?*" At least Madi is appropriately shocked. But it guts me that she doesn't even know why I'm here or what I'm up to. She doesn't know anything that's going on in my life right now.

"There's a good reason. I'll tell you all about it when we get together."

"Wait, no! Tell me now. I have to know."

"I would, but I'm here working now, so...I can't really talk."

"Oh, my God! What is this about? Now I'm dying."

"Good. Then I can be sure you won't cancel our date."

"Aubrey, I'm sorry about last time."

"No, no. It's all good. We'll chat next week. Ooh–you know what? There's a good eighties cover band playing at All Night."

Eighties music is my favorite. I'm obsessed with the

5

whole decade as a result of my parents' taste in music. In college, Madi and I had a Go-Go's cover band, and we played at All Night.

"Perfect. Let's meet there."

I perk up. It will be like old times. "Yay! I can't wait to catch up."

"Okay. Me neither. Love you!"

That wrenches a smile from my lips. "Love you, too. Bye."

I check the timer on my phone. Twenty-six minutes.

The download should almost be complete now.

I slip back into the stairwell and jog down to the tenth floor again. The drive is copied. I quickly disconnect it and tuck it back in the front pocket of my overalls then head back to the staircase.

I'm two flights down when a door opens.

Fuck. It's the security guard. "Hey," he says sharply. Then he recognizes me. "Oh, it's you." His brow furrows. "What are you doing in the stairwell?"

Sweat makes my palms clammy. I resist the urge to touch the pocket of my overalls to make sure the drive is out of sight. "Oh, I'm just leaving now. I'm done for the night!" I chirp.

"But why are you in here? This is the fire escape."

"No, I know. I actually have a bit of claustrophobia, so I prefer taking the stairs to the elevator. Especially at night when there'd be no one around to hear me scream."

He blinks at me.

Fuck. Am I a horrible liar?

"I would hear you scream."

Was that a threat? Does he want to hear me scream? Is this guy a serial killer? I spin out of control as my heart chokes my throat.

He relaxes into a grin, and my knees nearly buckle with relief.

"But I get it. I just like to take the stairs to stay in shape."

"Right! That too." I sound out of breath. A little crazy. "Well, I'd better get going! It's late." I rush past him, taking the stairs at a jog.

For a few moments, I feel him watch me, but I don't look up. I just keep on running all the way down eight flights of stairs until I get to the ground floor.

I throw the door open to the lobby and suck in a deep breath.

The security guard at the front desk gives me a startled look. "Where'd you come from? Is something on fire?"

I force a laugh. "No fire. I just ran down the stairs for, um, exercise. I'll see you tomorrow!" I call out as I sail past him.

Fuck, fuck, fuck. That was close.

I suck in a deep breath of cold spring air as I truck to the subway.

I'm halfway down the block when I start to giggle. And then my giggle turns into a full-bore laugh. I'm laughing hysterically when I get on my train to Brooklyn.

I did it—my first corporate espionage job is complete.

Hopefully, the information I got was worth the risk.

Chapter Two

B*illy*
I stare at an Instagram page on my phone. A siren in the shape of a human smirks back at me in front of a giant mural. I've seen the mural firsthand. It's decent. The artist is *not* decent. She's a menace to society.

For the thousandth time, I study her silky brown skin. The high cheekbones and full, pillowy lips. Black hair that falls in wild gold and scarlet-tinged braids down her back. Her hair is more colorful than the last time I saw her at Brick and Madi's engagement party.

The time she fed me more of her insolence and flipped me off.

The desire to take her to task for that sass makes my dick hard, also for the thousandth time. I'd love to bend her over the counter of the Bohemian cafe where she works and listen to what sounds she makes when I'm smacking her ass.

The fact that I have an errant desire to touch a human is insane. What makes it even more disgusting is the fact that I haven't touched a female–wolf or human–since said engagement party.

"Mr. White?" Annabeth, my executive assistant, interrupts through the intercom. She's a redheaded she-wolf and extremely efficient, which is why I employ her.

She usually knows better than to disturb me.

"What is it?" I snap, hurriedly closing the phone.

"Your–uh...Mr. White the Second is here to see you."

The second.

As in, *my dad*.

What the fuck does he want?

I stand from the desk, instinctual respect too beaten into me to deny him that courtesy. Not that he deserves it. "Send him in."

My dad strides through the door.

Just the sight of him brings on a self-loathing rage. This is the asshole I was born to. I carry his odious DNA in my blood.

William, Bill, White II is a tall wolf–six foot two, and despite the greying at his temples, he still looks every inch the alpha of his pack. He reeks authority. Cruelty. Entitlement.

I never quite reached six feet despite the synthetic growth hormone he fed me during my childhood. But I did grow strong. Not because of all the beatings and tests he put me and my wolf through but despite them. My sister helped me survive him, and I chose to thrive. To escape.

Now, I stay behind my desk rather than come out to greet him. It gives me a position of power in the wall-to-wall windowed executive office.

That's right, asshole–the son you tossed away is a Wall Street billionaire now. Second in command of the largest and most powerful pack in New York. A far cry from your backwoods Maine pack now.

I've worked at Moon Co since we helped Brick start it

10

while still at Yale, but my dad has never been to Manhattan to see me here.

Until now. What does he want?

He takes in the office and my power position with a sneer.

"What are you doing here?" I skip the niceties.

"Your mother wanted me to say hello."

My mother. The meek rabbit he mated to solidify his position as alpha. Her dad was the previous alpha. Another cruel leader, as I recall.

It certainly wasn't a fated match. Their union was arranged. A strategic union for both my dad and my grandfather. My mother had absolutely no say in the arrangement.

Medieval much?

"What are you doing in New York?"

"I had some business to attend to."

Something about the vagueness of his comment sets off alarms in my head. What business could he have here? Something that had to be done in person.

I draw in his scent through my nostrils, knowing full well it will trigger a trauma response.

It does. My body goes into a kind of shock, ready to fight or be beaten.

I have years of practice in working around my triggers, though. I examine his scent for traces of others in it. I catch the stench of New York—car exhaust and hotel lobby. Humans out on the street.

Nothing else.

Fine, I'll bite. "What business?" I demand.

My dad casts a cruel smirk at me. "You gave up the right to inquire about my business when you abandoned your pack."

11

"I found a better one." My voice and my gaze are dead. "I don't recall you ever missing me."

My dad lifts his upper lip in a sneer. "I had no use for a traitor. But that could change."

Oh, for fuck's sake. He must be joking.

"What? Now that I have money, I'm worth something to you?" I saunter out from behind the desk and then lean casually against it, folding one of my legs across the other. "Or is it Brick's power you want to use?"

"Brick is not as powerful as you think," my dad sniffs. "That human mate of his will be his destruction. You should jump ship before it's too late."

My dad despises humans. He has made a powerful place for himself as the leader of hate-mongering focused on humans. I was raised completely apart from humans. I never mixed with them, never interacted until Brick, Nickel, Jake, and I had to live amongst them in boarding school and later at Yale.

My father taught me at a young age to fight for my survival, so that's what I did. I latched onto the bluest blooded wolves on campus and made myself indispensable. During our first year at Yale, Brick's mother poisoned his dad, and the Adalwulfs ripped his wealth from him. He needed a right-hand man to help him exact revenge and fight to regain everything the Adalwulfs stole. I had enough vengeance within me to power all the electricity in Manhattan.

I now know we all trauma-bonded. Nickel–a royal wolf from England–had also been escaping family trauma and political machinations. Jake was a quiet loner who'd never had a pack to rely on until Brick brought him into the fold. The four of us became a found family, united around a single cause–to rebuild the Blackthroat pack's wealth and status, so Brick could maintain leadership.

"The pack has accepted his luna," I say stiffly.

Granted, I wasn't exactly in Madi's court, and I fought Brick on his decision to mate a human, but I'm not about to tell my dad that. I would never let him see any chink of weakness in my pack or my alpha.

My dad watches me closely. "I heard it was a bloodbath. He had to kill hundreds of his pack members to maintain dominance. His pack will organize the next coup better."

His words send a chill up my spine. If I were in wolf form, my hackles would raise, but I'm careful to show no emotional response. I don't like that he's given so much thought to our pack's defenses. I don't like his cruel attention shining on the Blackthroat pack in any form. My dad is dangerous and unpredictable. I've spent a lifetime learning to control myself and my surroundings to prevent the destruction he wages.

"I expect I'll have a chance to assess things for myself at the wedding," he continues.

What? "You're not invited."

"Not yet." My father fiddles with his cufflink. "But I expect you can put a word in with your alpha to change that. I am a blood relation to his second, after all."

Figures my father would spend the first half of a conversation tearing my pack down, and the second half angling for an invite to what he sees as the most prestigious event in our pack's history. I shouldn't be surprised at the hypocrisy. In my father's eyes, the Blackthroat are the wealthy bluebloods of the shifter world, and he wants proximity to all their wealth and power.

I raise a brow, acting cool. "I'm surprised you want to be

there, since he's marrying a human. I know what you think of them." He drilled that hatred into me as a pup.

For a moment, I'm back in Maine, standing with the pack on our land. I can hear my father shouting, "It's time to hunt the human." I remember how my sister held me tight, as if trying to protect me from the wolves around us and the violence they would wreak.

My fangs grow sharp in my mouth. The thought of allowing him near my luna makes my blood run cold.

But I keep my expression controlled. *Never show weakness.*

"It's the wedding of the century," my father is saying. "Surely you can swing an extra invite—"

Fuck this. I've got to shut him down. "Don't hold your breath." I match him, sneer for sneer. "I can tell you now— there will not be another coup. Madison Evans isn't just a human mate. She's a true luna. She claims and holds a power that the pack recognizes. No amount of hate-mongering can override nature's law."

It's true. Even I have conceded her position and power at my alpha's side.

I've accepted my punishment for trying to keep them apart. A punishment that now involves me playing fucking ambassador to the humans.

This reminds me—I should visit Cafe Girl to discuss those duties.

Bill White II lets out a derisive scoff. "My own son is now a human lover."

His words knot and twist in my gut. One part of me snaps and roars at the implied weakness he projects at me. The other part hates any of it that might be true.

I refuse to think about Cafe Girl or her nutmeg and honey scent. The way her hair would look wrapped around my cock. The noises she might make if I fucked her hard from behind.

"Your own son wants nothing to do with you." Again, my voice and gaze are dead. I show no emotion and project strength, as he taught me to do. "Tell my mother I'd prefer a visit from her rather than you as her messenger."

My father's nostrils flare with anger. I don't know what he thought he'd accomplish by visiting me, but he didn't get whatever it was he wanted.

Good.

"You're a disappointment." Neither his words nor the bitterness in my father's tone are anything new.

"I'm everything you are not," I say. It's taken me time to realize that's a fact worth celebrating. I've had to be ruthless and work my ass off, but Brick Blackthroat, the most powerful alpha in the country, finds me indispensable. I have a place beside the king. My father is nothing to me now.

"That's for sure," my father snorts as he turns on his heel and walks out.

I pick up the stapler on my desk and crush it into a tight ball, then hurl it at the closed door. It embeds itself in the wood and remains there, suspended.

Chapter Three

ubrey

A   I work all Saturday at La Résistance, which has been my home away from home since I was sixteen. Working there isn't work at all. It's hanging out in a hip coffee shop with the people I love.

Right now, it's evening, and I lean on the counter, nursing a mug of chai. The place is quiet, and I'm lost in my thoughts to a dreamy soundtrack. The song is a Bossa Nova cover of "Take on Me," and it reminds me of my 80's night date with Madi next week. I can't wait.

I miss her. This is the sort of night she'd come by the cafe, and we'd chat between customers. Now I'm lucky if I see her once a week.

I don't want to resent her new relationship, but it's changed everything. I should be happy for her–and I am. She's in love, and I've never seen her so aglow. It's amazing. But I feel totally shut out of her life now. At least at the beginning of the relationship, she would share all the gory details. Now I get nothing.

"Hey, chica," my boss Caroline beckons me back to the

office, where her wife Jan is waiting. I greet them both. Caroline is a petite, white spitfire–barely over five feet–and the fiercest and most loving woman I've ever met. Her wife, Jan is tall, black, and slender with a close-cropped afro.

These two are like second and third moms to me. They co-own the cafe. Jan is a Legal Aid lawyer, and Caroline runs this place full-time. They've staged many a revolution within these walls over the last thirty years.

"We're meeting with Jamie, right?" I ask. Jamie is the whistle-blower from Sentience.

"Yes, she's running late," Jan says.

I have a flicker of unease at that–Jamie isn't the sort to be late to a meeting. She's a starched shirt sort of person. But it's probably nothing. I'm just a little nervous–the drive I procured from Sentience is burning a hole in my satchel.

"First, I've got something for you," Caroline is rummaging around in the coat closet. "Well, you and Madi."

My heart contracts a little at my best friend's name. The pain surprises me. It's not like Madi has died. She's just busy. Too busy for me.

"Ta da!" Caroline whirls around, holding up a gorgeous turquoise-colored jacket.

"Are you serious?" I move closer to study the jacket. It's made of leather, and cropped, but in an older style with wide lapels. "This is amazing. It looks just like–"

"Janet Jackson circa Rhythm Nation?" Caroline makes the jacket boogie while singing part of the chorus.

"Yes!" She hands it to me, and I hold it up, admiring it. It's in pretty good shape but obviously has been worn before. "Is this...vintage?"

Caroline and Jan both shudder. "I hate that word." Caroline points to me. "One day your clothes will be considered vintage, and you'll cringe too. This is second hand," she emphasizes. "For you! For the next time you and Madi play at All Night."

I take the jacket and hold it up to me. "Oh my God, I'm *obsessed*."

"Rhythm Nation came out in 1989," Jan points out, ever attentive to detail. "So culturally you're pushing into the 90s."

"It still counts." Caroline waves a hand. "And it's Janet Jackson."

"*Miss Jackson if you're nasty*," Jan sings, and for a moment, I can imagine her out of her lawyer suit and in a leather lieutenant hat. She once showed up to karaoke dressed like Grace Jones on the cover of Nightclubbing, so I know she probably has a closet full of club outfits herself.

"I also have these." Caroline produces a pair of white go-go boots. "If you and Madi want to add a little Nancy Sinatra to your set."

"Oh wow," I laugh. "Why not? Can I borrow these?"

"Keep them," Caroline says at the same time Jan says, "They're yours."

"Are you sure?" I ask. "You're not going to want them back to wear? You know, just for a night on the town?" I waggle my brows at Caroline, who grins.

Jan snorts. "Those days are over."

"Well, anytime you want them back for karaoke or something, say the word." I gather up the amazing jacket and go-go boots, imagining the outfits I could wear on stage. I'll show them to Madi on Thursday.

Jamie turns up, and the mood turns sober. She looks more haggard than when I first met her, with dark circles under her eyes. Her clothes are rumpled, too. Whistle-blowing is stressful, and on top of that, she hasn't found a new job. Even if Sentience hasn't retaliated further, she must be lying awake at night wondering what will happen next.

"Here's the hard drive." I produce the computer drive from my satchel and put it in the center of the round work table. This back office is where Jan works weekends and evenings, and this table has also been the planning ground for at least a hundred social protests, starting long before I picked up a marker and created my first protest sign.

"What is this?" Jan asks.

Jamie picks it up. "This is a copy of my work computer's hard drive. From this, I can produce all the evidence you need."

Jan looks between me and Jamie. "But how did you get it?"

I shrug. "I might have stopped by her old office while I was painting a mural for Sentience."

Jan's eyes widen. "You know I can't use anything obtained illegally as evidence in a trial, right?"

"Then we can send it over to the *New York Times*," I point out.

"But you can't use it in a lawsuit?" Jamie asks.

Jan shakes her head. "Any bit of info you provide can help us subpoena the company's executives, but we can't use this as evidence. Not unless you find a way to legally be in possession of this information. But maybe you have a copy of something you'll find on here." She flicks her brows at Jamie.

"Got it." Jamie nods. She sends me a grateful look. "Thank you so much for getting this. You risked a lot."

"I hope it yields something." I sure as hell don't want to take the risk again, but I will if I have to. It takes courage to fight against giants.

I catch the sound of someone ringing the bell at the cash register, and I jump up. "I'll get it." I hustle out to the cafe and then immediately slow my roll when I see who it is.

This is not a man I will hustle for.

Ever.

"Are you lost?" I repeat the question I asked the first time this entitled alpha-hole came in here. The time he stole the photo of Madi and me right off the bulletin board behind the counter and used it to get Madi fired.

Irritation–a habitual expression for this jackal–flicks over William White the third's face.

He looks down his nose at me. He's not quite as tall as his best friend, Brick, but still close to six feet. Broad-shouldered. Dressed in a billionaire's suit. He's the type of man women cream their panties over, but his rank personality spoils the look.

Instead of going behind the counter to serve him, I stroll around to the front. His business isn't welcome here.

As I get close, he turns to face me, his expression screwed up like I smell bad.

"What do you want?" I demand since he still hasn't answered my first question.

A sour look mars his otherwise beautiful face. "We need to talk."

Color me surprised. I can't imagine what he thinks we need to talk about. Brick and Madi are happily engaged. He doesn't need to offer me half a million dollars to get her to see him like he did the last time he stepped in La Résistance.

"Do we?" I keep my voice cool.

There's something about his large, imposing form and the force of power that emanates from him that has me wondering what it would be like to be underneath him.

Would he be rough? Cold? Would he want his date on top doing all the work?

Or is he the kind of guy who just pays for blowjobs to keep it completely unemotional?

I'm curious about what his type is. When he picks a woman—and I'm sure he could pick any woman in New York—does he go for the vapid model type? A long-legged blonde with zero brain cells and a shopping habit? Or a blue-blooded Harvard type—smart and horse-faced with a pedigree that goes back farther than his?

"You and I are..." He trails off, and I cock my head.

I can't wait to hear what comes next. I can hardly believe he would start any sentence with "you and I."

"Responsible for things. For this wedding. You're the Maid of Honor, and I'm the Best Man."

My brow furrows. Of all the things I thought he might say, this wasn't one of them.

He waves an impatient hand. He has broad wrists. I don't know why I find them sexy.

"I don't know what they are. I haven't done this before."

"And you think I have?"

"Well, you're—" He cuts off whatever it was he was going to say.

"A woman?" I prompt, trying to follow his line of thinking. "Human?"

His brows rise like he's shocked by my second word choice.

"Someone in possession of a beating heart? Someone who actually cares about her friends?"

He relaxes. "Right. That." He glances at the bulletin board with the photos on it, like it might hold some clue to real friendship.

"You still have my photo."

I expect him to be dismissive, but he nods. "I'll bring it to you."

"You said that last time."

His jaw clenches. "Listen–can I buy you a cup of coffee? Or dinner or something? So we can talk?"

This guy keeps shocking me. "You want to buy me *coffee* or *dinner* or something?" WTF? Is he out of his mind? "No. We aren't friends. We're not going to be friends. I don't know why Brick even asked you to be his best man when you're the guy who broke them apart in the first place."

That sour look returns to his face. "It's my...punishment." He mumbles the last word.

Laughter rockets out of my mouth. "Your *punishment?*"

He looks dead serious, though. Like Brick is actually punishing him by making him... OMG, I think he *is* serious!

It's torture for him to have to do the cheesy wedding stuff. To be a decent best man and stand up for the groom.

A slow grin spreads across my face. "Oh my God, this is hilarious!"

Irritation crowds his expression. He frowns at me.

"I'm in." I'm delighted. If Brick wants to punish him with forced wedding festivity, I will gladly join up and heap on the punishment. Even better if part of his punishment is making nice with me. I'm going to eat this up with a spoon!

He arches a brow. "You're in? What do you mean you're *in?*"

I smile glibly. "I'm happy to punish you, Suit. In fact, it might become my new favorite pastime."

Billy isn't nearly as amused as I am. In fact, his expression turns downright stormy. It's a look I could love.

"Yes, let's start with dinner," I say brightly. "There's a great sushi place around the corner."

His eyes narrow, but he doesn't protest.

I head to the back room to let Caroline know and say goodbye to Jan and Jamie, pick up my jacket and satchel, and reemerge.

Billy snatches my jacket from my hands with his signature irritation, and for a moment, I think he's going to throw it on the floor or something, but he opens it, and holds it out for me.

I stare at my opened coat, dumbfounded. I'm twenty-three years old. I grew up in Jersey and live in Brooklyn. I've dated musicians and artists. Social justice warriors. Nice guys with big hearts. But I've never once had a guy hold my jacket for me.

The feminist in me wants to demand to know whether he thinks I'm incapable of putting on my own coat, but that would be silly.

Clearly, no man holds a coat for that reason. Just like they don't hold doors open because we're too weak to pull a handle. It's a courtesy. Good manners. Chivalry.

And I don't hate it.

Especially from a guy who looks like he'd rather suck a lemon than show deference to anyone. I rather like seeing the manners bred into him through fancy prep schools and a Yale education. Almost like something he's compelled to do rather than *wants* to do. Like this wedding stuff.

So I accept the gesture, sticking my arms into the jacket and letting him lift and drop it onto my shoulders.

He inhales deeply and then holds his breath.

What the hell? He's probably only smelled richly-perfumed women in his privileged world.

I twist to look up at him. "Do I smell bad?"

He rubs his nose and gives a quick dismissive shake of

his head. "You smell like nutmeg," he mutters. He puts a hand on my lower back and propels me toward the door.

Nutmeg?

"And honey."

"So...not bad?" I stop in the open doorway to look up at him again. We're close–our bodies colliding as he stretches a long arm out to hold the door open for me.

It must be some bizarre biological reaction to his size and sheer power because I'm suddenly turned on. My nipples get stiff, and heat travels south between my legs.

He gives me a formidable scowl. I'll bet looks like that make the people who work under him run for cover.

I don't move from my position, wedged in the doorway with him, his arm extending beyond my shoulders to hold the glass door ajar. My lips stretch into a slow smile–my response to his unhappy expression.

Making him scowl is my new favorite pastime.

* * *

Billy

Nutmeg and honey. Cafe Girl's scent is no less potent now than the first time I met her. The way it hits me in the chest and travels south to my groin is both a painful and ecstatic experience.

I want to sink my teeth into her skin and–

No, that's not right.

I definitely do not want to *mark* her. Is that what I was imagining?

Fuck no. There's no way I'd mark a human. Especially not a waste-of-oxygen-nobody like this female. Why would I even picture that?

That's...so *wrong*.

Everything about her is wrong. Her feisty attitude, for one. She's never met anyone she wouldn't challenge. I doubt she bends a knee for anyone, even if they're more powerful than her. She's reckless and willing to put herself in danger for what she believes in. In my dog-eat-dog world, that can be suicide.

It also turns me on. Makes me want to savage her. To shove her against this door frame and wrap my fingers around that long, slender neck. Kiss her with bruising force before I tongue-fuck her mouth.

I want to teach her to drop to her knees for me. To learn to please me.

Fuuuuuuck. The image of her gazing up at me in submission with my cock between those pillowy lips nearly makes me jizz in my trousers.

No.

Erase, erase, erase.

Fuck. I can't get the image out of my head.

To my utter shock, she reaches for the lapels of my suit jacket and smooths them. "This is going to be fun." She gives me a bright, disingenuous smile.

Something twists in my gut. Misgiving about the meaning of that smile coiled with something more sinister.

Something I can't even fathom.

The desire to win a real smile from her pouty mouth. The desire to have her hands on me for other reasons.

I want to spank her ass for creating such a riot within me.

Internally, I'm snapping at her to move her ass out of the doorway, but the only words that choke out of my throat are, "Is it?"

Her smile grows wider. The silver nose ring she wears

glints. It would sear my skin if I touched it. "So fun. Let's go, Suit."

She finally releases her invisible hold on me by moving through the doorway. I suck in a deep breath of not-her to try to regain some of my brain cells. She sashays ahead of me, strutting in her white patent leather Doc Martens like they're a pair of six-inch heels. I stare at her ass as she walks.

Spankable.

Very spankable.

Fucking gorgeous. I can't wait to see it bared.

No, wait. That's not happening. I'm not going to fuck this human. She doesn't deserve my attention. She isn't worthy of my time.

Plus, it would be messy. I'd want to do horrible things to her, and she'd cry to Madi, who would talk to Brick. I'm already in the doghouse with him.

I want to go back to being his most trusted advisor and friend. I seriously miscalculated when I tried to get rid of Madi. It's a failure that still keeps me up at night.

I hate failures.

Aubrey leads me to a sushi place around the corner. I look around doubtfully. The place is clean but tiny and low-budget.

"You've eaten here before?" I ask doubtfully.

Shifters generally don't get food poisoning, but the idea of her getting sick on raw fish puts me on edge.

She rolls her eyes. "What? Do you think good sushi has to cost a hundred bucks a roll? This is good food."

I shrug. "Fine."

I need to just grit my teeth and get through this meeting. Find out what's required of me for the wedding and be done with it. Coming here to meet with her in person was a mistake.

And yet, even as I have the thought, I'm certain I'll be making the mistake again.

We order at the window and take a number to our table. I sit down and openly study the human.

She quirks a "what?" eyebrow to show me I'm being too obvious.

"So tell me." I spread my hands. "What do I need to know about this wedding thing."

"Well. You're in charge of the groom's shower and the bachelor party."

I frown. "*Groom's* shower?" I've heard of bachelor parties, but a *groom's shower* doesn't ring any bells. Granted, I don't run in human circles, so it could be something new.

She nods. "Yes. You have to host a brunch with mimosas and invite all of your male relatives and hers to bring gifts and play games."

My upper lip lifts in a snarl. "*What?*"

"What?" There's something overly innocent in the way she's looking at me.

"You're fucking with me."

She flashes a smile that goes straight to my dick. Her lips have a purple-mauve gloss on them that makes me wonder what shade her nipples are. What color her nether lips turn when flushed with blood and arousal.

"Yes, Suit. I am. It's way too easy."

My cock is unbelievably hard. I spread my legs to make room for my erection. I don't know why I seem to *like* her fucking with me. I'm glad we're sitting down, so she can't see the tent in my pants.

"So no groom shower?"

Her laugh is low and throaty. A husky sound that brings to mind a fresh image of her on her knees. This time she's naked. Hands tied behind her back, so those big breasts are lifted and spread for me. "No groom shower. But definitely a bachelor party." She narrows her eyes at me. "Is Brick the strip club type?"

Now I'm picturing Aubrey swinging topless from a pole. That image makes my dick happy, but my wolf gets pissed at the idea of a room full of men seeing her tits. A snarl of jealousy tangles up around my throat.

I will not make it through this dinner. I force a shrug. "No. Not really. Especially not since Madi. He wouldn't look at anyone else."

Aubrey relaxes. I'm not sure why she seems surprised by that news. But then, she doesn't understand that Brick is a mated wolf. She's not part of our world.

"Well, maybe we should think about a coed party. I know Brick is sort of jealous, so he probably wouldn't want me taking her to a *Magic Mike* show, right?"

"A coed party?" I can't keep the skepticism out of my voice. All of this sounds abominable.

"A joint bachelor/bachelorette party. You might have heard it called a Jack-and-Jill party. Often a destination event—like we all go to Vegas together."

"Done," I say. "How's this for a deal—you arrange everything; I foot the bill."

I'm used to throwing money at problems. It's the advantage of being a billionaire—I hire out any task I don't want to do. But stupid me. I forgot how much this female hates money. I made this mistake with her before when I was trying to save Brick from moon madness. Offering money only incenses her.

Her cinnamon-colored eyes flash. "I don't think so, Suit. This is your punishment. That means you have to play."

29

Something about her words excites me. Oh, yeah. I know which words. *Punishment. Play.*

How would she respond to punishment? Fuck, I'd love to bend her over and warm her ass until her pussy is dripping.

Except...I think *she's* turned on by the idea of punishing *me*.

And somehow, I don't mind that, either. She could strut around in a latex catsuit and point her crop in the center of my chest. Command me to lick her pussy until she can't take any more pleasure.

Would I grovel for her? Never in a million years. But I'd eat that pussy.

Yeah. I'd definitely lick her clean.

I tug at my tie to loosen it. I'm way too hot around the collar. "Fine. You want to play with me? Let's play."

Her pupils dilate, and her scent thickens. Yep. She's definitely turned on, too.

Damn. That thought sends my brain on a race around the moon and back.

Okay, the bratty female wants to spar with me. I'm in.

She backpedals a little. "I should check with Madi first to find out what she wants. That's what really matters. I won't see her for another week, though, and it's hard to get her on the phone these days." There's a note of bitterness in her voice.

Even more disturbing is the tinge of sadness to her scent.

Understanding hits me hard. Just like I've lost Brick, she's losing her best friend. Or perhaps she's already lost her. It makes sense. Not only are Brick and Madi inseparable now, but Madi can't talk to her human friend about what we are. She can't bring her around or invite her into our world.

My wolf doesn't like this scent of defeat on the human.

I whip out of my phone. "I'll arrange a joint meeting," I say before considering what I'm suggesting. I'm going to torture myself with another face-to-face with this vixen? It's a terrible idea. But I'm already typing out a text to Brick. "The four of us can sit down and talk about it together."

I fire off a text to Brick:

Aubrey and I need to meet with you and Madi re: bachelor party.
Tomorrow night, my place.

I'm disgusted that I typed the words "Aubrey and I." There is no *Aubrey and I*. That's fucking absurd. But I don't hate the idea of having her in my penthouse. Getting her scent on my sofa. In the rugs. Of course, that would involve me putting her on her knees on the floor. Better yet, face down on her belly, legs spread wide.

Damn, my cock's so hard it's going to break off.

"Does tomorrow night work for you?" I demand belatedly. I've already sent the text.

Surprise registers on her face. "Uh...yeah. I mean, if that works for Madi." I catch the sadness to her scent again, and my hard-on droops.

I rub my forehead, contemplating the problem. I am an extremely good fixer. It's how I made myself indispensable to Brick early on. Give me a situation, and I will strategize the hell out of it. And I'm not afraid to make the hard or dangerous decisions. To put myself at risk to achieve the desired result.

What's bizarre is that I'm analyzing an *emotional* problem. A *human female's* emotional problem.

It's definitely a first for me.

The server arrives at our table to deliver the platters of sushi and take our number away.

I have to admit the food looks good, but I'm still gnawing on Aubrey's situation.

"You miss Madi," I say out loud.

Her chopsticks pause halfway to her mouth, and those purple-mauve lips part.

I get an even bigger blast of her sadness, which does something strange to my chest.

"I..." There's a flash of vulnerability on her face that simultaneously gashes my chest open and makes me wish I hadn't asked. I don't like to see her made vulnerable.

Not this way.

Only naked and tied with my rope.

She shrugs. "I mean, yeah. We didn't see each other all that much when we lived together, but it was fun. And we used to talk on the phone more. But...she's even busier with Torrent than she was with Moon Co., and the rest of her time is apparently spent in bed with Brick." She flashes a forced smile, attempting to lift the mood.

I pick up a roll with my chopsticks and pop it in my mouth. "Yes it is," I agree, chewing.

Aubrey was right–the food is delicious. Not that I'm going to tell her that.

"They're disgusting."

Aubrey's light laugh is genuine, and my wolf relaxes a bit.

We eat in silence. Apparently, Aubrey is starving because she inhales the food. I let her eat until she slows and then move in to kill the rest.

"So a coed party. No groom shower. Anything else?"

"You'll have to get Brick to the ceremony on time and hold the rings. And you'll make a toast at the reception."

"Pass," I say immediately.

"It's *required*." Aubrey makes her voice hard. I can't decide if she's fucking with me again or not.

"Are you doing one?"

"Yep. I'm going to talk about how hard everyone worked to keep them apart, and yet, they persevered." She gives me a pointed stink-eye.

I wipe my mouth with a paper napkin and sit back. "And I'll describe the half a million dollars I pledged to try to get them back together but was completely shut out by her so-called Maid of Honor."

Her eyes narrow. "You think you can solve everything with money, don't you?"

I hesitate because, honestly? Yeah. Most problems in my life can be solved with money. But this is the female who wore an "Eat the Rich" t-shirt as a teen. I know because I stole the photo to prove it.

"I think money is a leverage point for a lot of people. Not all. Not you, as I learned."

The defensiveness ebbs from her shoulders. People like to be seen.

I don't know why I want to see more of this particular person. She both fascinates and disgusts me. She embodies nothing that I value. And yet, I want to throw the doors to her closet open wide and examine what's inside. Look under the bed and find her darkest, dirtiest secrets. Know what makes a money-hating artist want to study something like Women's Studies and work in a hippie cafe.

"What are your leverage points, Aubrey?" My voice is soft, and saying her name in that tone sounds too familiar. Too intimate.

33

Aubrey's face takes on a rosy glow.

She stands. "You'll never know, Suit." She tosses her napkin on the table. "Thanks for dinner. It's been illuminating."

My brain stutters on the word *illuminating*. What does she think she learned about me?

Nothing. I've shown nothing. I never show anything. That's how I can be ruthless.

"My place. Tomorrow night."

Her nose wrinkles, but I would swear that I catch the faint scent of female arousal. As if my demanding words conjured up some scenario other than meeting with our engaged friends.

My wolf fucking loves it.

"I suppose you live on Billionaire Row?" She cocks a hip.

"Same building as Brick and Madi. Apartment 44. Seven p.m."

"Did Brick even respond?"

"I'll make sure they're there. You just show up."

Her eyes narrow as she considers me for a moment, then she holds out her hand. "Give me your phone."

My dick twitches. I like it when she demands. I imagine her in that catsuit again. Crotchless, of course, so my tongue can reach the places it needs to reach.

I unlock my phone and hand it to her, watching without expression as she texts herself:

WWIII.

My initials–or World War III–depending on your interpretation. I'm surprised she knows my full name.

Pleased.

She thrusts my phone back at me. "That's my number. Text me if things change."

No chance. I don't give a fuck if a real World War III breaks out tomorrow.

Aubrey Jane Cook will be in my apartment tomorrow night.

Preferably naked and strung up from my ceiling.

Chapter Four

Aubrey

A I exit the subway at 57th Street with "Strut" by Sheena E playing in my ear buds. The tunes give me the boost I need to find my second wind. I had a long day of classes. I am just a few weeks away from finishing my bachelor's degree in Women's Studies. My original plan was to study law and become a social justice lawyer, fighting for the cause, like Jan, but that's mostly because I've dismissed art as a viable career. It probably still is, unless I want to be a sell-out to corporations like Sentience, but I honestly don't want to go on to graduate studies anymore. I'm burned out on school.

I hum along to the music. I blame my parents for my eighties music addiction, but who knows? Maybe I died young as the leader of an 80's girl band in my last lifetime. All I know is it makes me happy, and this particular song embodies the energy I'm bringing to throw at William White the Third.

He is a real piece of work–the kind of guy contributing to everything that is wrong with this world. Which is why I enjoy sticking this whole bachelor planning thing to him. I love that Brick is punishing him. I mean, it's also weird– aren't they best friends? But Brick is his boss, so I guess there's a hierarchy there.

As I walk, a text comes through from the group chat Jan set up between me, Jamie, Caroline, and her about Sentience.

Jamie–did you find anything useful on the drive?

It shows up as read, but Jamie doesn't answer.

Maybe she's busy, but a niggling of foreboding runs through me. I'm probably just paranoid, but what if someone got to her? Or got her phone?

She was pretty paranoid about them exacting retribution beyond the firing.

Corporations like Sentience might be dastardly enough to hire someone to "fix" her entire situation.

No. I'm being nuts.

I walk the few blocks to Madi's building on Billionaire Row. I've been here only twice before, which is weird, considering I used to see Madi daily before she moved out. We grew up living in the same building in Jersey and then moved in together in Brooklyn last fall. While we never went to the same schools, I was used to seeing her evenings and weekends. Now I'm lucky if I see her once every three weeks.

The front doors are locked, but through the smoky glass, I see a doorman or security guard guy–a huge man with muscles that stretch his suit jacket behind the desk. He strides swiftly to open the door.

"I'm here to see Madison Evans," I say. I texted her earlier to make sure this thing was really happening because there was no way I was coming all the way over to Central Park if it wasn't a sure thing. She said she would be here.

"Are you Ms. Cook?"

I startle. "Yes?" Madi must be running late and called to tell him. Damn. I am five minutes early.

"Mr. White is expecting you." His voice is gruff and deep. Less suave butler and more mafia bodyguard.

Mr. White. Not Madi. And jeez–so formal.

"William White the Third." I mimic his formality with a lash of sarcasm on my tongue. "Yes."

"Right this way." He escorts me to an elevator and uses his keycard to punch the button for the fortieth floor. "Number forty-four." He steps out of the elevator, and the door closes.

I take the elevator up to Billy's apartment. I don't know–in buildings on Billionaire Row, do you even call it an apartment? Are they all penthouses? Do they each have their own floor? I know Brick and Madi do.

I don't love that I'm not going to Madi's place first. Being in her apartment building without her makes me feel adrift.

A little...abandoned.

But that's ridiculous. I'm a strong, independent woman. I can go to a billionaire's apartment without her.

It's not like I'm afraid of William White.

Except my heart races at the prospect of being near him again. Being under his harsh, judging blue-gray gaze. The one framed by thick, angry brows and an air of total disdain. I remember the way we bumped into each other in the doorway at La Résistance. Because he was holding the door open for me.

I don't want that kind of man. The kind that holds doors

and throws money around like he grows it on trees and owns twenty orchards. I'm not interested in Billy White.

Only in making him suffer.

I toss my tight curls and lift my chin as I march out of the elevator and look for number forty-four.

The door is slightly ajar, like he left it open for me, and that does something to my belly. Makes it drop out at the familiarity of it. Like I'm Billy's girlfriend coming home to him after a long workday.

Or, in Billy's case, the scenario would more likely be a call girl showing up to service him.

And that idea causes a squeezing of the flesh between my legs. A lifting and holding. Heating.

I shake off any sick attraction I have to this guy. It's probably just the "other" thing. He's different from my usual type. That makes me morbidly curious, that's all.

I throw the door open without knocking. He left it unlatched, after all.

"Honey, I'm home!" I call out. It's not that funny, but it was the first thing that came to mind.

Billy stands behind a long gorgeous marble-topped kitchen island, pouring a gin and tonic. The look of utter horror he sends me makes my not-funny jab worth it.

I slam the door behind me to add to his annoyance and love that he visibly tenses. I'm pretty sure I can see the muscles around his jaw tightening in real time.

He's probably grinding those white molars down just having me in his place.

I look around. The apartment is different from Brick and Madi's exposed brick industrial look. This one is all plastered walls and windows, but the entire palette is gray.

Dull gray.

Billy comes around from behind the counter holding his drink as I shrug out of my acid-washed crop jean jacket. It's my favorite 80's throw-back, with rows of rainbow jewels stitched onto the pockets and around the cuffs. I toss it on the gunmetal grey leather couch at the same time he reaches to take it.

"Who decorated your apartment, a prison guard?"

His upper lip lifts in a snarl. "What do you mean?" He picks my jacket up from the couch like it's a dust rag that got left out by the maid.

"I mean, why is everything grey? Are you depressed? Maybe you should see someone about that."

Billy carries my jacket to the front hall closet and hangs it up without responding, so I persist.

"Have you ever heard of color? Art?"

"Lori Ann Beiber decorated the place."

I look at him blankly. "Should I know her? Is she an ex-girlfriend? She has terrible taste."

"She owns the top interior design firm in Manhattan." His voice is dry and condescending, as if to imply that I know nothing about art or culture.

I send him a mock-sympathetic look. "A little therapy goes a long way."

His jaw muscles flex again.

"Aren't you going to offer me a drink?" Because my intention is to annoy the hell out of this guy—working with me on this wedding is his punishment after all—I take his drink from his hand.

His gray eyes flash, almost looking ice blue for a moment. His gaze follows as I bring the glass to my lips and take a deep swig.

"Mmm." I'm surprised by how smooth the drink is. I suppose I'm not used to top shelf alcohol. How much do you have to pay for gin that coats your throat with cool warmth like that? "That's good."

"Keep it." His voice is rough, his gaze still pinned on my lips.

Something about his gaze makes my skin tingle, but I can't quite say why. Danger? Attraction? It's unclear.

I look around again to dissipate the electric moment. "Where are Madi and Brick?"

Billy walks back to the kitchen. "Probably fucking," he says with disgust.

I can't quite laugh, but I let out a huff of agreement. Considering how much sex my former roomie gets these days, I'm sure he's right.

He pours himself another drink, and I follow him around behind the island to make myself a pest, loving when he looks askance. I take it a step further, boosting myself up to sit on his counter beside the cutting board with limes.

The marble slab that comprises the island is even more magnificent up close. It's grey–like everything else, but veined with white, silver, and purple and rather than being slabs put together with seams, it seems to be one long, gorgeous piece. I trace a purple vein with my finger.

He turns from the ice machine where he was filling a fresh glass and takes in my new position. His eyes turn icy blue-grey. He strolls toward me. "You sit on my kitchen counter, I'm going to assume you're offering yourself to eat." His tone is so dry I take a half-second to register the overt sexual nature of his words.

Oh. *Damn.*

Heat pools between my legs at the suggestion.

I hadn't pegged him as the kind of guy who eats a lot of pussy. I figured he hired sex workers and forced them all to sign NDAs. It's hard to imagine the cold, reserved asshole giving anything back to anyone–even a lover.

A shiver races down my legs at the vision of him pushing my thighs open and lowering his head to find out what I like.

And that's when a flood of awareness rushes through me. This is a guy who is good at what he does. He holds doors automatically, even when he doesn't appear to want to. He knows proper etiquette. Which means he must know proper etiquette in bed, too.

Maybe, maybe not. But something in me desperately wants to know.

I pick up one of the sliced limes and bring it to my lips, biting the tart flesh and sucking. "You wish."

* * *

Billy

Do I?

Do I want to use this knife to cut every ribbon of clothing from this smart-mouthed girl and shut her up with her own moans?

Fuck. Yeah, I do.

I set the glass with ice down and swiftly turn to grip her waist, picking her up from the counter, and setting her down on her feet.

I move so fast that she doesn't have time to react. Hopefully not to process how strong I am to be able to lift her from the counter like that. Once she's on her feet, I don't want to let go, though. I like the sensation of her soft waist in my hands. I want to touch the other places that are soft. I want her out of these fucking clothes. The light purple cropped sweater has a wide square neckline that gives me a view of her cleavage, and the knit fabric hugs her breasts and waist. She's wearing wide-legged jeans that are the fashion now and a pair of chunky heeled boots. I wonder what she'd look like in just panties and boots.

Lust makes me mean. "Stay off my furniture," I growl like she's a bad dog who needs scolding.

Her eyes narrow, and she shoves me away. The silver nose ring she wears renders her unkissable, not that I was thinking about claiming those pouty lips.

I release her reluctantly, already regretting being such a dick. I should apologize for touching her without permission.

Even as I consider apologizing, I want to do it again. To pick her back up. Put her on that counter and make good on my offer to eat her pussy.

She nabs the paring knife from the cutting board and slashes it toward my throat. It's for show–she's a full foot away. I know she's not actually trying to defend herself. I smell anger on her, but not fear.

"Touch me again without permission, and you're going to get hurt."

My lips twitch. I don't mean to smile. I should show her I'm taking her complaint seriously. But I like that I've gotten under her skin. I enjoy her flushed and angry, ready to fight.

I school my face. "Noted. And..." Fuck. I can't believe it. Am I going to apologize? I have to force the words out of my throat. "Sorry," I say stiffly, but add, "The next time I touch you, I'll ask first."

Because I *do* plan on touching her again.

I need to.

I need to work this...*curiosity*–nothing more–out of my system.

A brow arches as her pupils dilate. She's definitely not

afraid–she's turned on. My suggestion that I'll be touching her again registers with her body, whether or not her mind agrees. Like me, she must feel the chemical attraction between us. She must know that her animal body is drawn to the animal body of someone completely unsuitable. Someone she could never be with.

My hands twitch to pick her up again. Wrap those thick thighs around my waist and carry her to the bedroom where I can tie her to the headboard and make her weep with pleasure.

A knock sounds at my door. Aubrey and I lock gazes. She's still holding the knife out defensively.

Brick will cut my dick off and feed it to me if he thinks I threatened his mate's human friend. All the gains I've made in the past months will be lost again. Maybe forever. If he thinks he can't trust me to behave with his mate's human family and friends, I will be cut out of his inner circle.

Fuck.

Chapter Five

B *illy*

Aubrey cocks her head at me, knife still outstretched. "Do that," she says lightly. She's already recovered. She tosses the knife on the cutting board and whirls as Brick opens the door and ushers his mate inside.

"Hey, girl!" Madi ignores me and comes straight for Aubrey, who picks up my drink and sashays out to meet her.

I pick up my abandoned original drink and torture myself by sipping from the same place her glossy lips marked as the two women hug then open a bottle of Madi's favorite prosecco. She's my luna now. As much as I would've hated to say it a year ago, I serve her as much as I serve my alpha. I pour four glasses in case everyone wants to partake.

Brick saunters up to the other side of the kitchen island—the position any normal guest to my place would take.

Fuck, what would possess that little human to come into my space and make herself so at home? To walk in without knocking? To sit on my countertop like she's my lover, not a near stranger who has yet to exchange any polite words with me?

"For fate's sake, you two couldn't shower before you came down?" I mutter when I catch the scent of sex on Brick.

"No."

Of course not. He loves having the scent of his cum all over his mate. She bears his mark, but he makes sure she smells like she's been freshly marked every waking moment.

He picks up a glass of prosecco and drains it. As he sets it down, he studies me. "You're taking your assignment seriously."

"Yes, Al–" I bite off the word *alpha* before I speak it in front of a human. "Yes."

I want to say, "I take all your orders seriously," but I don't want to sound cloying. Besides, he knows that. I've proven it a hundred times. He just needs me to prove it again in this most demeaning way.

I frown in the direction of Aubrey.

"She thinks you'll want a Jack-and-Jill party."

The women enter the kitchen. Madi was barely an adult when she started at Moon Co last fall, but after she claimed her position as luna, I stopped seeing her as a child. Aubrey never came off as anything but a self-possessed woman, but now, with them together, laughing and talking fast in some kind of girl code, the age difference between the two of them and Brick and me feels like eons.

My conscience pricks over what a dick I've been to her.

Not that she couldn't take it.

"Ooh, prosecco. You know what I like." Madi breezes in and takes a glass from me. "Thank you." She makes the

48

point to meet my gaze, and there's a sincerity to her tone that makes prickles race across my skin.

The power of a pack luna radiates from her. My need to protect and serve her is physical. No matter how much I wanted them apart before, now I'd fight to the death for her.

Her human friend, though, is a different story. I pick up a second glass to offer to Aubrey, who ignores my outstretched hand and sips my cocktail while holding my gaze.

I don't hate having her lips where mine have been.

Having her drink from my cup gives my wolf a masculine pleasure.

It occurs to me that she's trying to get to me. She lit up when she learned that working with her was my punishment. That must be why she climbed up on my countertop and insulted my decor.

"What's a *Jack-and-Jill party*?" Brick uses the same semi-disgusted tone I did when Aubrey mentioned it.

Aubrey answers before Madi can. "It's a joint bachelor / bachelorette party–often at a destination like Vegas." Seeing Brick's frown, she continues, "Unless you want me to take Madi out to the male strip clubs for her last hurrah."

"*What?*" My alpha's voice grows sharp and dangerous. "Fuck, no."

Aubrey folds her arms across her rather perfect breasts with a smug look. "That's what I thought."

Brick glances at Madi. "Jack-and-Jill, it is. Whatever my bride wants."

Madi's intelligent expression goes soft at his words. "Sounds fun to me. So...Vegas?"

"How about Monte Carlo?" I suggest because Vegas is so base. *Not* because I want to share a long, international flight in our private jet with her annoying maid of honor.

49

Renee Rose & Lee Savino

But the moment I think of it, I picture handing Aubrey a glass of champagne where she lies in the sleeping pod, naked except for a tangled sheet around her luscious body, her body relaxed from the hard fucking I just gave her.

Yeah, I wouldn't mind that scenario. As a one-off, of course.

Aubrey immediately rolls her eyes. "Oh, please. Why? Because it's expensive?"

"It has the best nightlife in the world," I answer evenly.

Again, Brick looks to Madi, who says, "That sounds amazing. I've never been."

Yeah, no shit. I doubt she'd ever been out of the country before she met Brick. She tries to hide her lack of sophistication and normally has a decent bluff, but it was painfully obvious when he brought her to the Blackthroat Family Foundation Ball as his date.

Because I'm a first-class asshole, I cock my head and ask Aubrey, "Have you been?"

* * *

Aubrey

I suck in a breath and will away the flush Billy's words inspire. He is the biggest dick ever.

I still feel where he put his hands on me, spanning my waist as he picked me up from the counter. I guess there are some decent muscles under that button-down designer shirt.

How and when does he work out? He's not as pasty-white as you might expect from a Wall Street suit. I see freckles and signs of weather on his face, like he spends time outdoors on the weekends. Probably in the Adirondacks with Brick and Madi.

50

I force myself to stop imagining him in workout clothes and return to the game of verbal chess we're playing.

He's obviously trying to point out my lack of worldliness. I don't care what a douche like him thinks—not all of us were born with silver spoons in our mouths. But I guess his point has been made—I can hardly reject Monte Carlo when I've never been there. I've never even been to Vegas, for that matter. Atlantic City is the farthest I've ever traveled.

"No." I meet his gaze, refusing to let him fluster me. "So, I guess you'll have to take the lead on all the arrangements." I give him a mock-sorry look, then add brightly, "You already promised you'd foot the bill, right?"

It was the wrong tack to take. I forgot my aim was to force him to work with me on every tiny detail. He gives a dismissive wave of his hand. "Done. Get me the number of people, and I'll have Annabeth arrange everything."

I bristle. "Oh no, Suit." Because I've sucked down most of his drink and because he's already laid hands on me, my normal inhibitions are gone. I poke him in the chest with my index finger. "We already talked about this. You don't get to throw money at this thing to make it disappear. And I'm not your assistant who you give orders to. We're working on this party together, remember?" I don't toss in the reminder that this is his punishment because I suspect humiliating Billy White in front of Brick would be dangerous.

As it is, his eyes do that strange trick of glinting icy grey. He snatches my hand with the outstretched finger and pulls it to his mouth, biting my knuckle.

I shriek. He didn't bite me hard; I'm just shocked.

As quickly as he snatches my hand, he lets it go. I pull it to my chest, wrapping the other one around it protectively as I stare up at him.

He looks back impassively. I can't read his expression at all. Was that bite a challenge? Punishment? An assertion of dominance?

Whatever it was, it turned me on. My nipples scrape against the inside of my bra, and tingling ignites between my legs.

I sense Brick and Madi staring at us, but can't seem to move or think of anything to say.

Billy's inscrutable look changes to one of scorn, like "asshole" is a persona he's donning. "I remember," he says, like working with me is utterly distasteful.

I am one part offended, one part glorying in the punishment aspect of it–that I'm forcing him to be with me when he hates it. Except I'm uncertain he *does* hate it.

I think...unbelievably...that he might be attracted to me.

And that he probably hates *that*, too.

I give him my sweetest smile. "Great. So should we talk details?"

Billy takes the empty glass from my hand and replaces it with a crystal champagne flute filled with something bubbly–*prosecco*, Madi said. I've never had prosecco. It looks like champagne.

Like when he held my jacket and opened the door for me at La Résistance, I find his attentiveness at odds with the dickish personality. Also a bit disconcerting.

Like, I don't *want* to enjoy being the object of his attention, but I do.

He sweeps a hand in the living room's direction like a proper host. "Let's talk."

I trail behind Madi and Brick, maddeningly aware of Billy at my back. Brick sits in a large armchair and pulls Madi onto his lap.

That familiar wave of sadness hits me again–grief over

my changed relationship with Madi. I was excited to come here tonight and see her sooner than next Thursday. But even though we're in the same room now, she's very much wrapped up with Brick.

For the four hundred and fiftieth time, I mentally kick myself for not being happy for her. For not getting over myself. For feeling so abandoned.

I drop onto the sofa beside them and suck down half of the bubbly drink Billy handed me. It's nice–light and refreshing. I drain the glass and set it on the gleaming chrome coffee table.

Billy does not sit down yet. He seems to be considering the three of us. "Aubrey says it looks like a prison guard decorated my apartment."

The alcohol must be going to my head because it takes me a second to note how odd it is that Billy would offer that up as a conversation starter.

Madi laughs. "Right?" She catches my eye, and I'm relieved at the familiar camaraderie. The reassurance that we still share similar beliefs and values despite the drastic changes in her financial and social status. That we still have common ground. "It's completely devoid of color." Madi glances at Billy. "You need art in this place. You should buy one of Aubrey's paintings."

"I'm not sure an Occupy Wall Street mural works with my vibe."

Billy's tone is dry, but it starts a curl of pleasure in my belly to hear that he knows about my work. I shouldn't care–I don't need his recognition. But there's no denying the hum of warmth inside me.

"Speaking of your murals–you have to tell me what the deal is with the Sentience mural," Madi says.

"Oh, right." I glance over my shoulder at Billy, who, for

some unknown reason, is still standing. I guess he likes to be the master of his domain. "I, uh–let's talk when we go out next week. I'll give you the whole scoop."

"You're painting a mural for Sentience?" Billy's voice carries disbelief.

Again, I'm just a teensy bit flattered that he seems to know me–or think he knows me–well enough to comprehend that the job is out of character for me.

I wave a dismissive hand. "I finished it."

"For *Sentience*."

"They pay well."

Billy suddenly man-sprawls on the sofa beside me. It's a nice leather couch, so it doesn't dip too much, but his large presence registers in every cell of my body. He leans back with one ankle crossed over his knee, his arms stretching out on the back of the couch in each direction, one behind my shoulders. "How well?"

Jeez. I didn't expect the sudden interest. I might have underestimated Billy. I considered him a self-centered prick. But here he is, sniffing into my business like he can smell my deceit. That actually takes a level of empathy and human understanding.

Maybe that's how he got to the top in Brick's company. He is a self-centered prick who is savvy enough to manipulate those around him. That's my new working theory.

"Twenty grand." Obviously, I'm not doing it for the money. Madi knows that. It seems Billy knows that, too, but I'm not about to tell him what I'm really up to over there. It's none of his business, and he wouldn't understand.

"Thought you didn't care about money." It's a jab, but I feel him watching me, like he really wants to figure out the puzzle.

Damn.

This could be a problem.

"I needed to pay off my student loans," I toss out, which is not a lie.

Brick's fingers trace down Madi's thighs, and she squirms in his lap. They probably won't last another five minutes before they disappear to fuck again.

"Fifty grand," Billy blurts.

I slow-turn to give him a withering look. "Fifty grand what?"

"I'll give you fifty grand for a mural in here."

The Champagne–or prosecco–has definitely gone to my head. I snort. "Why?"

His blue-grey eyes are fathomless as he stares back at me coolly.

"I don't understand," I say, honestly. He would hate my art. It doesn't make sense.

"Aubrey's work is incredible." Madi starts selling me, even though my services aren't for sale. "She could transform this place."

I look around doubtfully. What I paint would look horrible in here. I paint with bright colors–and it's mostly protest art. I'm about social change, not billionaire bros. But it would be fun to be in his space, tormenting him on a daily basis. I could insist on working nights, when he's home.

I'd get to see Madi on a daily basis again. That would be nice.

"But no color," Billy adds.

I smack my lips. "Hard pass."

Except my mind was already enjoying the idea of the job. As I speak the words, I'm a little sorry at my haste in refusing.

I steal a look at him. He's sitting too close to me for me

to fully face him, and I'm suddenly hyper aware of the six inches that separate our legs on the couch.

Billy's posture is relaxed. There's a smug expression on his face. Why on Earth does he think he's won something here? I just said, *hard pass*.

"Anyone can make a big splash with color. It takes nuance and subtlety to find the life in the gray area."

"Is that where you reside?" I make the mistake of looking at him again. I'm suddenly trapped in his blue-grey gaze. "In the grey area?"

I suddenly wonder just how grey he goes. What rules does he bend? In what aspects of his life?

He gives a barely perceptible nod. "Yes." There's a purr to his voice that unnerves me. I don't know why or how he thinks he suddenly got the upper hand, but we flipped from me goading *him* to him provoking *me*. He's issuing a challenge, and his eyes glint with the knowledge that I'm going to accept.

No, I'm not. That's insane. Why would I?

I glance at Madi, and she gives me an encouraging flick of her brows. Like she wants me to negotiate this deal with him. And as much of an outsider as I feel with Madi and her new life, the idea of having this entry point appeals to me. We'd have shared experience again. Common ground.

"One hundred thousand for *two* murals." I throw out because that's the number that would make me feel okay about giving in. I don't lust for money, but things are definitely shoe-string tight. The reason it's taken me five years to get my degree is because I work almost full time in addition to school. The Sentience job allowed me some breathing room, but that money feels dirty. Plus, Madi's still footing the bill for her half of our apartment, and while I love having her former bedroom as a painting studio, I don't like accepting her charity.

"She's worth it," Madi pipes in.

"I don't need two murals," Billy counters.

"One grey" –I sweep my hand to indicate the wall behind the couch– "and one color." I point to the larger wall directly across from it. "That's my only offer. Take it or leave it."

Billy considers me. "I approve the design before you begin."

Wow. He's accepting my bid? Surprising. I thought he'd hardball me. I dismiss his stipulation. "No deal."

"Concept," he immediately counters.

Fireflies dance inside my entire body. I'm lit up by our negotiation–both physically turned on and mentally thrilled.

I consider his counter-offer. There's a lot of grey area with an approved concept. "Okay," I agree.

He grows more smug. I'm not sure why he seems to think he has me where he wants me. I'm charging a fortune, and I plan to make his life miserable with this venture.

"You pay all expenses," I throw in as an afterthought.

"Done."

A frisson of excitement pulses through me, even as some wary part wants to throw on the brakes. But I have nothing to fear. If it doesn't work, I can always walk away. Billy likes to push people around and bend them to his will with power, status, and money.

I'm immune to all of it. I can't be pushed around when I don't care about any of those things. I'd rather have my dignity than his money.

William White III will soon find that I'm not afraid of the Big Bad Bully.

Chapter Six

illy

B What in the hell am I doing? I must be out of my mind.

I hate having people in my place. It messes with my control over my environment. Even my housekeeper and chef annoy the hell out of me–and they're shifters in the Blackthroat pack. Respectful and trustworthy to the bone.

Why would I subject myself to having a *human* in my apartment? A mural must take weeks to paint. Maybe more. And she wants to paint *two*.

Two murals. One in color. Ugh. It will be ghastly. But whatever, I can have someone paint over it in a day.

The point is, I'm going to have Aubrey Cook in my apartment for months.

I. Will. Go. Mad.

Except, smug satisfaction emanates from my wolf at the idea of having her here. I have no doubt he manufactured this outcome. He wants to fuck the little human.

It's a strange impulse for a pure-blooded wolf from an

alpha line. I *can't* be going down the road Brick did—wanting to claim a human.

Not even one who smells as enticing as this one.

Fuck no. Humans are weak. Inconsequential.

I had that drilled into my head since before I could walk. Back when I was a runt who my father hid away from the pack out of shame.

I've spent my entire life scraping and scratching to get to the top. First, to prove I was worthy of the White name, which I now fucking reject. Then to prove I was worthy to be Brick's second in command.

I was born small and stayed small as a pup. My transition came late—I didn't shift or hit my growth spurt until I was fifteen—long after my dad had abandoned me at boarding school.

Long before then, I learned to fight ferociously, besting kids twice my size. I learned cut-throat strategy.

And when I finally hit my transition and shifted for the first time, I *willed* my way to rapidly grow to this size.

So I can screw this ridiculous human who smells like nutmeg and honey, but after that, I need to cast her aside. My story doesn't end with a human in my life. Full stop.

Madi claps her hands in delight and reaches for the bottle of prosecco to pour another round.

Aubrey picks up her refilled glass and drinks from it. It's hard for a wolf to even get buzzed because we metabolize alcohol so quickly, but I can tell Cafe Girl's on the border of drinking too much. Her movements are getting jerkier and reactions slower.

Part of me doesn't mind seeing her with lowered inhibitions. But it riles my wolf as if she's in some kind of danger here.

From me, perhaps.

Certainly not Madi or Brick.

"What else do you need from us?" Brick cuts in. He's got his hands all over Madi. I'm sure he wants to get her alone again. With the amount of sex those two get, it's a wonder she's not knocked up already.

"Help with the guest list," Aubrey answers. "And we need to set a date. Do we want it right before the wedding?"

Madi muses. "Yes. Let's do it the week of the wedding, arriving back home at least two days before the ceremony. I'll put together my guest list this weekend and get it to you, but I think it will just be you and Brick's two sisters."

Brick's fingers slide along Madi's inner thigh, inside the skirt of her form-fitting dress. She lets out a soft moan.

Aubrey covers her eyes. "God, you two. Unless you're angling for a foursome, I think you'd better take it upstairs."

My wolf bristles. The idea of Cafe Girl participating in *any* orgy–even one involving me, seems to piss him off.

Brick lifts Madi from his lap and rises at the same time. "Billy. Aubrey." He gives me a solemn nod.

He's satisfied with me. He doesn't say it, but I register my alpha's approval as much as my body would register alpha command. I'm starting to win my way back into his good graces.

The sense of victory makes me want to pounce on the helpless human. To claim her for a victory fuck–fast and furious. Just enough to work the aggression out of my system, so I can toss her away.

Aubrey also stands. "All right. We'll be in touch. Madi, I'll see you Thursday night." She hugs her friend, and for a moment, something dark and seething swirls in my gut. A familiar feeling from my childhood. That sense of wanting something given to someone else.

"Can Tony run Aubrey home?" Madi asks Brick.

"Of course." Brick pulls out his phone.

"No, I'm good," Aubrey says quickly. "Limos are not my style."

"You've been drinking." My words come out in a harsh growl.

She sends me a sharp, offended look, accompanied by a frown. "I didn't *drive* here."

She thinks I'm accusing her of drunk driving.

Madi tugs her toward the door. "They think the subway is unsafe. Take a cab, or they'll stuff you in the limo," my luna advises her friend.

For fuck's sake. In what universe is taking a limo to Brooklyn a hardship? Apparently in Aubrey Cook's upside down artist-activist world.

"Fine, I'll take a cab," she says quickly. "Thanks for the bubbles, Suit!" She precedes Brick and Madi to the door.

I follow, not sure why I'm so annoyed. The ridiculous human seems to keep me in a constant state of annoyance, though.

She finally turns to make eye contact after she's through the door. "I'll be in touch." She holds her thumb to her ear and pinky to her mouth to mimic a phone.

"I'll brace myself," I mutter.

Chapter Seven

ubrey

A They wanted to send me home in a limo.

That fact alone should tell me that Madi and I live in completely different worlds now. And she's not coming back to mine. Even if things don't work out with her marriage–which I couldn't imagine–she recently discovered her paternal grandmother is also a billionaire who wants her to take over the cosmetic company when she dies. So Madi's never going to be like me again.

Maybe I should just grieve the ending of what we had and move on.

Taking a painting job with a douchebag I can't stand just to stay close to her seems absurd now that I'm out on the street.

And fuck a cab.

They think the subway is dangerous?

I've been riding it alone since I was twelve. I grew up in Brooklyn. Why should I be afraid of public transport?

I walk to the subway station and board the train.

I snag a seat as my phone rings. It's Jamie.

I'm not sure why she's calling me rather than Jan, but I pick up.

"Hey Jamie."

"Don't use my name," she utters urgently into the phone.

I have to press my ear to the receiver to hear her over the noise in the train. "What's going on?"

"We can't text anymore. I think I'm being watched."

Alarm bells go off. No wonder I got a weird vibe earlier. "Shit," I mutter. "What makes you think that?"

"I saw a guy across the street just sitting in his car. I can't meet in person again. Listen, I looked through the hard drive, and it has all the pirated artwork still in the folders, but the email chain where we were ordered to pirate the artists' work isn't there."

I wish Jan were in this conversation. "Well...it still might be enough, right? Have you talked to Jan?"

"No. I know where to find the stuff on the server. I have a hacker friend. If he can get access to the server room, he can install a backdoor entryway for me."

"A what?" I'm imagining a back door carved into the side of the Sentience building.

"Like...a way into the servers." Jamie sounds like she is too impatient to explain the technical details of the plan. "He's willing to break into the server room to do the job, but it's on the lower level–sub floor 3, and he'll need a keycard to get in there."

"You gave me a keycard–"

"Mine won't work anymore. I need a new one."

A new key card. This is getting complicated. I don't like that she's involved another person in our conspiracy, even if he is a hacker willing to help us. And now I have to steal another keycard?

"I finished the mural already. I mean, we have the grand opening gala, but I'm not there after hours anymore."

"Can't you say you have to put a top coat on it or something?"

I swallow, hard. My heart thuds as if *I'm* the one being watched. "Um, maybe. But even so, how will I get this new keycard?"

"I don't know. But without the email chain, they could just say I was the thief. The risk you already took would be for nothing. If you can just get a keycard, I can take care of the rest."

Fuck.

"Okay," I say. "I'll arrange to get back in there this week."

Except it's midterms, and I've now agreed to paint two murals in a billionaire's penthouse.

Well, Billy White can wait. I'm fighting for justice here.

When I get off at my stop an hour later and climb up the stairs, a sleek cobalt blue electric Porsche is double parked across the street. It's blocking traffic and cars are honking at it.

"Move, asshole!" a taxi driver yells out his window.

Some guy is behind the wheel looking my way. I remember what Jamie said–that a guy in his car was watching her.

Am I being watched, too? My heart rate kicks up again.

I stop walking and stare, and the car suddenly zooms off, making gooseflesh rise on my arms.

Except the guy looked like...Nah.

Couldn't be.

Someone bumps into me from behind, and I start walking toward our...I mean, *my* apartment, shaking my head.

Of course, that wasn't Billy. I just have billionaire bullies on my mind now. One second you don't know any billionaires, the next minute it feels like they're everywhere because they're in your consciousness. You're thinking about them.

There have probably been expensive cars parked in my neighborhood before, but I just didn't notice.

I walk the few blocks it takes to get to my place and enter the building, trying not to think about Billy White the Third.

The next time I touch you, I'll ask first. His words rattle around in my head, causing my nipples to stiffen in my bra.

Um, excuse me?

Who says there will be a next time?

As I walk up the stairs, I recall the way his hands felt on my waist when he picked me up. Searing hot. Large. Deadly strong.

I usually think of Wall Street guys as thin, pasty-white, and too manicured to be manly, but under that five thousand dollar suit, Billy White might be a beast.

No. I shouldn't think that.

Why would I be turned on by that thought? It's all wrong.

Except I'm suddenly imagining that cut-throat businessman getting rough. Tearing my clothes off. Tossing me in the center of his bed. Ravishing me.

I'm flushed with heat by the time I reach my door and not just from the exertion of climbing the stairs. I open the door and grab ice from the freezer. I walk over the window, rubbing it along my forehead and neck to cool down.

There, across the street, is the same flashy blue Porsche. The driver's side window is down, and his face is angled in the direction of my window.

Fear flashes through me a split second before I identify the driver.

It's not a fixer from Sentience.

Not unless they hired Wall Street tycoon William White III to do their dirty work.

What in the actual fuck?

The adrenaline from thinking I was being tailed morphs into anger, and I whirl and storm back downstairs. I'm flying out the door as his car pulls out. "Hey!" I yell. "Stop."

The car on my side of the road stops and honks at me as I rush in front of it. Billy also throws on the brakes, causing the driver behind him to lay on the horn.

"What in the hell are you doing here?" I shout, reaching his window as he swiftly backs into the parking spot he'd snagged along the road.

His window is down, and he narrows his eyes at me, his mouth screwed into a tight scowl. "You said you'd take a cab," he snarls back.

As if that makes any sense.

"So?"

His nostrils flare, and his eyes glint light grey under the streetlight. He gives a quick look around, like he's in the secret service checking for snipers. "What are you scared of?"

I look around as well. Do I look scared? I'm pretty sure I shook that off the moment I realized my tail was this billionaire bro. "I'm not scared." The slight catch in my voice makes it sound like a lie.

"Were you scared of *me*?" Billy sounds pissed.

"I saw a car following me. So yeah. That was scarier than anything that happens on a subway ride."

Billy shakes his head and hits the window button, causing it to roll up.

I catch the top of the glass with both hands, trying to stop it. "Hang on a second."

He reverses the window. "Are you trying to break my window?"

"Seriously. What are you doing here?"

Billy's expression is inscrutable. He stares back at me for a beat, then looks pointedly down at my fingers, still covering his window to keep it from closing.

I persist.

"Did you actually follow me to make sure I made it home safely?" It sounds crazy when I say it out loud.

Billy's gaze deadens. "You are my worst punishment."

A slow smile spreads across my face.

Wow. I'm his punishment. I love this.

Torturing Billy White is going to be even easier and more satisfying than I imagined.

Chapter Eight

B *illy*

"Get the financials on these three newcomers in superconductor and battery tech I identified for possible acquisition." I give Noah, one of our top analysts, a handwritten list. "Prepare a full analysis for the next executive meeting."

"Yes, sir," Noah answers.

He's a wolf, but he's not part of our pack. He secured a job at Moon Co the conventional way–through an Ivy League degree and excellent references. Once he was in, we recognized him as one of our kind by his scent. Sully, our head of security, ran a thorough background check to make sure he wasn't one of the Adalwulf's spies, but we found no connection to our enemy pack. After that, he rose quickly through the ranks. There's nothing this company appreciates more than a bright, competent young employee who is also a wolf.

That's why I would never fuck Annabeth, my assistant, even though she's gorgeous. She's too valuable to the company.

Noah won extra favor this past winter with Brick for lipreading a video of Aiden and Madi that proved me wrong about their meeting, a mistake I'm still paying for.

Still, Noah isn't part of our inner circle. Brick hasn't even asked him to join the pack–something about him being pissed that Noah didn't present himself to join immediately when he came to New York. Brick takes it as either a sign of disrespect or that he was playing both sides and was going to join the Adalwulfs if they offered him a job.

I was suspicious at first, but now that I know the guy, I think it was out of integrity. He didn't want to use wolf connections to get a job on Wall Street. He might be someone determined to prove himself after facing discrimination at some point in his life for being deaf.

Now that I'm sure he's trustworthy, I've come to rely on him because he's smarter than most of the people who work here and observant as fuck. I ordered my team to learn American Sign Language and took lessons with a private tutor until I was fluent myself.

I'm tempted to open the topic of him joining our pack, but it's a rocky time right now. The pack is still settling after all the challenges to our Alpha.

"That's all, thank you," I sign to Noah and follow him out of my office to stand in front of Annabeth's desk.

"I need you to arrange Mr. Blackthroat's bachelor party in Monte Carlo," I tell Annabeth.

She looks up at me, startled. There's a trace of fear in her scent. She's competitive like me, so she doesn't like surprises she doesn't know how to handle.

"I know you know nothing about these human rituals."

She's already recovered, picking up a pen and angling her notepad to face me. "I can research it. Of course," she assures me. She writes "Bachelor Party" at the top of the yellow notepad.

"It's a joint party with Ms. Evans. Her maid of honor will want final say on everything."

Annabeth nods. "Would you like me to reach out to her now to start the process?"

I hesitate. I should say yes and wash my hands of this. But I know Aubrey wouldn't let me off the hook so easily. She didn't want me to offload this project or make it go away with money alone.

I was a fool to disclose the fact that this is punishment for me. She loved the notion way too much.

But then, I like seeing her turned on by something, even if it is torturing me.

Of course, I intend to torture her right back.

At this point, just being around each other seems to be torture enough for both of us.

"No." I blow out my breath. "I'll be the intermediary for now."

Annabeth fails to mask her surprise.

"I'm Best Man," I say, as if that explains things.

Of course, Annabeth doesn't understand these human ceremonies any better than I do.

"Mr. Blackthroat wants me to liaise with the human side."

"*You*, sir?" Annabeth doesn't manage to hide her incredulity. She knows I was behind getting Madi fired because she executed my orders for the full security investigation I ordered. She knows I only surround myself with wolves. I'd rather have a wolf at my back than a human any day. I don't work with humans unless I absolutely have to. No humans work on my floor or my department.

"Me. As homage to our luna." The only reason I'm

explaining this for a second time to someone outside the circle of me is because I trust and expect Annabeth to protect my interests.

"Ah. Of course."

"All arrangements should be charged to my personal gold card. We're looking at the week of the wedding."

Annabeth nods. "Taking the company jet?"

"Yes." The one with enclosed sleeping beds.

I know nothing about bachelor parties, but I'm suddenly picturing the party starting on the jet. Champagne flowing. Music pumping. Aubrey removing her clothes like a stripper who pops out of a cake.

No. No, no, no. That's so wrong. Aubrey will *not* be the bachelor party entertainment. No one will be watching her strip.

Unless it's me. In the private sleeping pod.

"How long will you stay?"

"You determine what is ideal." Now I'm picturing Aubrey in a white string bikini, her skin sun-warmed on the beach. Her nutmeg and honey scent would carry a salty taste. My dick starts to harden.

I clear my throat and try to push the image out of my mind. "We'll need a few days to enjoy the beach, as well as the nightlife."

"Understood. Number of guests?"

"Ms. Evans will provide a list." I walk away before Annabeth sees me tugging at my tie to cool my neck.

Irritation spikes as I enter my office.

The desire to make the annoying human pay for being so colorful. So larger than life. So fucking all-consuming eats at me.

I pull my phone out and hit her number.

"William White the Third." She bites off the consonants in my distinguished name, loading it with sarcasm.

My cock gets hard picturing her tossing her hair and smirking like calling out my full name is some kind of insult.

"Cafe Girl."

"Is that what you call me?"

"I don't call you anything. But you can call *me* 'boss.'" She did take a commission from me, after all.

She scoffs. "You're not my boss. I'm an independent contractor. And I haven't even started."

"That's why I'm calling. I need to know when you're starting."

She hesitates. "I have to go back to Sentience tonight."

There's a thread of tension in her voice I don't understand. But it also doesn't make sense that she's painting a mural for them. They seem like exactly the kind of company she'd thumb her nose at.

"I thought you were finished."

"I just need to paint a top coat to make sure it lasts."

"At night?"

Something about this feels wrong.

"I'm a part-time student. Besides, I like being there when no one else is."

That part rings true and makes sense. But my wolf doesn't like the idea of her being there alone at night. Walking to the subway afterward. Walking home from the subway.

"How late?" I demand.

"What?"

"How late will you stay? How long will it take?"

"*Why?*" She sounds annoyed now.

"I'll pick you up."

"No, thanks."

73

I end the call, too irritated to negotiate further. I'm losing my touch. It's usually easy for me to manipulate any situation to get what I want. For some reason, I lose all rationale with this absurd female.

I cock my arm back to hurl my phone at the wall then restrain myself and grind my teeth instead.

I will have that little temptress on her knees begging for my cock by the time I'm through. I hold that vision as my end goal. This may be a long game, but it's a game I will win.

Because coming from behind to steal the entire game is where I excel.

My father never saw it coming.

Aubrey Cook thinks she is impervious. Immune. Uninterested.

She will soon find out just how wrong she is.

Chapter Nine

ubrey

A I don't know how long I can dawdle here pretending I'm still sealing up this damn mural. I mean, how many coats of invisible sealing does it really require?

That's what Jack, the security guard, just asked me.

"That was the last one." I wipe the brush on the side of the polyurethane can to clean it.

I didn't run my plan by Jan because I think she would've said not to do it. That's what she told me when I first volunteered to get the contents of Jamie's hard drive.

What I'm contemplating tonight is even harder. I have to steal a keycard? This is nuts. But it might be doable. Especially with Jack's omnipresence.

His keycard is hanging out of his pocket. All I have to do is distract him and pull it out.

"I'm going to get cleaned up here, and then I'll be out of your hair."

"Oh no, I don't mind you here at all," he's quick to say. "I'm just fascinated by your process here."

Or my ass. But whatever. I don't mind his interest. It's going to play in my favor in a minute here.

I put the brush on the paint roller tray with the roller and pick it up. "I'm just going to wash this stuff out, and then I'll be on my way."

"Sure. I'll walk you down."

Such a gentleman.

As I brush past him, I let the roller slide off the tray. "Whoops!"

He immediately stoops to pick it up. I bump into his hip, reaching at the same time with my right hand. As I jostle him, I tug on the lanyard hanging out of his pocket and tuck the card in my back pocket.

"I got it," he says, and we both straighten up, laughing.

"Thanks." I grab the tray to avoid locking gazes and having a moment with this guy. Guilt floods through me.

Hopefully, he won't get into any trouble over losing his key.

More importantly, I hope he never realizes I'm the one who took it.

I hustle off to the women's restroom and clean my brush, roller, and tray. When I return, Jack has folded my drop cloth into a neat pile and put away the step stool I borrowed from the closet.

He turns to look at me and draws a breath.

Shit.

He's going to ask me out.

I stoop to pick up the polyurethane can and set it on top of the paint tray.

He's hot, but I'm not interested. More importantly, I can't get involved with him now that I stole his keycard. It would put him in danger of losing his job—or worse.

I'm saved by his security radio going off. "Jack?"

He pulls out the walkie talkie and hits a button. "Go ahead."

"Is that artist still up there?"

He and I look at each other in surprise. He holds my gaze as he speaks into the mouthpiece. "Yeah, I'm with her now. What's up?"

"There's a guy down here who says he's her ride."

My ride.

Billy?

What the fuck? I snicker internally at the idea of Billionaire Billy acting as my taxi.

At least his arrival made for a perfect interruption. I smile brightly. "That's my...boyfriend." That will stop him.

The light and hope drain from his expression. "Oh, okay."

"You don't have to walk me down if you don't want."

"Nah, I will. Let me carry this stuff for you." He takes the paint tray from my hands and puts the drop cloth over the top.

A true gentleman. Even when he's been dissed.

The elevator ride is thankfully short, and I step out, taking my things from his hands.

Billy stands in front of the reception desk in the darkened foyer, his brows down, and a scowl on his mouth. As if I'd asked for a ride and was late or something.

The guy is an arrogant asshole.

"Thanks, Jack." I turn to walk backward as he steps out of the elevator, eyeing Billy.

Another rush of guilt runs over me, and I take two quick steps back and give him a hug. "You're a cool guy," I tell him.

He looks a little dazed but smiles.

I swear to God I hear Billy growl. Like, a literal *animal* growl.

"Bye, guys!" I call out, waving to both Jack and the other security guard as I bop on past Billy, ignoring him completely.

I hear another growl just behind me.

I don't stop or turn around, I just walk straight down the sidewalk. I should just keep ignoring him and walk myself to the subway.

Would he stop me?

Why is he even here? I said, *no, thanks*.

But it would be too rude to just walk away. My conscience won't let me. I stop and whirl, surprised to find Billy right behind me. He snatches the paint things from my hands, his scowl firmly on lock.

"Why are you *here*?" I demand.

He tips his head to the side. "Get in the car."

"Why should I?"

"Because I don't want you walking alone at night."

I don't want to like that statement. I hate that warmth crawls from the soles of my feet right up to my chest.

Dang.

It sounds like something my dad would say to my mom. Sweet. Unnecessary, but sweet.

But that can't be right.

Billy White is anything but sweet.

Now he's the one ignoring me, carrying my paint supplies to his car. He's illegally parked right in front of the building. This guy thinks laws don't apply to him.

But I guess there's no parking ticket he couldn't afford.

It's hard to imagine having the kind of wealth he has. The kind Madi will soon have. You could do so much good with that kind of money. Install green spaces around the city. Fund programs for the homeless. Back a political candidate who cares about their constituents.

Well, I will soon have a hundred grand to put to good use.

I've never even considered having that kind of money. I'll be able to pay off my student loans at City College. I could pre-pay my rent for the year and cut back on my hours at La Résistance, not that I don't love working there. After this one job for Billy, I can focus on my art. Or on studying for the LSAT, which was my original educational plan.

It's still a good one, but I don't find myself excited about the idea anymore. Making art is more fulfilling. Although creating change as a lawyer would probably also be fulfilling, just in a different way.

Billy throws the door to the passenger side open, somehow holding the paint tray with the half-full can of polyurethane in one hand. The guy must have bionic wrists.

I reach it, expecting him to move out of the way, but he stands there like a chauffeur. Is he actually going to *hand me into the car?*

It's absurd, but my body heats in reaction—just as it did with all the other gentlemanly gestures he's made. I stop right in front of him—too close—and lift my face to his. "What now, big guy?" I taunt.

His gaze dips to my lips. His eyes glint icy-grey. "Get in the car, Aubrey."

"I didn't ask for a ride."

"You're getting one," he counters.

One corner of my lips twitches. I hold out my hand. "Is this how it works?"

He's so smooth. His palm is already engulfing mine, a

firm, steady presence for me to lean into as I lower myself into the car.

I hold my hands out to take the supplies on my lap for the trip, but he slams the door, walking around and depositing them in the trunk before getting behind the wheel.

This suddenly feels like a date. Why is Billy really here? Is he interested in me?

Is that why he offered me the job?

The idea seems crazy, but I can't come up with another reason. Unless Brick ordered him to suck up to me or something.

But even sucking up wouldn't require him to play taxi driver to me–the lowly "Cafe Girl," as he calls me.

"What's with you and the security guy?" he demands as he peels out into traffic.

I lean my head back on the headrest and give a soft chuckle.

Well. I guess I have my answer. I wasn't imagining it. William White the III is interested.

In *me*.

The last guy in the world I would ever hope to attract wants in my pants. The antithesis of what I look for in a partner.

My lady bits tingle with sudden blood flow.

Huh. I'm turned on by the idea of screwing my "no way" guy.

If that's not the strangest and most unexpected twist in my life story, I don't know what is.

* * *

Billy

"Jealous?" Aubrey asks.

"No," I scoff, way too quickly. The second I saw Aubrey rise to tiptoe to hug the muscular security guard, my wolf went wild. Even now he's howling, demanding I pull her into my arms and replace the stranger's scent with mine.

But that's ridiculous. There's no reason I should be so possessive about this human. I grit my teeth and taste blood when the razor edge of my fang grazes the inside of my cheek. My canines ache, which also doesn't make sense. The only reason my fangs would sharpen is when I'm preparing to mark–claim–my mate.

And there's no way in hell this human is someone I would claim. I just need to get laid.

And let my wolf out. That's why I'm feeling feral–full moon is coming, and he'll need a run. In the deep woods, surrounded by pack and far, far away from any human. Even ones that smell like honey and nutmeg. *Especially* that kind.

Aubrey's delicious scent fills the car, making my mouth water. She's parted her legs, releasing a bloom of scent into the air. I bite back a groan.

"Hmmm," she hums, turning her head to hide a smile. The movement makes light flash on her silver piercing, and I have the urge to lean in and press my mouth against hers, tasting her flavor off her tongue. The silver would burn, but that would be part of the fun.

I shake my head as if that will jostle these thoughts out of my head. Kissing her is just a forbidden temptation, and I've always risen to a challenge.

My cock rises. I just need to remember that the goal is to make her beg for me.

"Why would I be jealous?" I force my shoulders to relax.

"No reason." She leans back in her seat, totally relaxed. The movement sends more of her scent wafting my way, and I grip the steering wheel tighter, as if that will help me hang onto my control. "You seem to be going out of your way to spend time with me."

"You're the one who took the job at my place."

"You're the one who offered." She turns to study me. I focus on the road, but my wolf preens under her undivided attention. "Or were you in the market for a mural before I came along?"

"No," I admit. I don't usually share my true feelings with anyone outside my inner circle, but this doesn't feel like a concession. I could be baiting a trap, luring the human in one confession at a time. "I like your work."

"Yeah right," she snorts. "Name one piece of mine that you like."

"The wall at La Résistance," I say, surprising myself. "Not the one outside, the small one by the bathroom. With the Brooklyn bridge in the background. That's your work, right?"

I sense her surprise. "One of my earliest public pieces, yes."

"I like it." I sound grudging, and I am. I don't want to like anything made by a human–especially not this one who drives me insane, but the mural is colorful and wild. "It has...heart."

"All right, Suit. I accept the compliment." She turns her smile towards the window, and I want to call her name. *Look at me. Smile at me.*

Ugh, I usually have better game than this.

Her stomach growls, and she doesn't seem to notice, but I go on high alert. The human is hungry, and I need to feed her.

"Have you eaten dinner?"

"I had a protein bar. Why?"

I swing into traffic. "Pick a restaurant."

"What?"

"You heard me." I glance at her and watch her weigh her options. "You're hungry. So let's eat."

"Are you asking me out, Suit? On a date?"

"Will it get us to dinner faster?"

"Who said I want to eat with you?"

Does everything have to be a fight with this female? "We can get takeout. Or eat at separate tables." Her stomach growls again, and I bite back my wolf's whine. "I'm just trying to feed you."

"I get that. I'm wondering why."

Some asshole in a truck cuts me off, and I lay on my horn, taking out my frustration on the rude driver. It doesn't help.

"Can't I just do something nice?" I mumble.

Aubrey chuckles, and I realize she's been playing me. "Dinner would be nice."

I decide to poke her back. "Just nice? Most people would kill to have dinner with a billionaire."

"A crypto billionaire," her lip curls. "And I'm not most people."

"What do you have against blockchain tech?"

"Oh, I don't know, the rampant waste of resources that exacerbate climate change."

"It's a dirty field," I agree. "Which is why Brick and I make sure all our companies run on green energy. We're carbon negative. But we need every business to take climate change seriously. As a species, we're not doing enough."

She blinks. She didn't expect me to say that. Then her

eyes narrow, and I hide my smirk. She wanted a chance to rip me a new one, and now she's annoyed.

Dinner is going to be fun.

I open my mouth to ask if she'd prefer sushi or tacos, when my dash lights up with a text. It's Sully, one of my pack brothers. *Need you at HQ now.*

I hit reply and dictate with a growl, *I'm with a client. Can it wait?*

No. Sully isn't big on words, but he's head of pack security, so when he calls an in-person meeting, I know it's important.

"So—now I'm a client." Aubrey's eyebrows rise.

I curse and do an illegal U-turn, heading back toward Aubrey's apartment. "Only so I can expense our time together." I speed through the streets, swerving around slow cars and delivery vans, and make it to Aubrey's door in record time.

I illegally park and hop out to get her door, but she's already sprung out by the time I get to her. "I'll get your things."

"No need." She waves a graceful, paint-stained hand. "You can put them in your apartment, save me a trip."

The thought that she'll be in my space soon calms me. I should hate having her around— why am I so annoyed right now at the thought of leaving her side?

I slam her door shut.

"Bye—thank you for the ride that I didn't ask for," she calls over her shoulder as she sashays away from me. Her ass is a work of perfection that I am dying to spank.

I don't bother with a response, but I suspect my eyes glint with my wolf. He wants me to follow her up the stairs and roll around in her bed all night. Naked. I'm hard as steel, imagining her soft skin coated in my scent.

I call the Italian restaurant I know Madi likes and order one of everything delivered to Aubrey's door. It makes my wolf feel better.

When I get to Sully's office, I practically tear the door off the hinges. "What is this about?" I snarl. My wolf is surly that we were called away from Aubrey's side.

Fortunately, Sully doesn't waste my time. He swivels in his seat, unfazed. "I was reviewing some footage and found this." He clicks a button, and the image of a street corner fills every screen. I recognize the building–it's the Adalwulf highrise, right across from Moon Co's office. "So what?"

"Watch." The footage rolls, showing a constant stream of street traffic exiting Adalwulf Associates. A few seconds in, a familiar face shows up. Sully hits pause and zooms in.

It's my dad. This video is proof that he took a meeting with my pack's sworn enemy.

I shouldn't feel betrayed by my father's actions, but I do. I knew he would do anything for power, but an alliance with our enemies? It hits hard.

"This was taken a few minutes before he entered our building and visited you," Sully says. "Is there any reason your father would be visiting the Adalwulf's?"

I curse. Damn him. Of course, he's fucking with my life again. I show my disgust on my face. "Knowing him, he's playing both sides. He showed up here, angling for an invitation to Brick's wedding. He also insinuated that Brick's position in our pack is weak."

Sully says nothing, just stares at me.

"Are you implying that I knew about this?" I ask.

"Not implying. I'm asking you outright."

"I don't control my father's movements." I return Sully's dead-eyed stare, incensed that he's grilling me like I'm a suspect in a crime. "If he met with our enemy, I had nothing

to do with it. The fact that you'd ask me makes me wonder–
is my loyalty being called into question?"

Sully leans back in his chair, in a deceptively casual
pose. He could easily launch out of his seat and into a fight.
"You've been at odds with Brick's decisions lately."

"Are you talking about my opposition to Brick claiming
a human mate? That was in the past. I want what's best for
the pack. Now that Madi is luna, I stand behind her and
Brick, just like you." Heat rolls through me, my anger
waiting to be unleashed. The fact that Sully would even
group me in with a dog like my father makes me want to
explode. "I have this pack's back."

"Good to hear," Sully says. His tone is mild, like we're
discussing the weather, not accusing me of treason. "Then
you'll have no problem with finding out exactly what your
father was up to when he visited the Adalwulfs."

"I know you have spies in the Adalwulf pack."

"But not in your dad's. You're our best bet at finding out
what he's planning."

I grit my teeth. "I'll be happy to spy on my father for
you, anytime."

"Wonderful. I'll tell Brick to expect a report within a
week."

Fuck, now I have to talk to my dad. My mood just went
from bad to worse.

My eyes are probably glowing. My wolf doesn't answer
to Sully–which is why he's careful to clarify that I'll be
reporting to Brick, not him. Still, the next time we're on a
run, I'm going to unleash my wolf on him. He needs to
remember that I'm second, not him. "Don't trouble yourself.
I'll tell him myself." I stomp out the door before I challenge
him to a dominance fight right in his office. Wolves and
security equipment don't mix.

I'm pissed I have to deal with this, but Sully is right. Any threat to our pack needs to be dealt with immediately. I have to hunt my dad down and eliminate the threat.

I pull out my phone, scroll to my second favorite contact, and hit talk.

"Billy?" My sister Boudicca answers, sounding confused. "Is everything okay?"

"Our father is here."

"What?" It takes her a moment to parse what I'm telling her. "In the city?"

"Yes." I grind my teeth.

She sighs. "I heard he was planning a trip. I would've stopped him if I could."

"I know."

When my sister turned twenty, she was exiled from our pack for mating a she-wolf. Because, of course, my dad is homophobic as well as a bigot. He can't stand to let people love who they love; he only wants to spread hate around.

Now she lives in New Hampshire with her mate, but she keeps tabs on the pack. She was always brave and strong and focused on protecting others. Protecting me. When she was exiled, she tried to take me with her, but my father and his enforcers wouldn't allow it.

Hearing her voice sends me back to an earlier, darker time. For a moment, I'm in the Maine woods of my father's territory. I can hear the pack shouting. I was five when they caught a hunter trespassing on pack land. I can still recall the stink of sweat and fear and the evil light in my dad's eye.

He made the pack gather and watch as his enforcers dragged the human forward. *"This human thinks he can hunt on our land,"* my father sneered. *"We'll teach him who does the hunting around here!"*

The rabid cheers fade away as my sister calls my name. "Billy? Are you still there?"

I shake my head to clear the memory. "I'm here. I need you to help me find out where he's staying." I know she's maintained relationships with the more decent members of my father's pack. She does what she can to help them to spite my father's tyranny.

"I'll do what I can," she promises.

I tell her I love her, and we end the call, but I'm still caught in the grip of memory.

I was only five when they found that hunter in the woods. At the time, my sister was my babysitter. She held me close while my father ranted and raved about humans and how weak they are.

"They think they can take over the earth! But they're weak." The disgust in his voice made me cower. If I was in wolf form, I would've tucked my tail.

I could feel the anger and triumph in my father, and that was never a good sign. I was a small child and often bore the brunt of my father's hate.

And he was whipping up the pack, getting them ready for violence.

At one point, I whimpered. I didn't mean to make a sound, but once it was out, it was too late.

My father heard me.

"Bring him here," he ordered my sister. She shook her head. Only twelve, and she was brave enough to stand up to him, even when he beat her for it. She tried to protect me.

I didn't want her to get hurt. I pushed away and made myself go on shaking legs to stand before him.

"This is a human. He thinks he's strong but take away his gun and..." my father raised a hand, and the man shrieked behind his gag. I didn't need to hear what he was saying to know he was begging for his life.

My father and his cronies laughed. "See?" My father shouted. "Weak. Come here, boy.' He gripped my shoulder, and his fingers dug into the muscle and bone. It hurt. I bit back a cry. "You're a wolf like me. My son. You don't want to be weak. Right?"

"N-no..."

He slapped me. "Louder."

"No, sir," I shouted. I could sense my sister's distress behind me. I had to be strong. I could do this.

"Good boy. So you're going to stand here, and you're going to watch. One day, all of this will be yours. And it'll be your job to take care of any threats."

I stared at the human. He was shaking, and tears tracked down his cheeks, dampening his gag. He didn't look like a threat.

"We're wolves," I pointed out. "We're stronger."

"That's right." My dad slapped my back. "He gets it. And now... it's time to hunt the human!"

They let the man go. He ran, but he didn't get far. They turned into wolves and herded him back.

"Don't look away, boy," my father snarled before he turned into a wolf to go in for the kill. And I didn't.

I stood very still and kept my eyes open until the human's blood sprayed in my face.

And now I've grown into everything my father wants me to be. Cold, cunning, controlled. Helping lead a powerful pack.

But I am not my father's son. I want him out of my city and my life, but mostly I want him far away from any humans he might hurt.

And it's up to me to stop him.

Chapter Ten

ubrey

    I walk to the subway from La Résistance after I finish my shift. Saturday mornings are my favorite time of the week to be there. The coffee shop is packed with regulars who have time to sit and visit with each other. La Résistance isn't just espresso drinks and cafe food. It's music and poetry. Community and love. I grew up in a loving home with amazing parents, but even so, La Résistance has been a home away from home since I got my first job there as a teen.

I call Madi on Saturday as I walk. "I'm on my way to your place. Please tell me you're around this weekend?"

"Gah! Why didn't you tell me sooner? We're already in the Adirondacks. Are you going to Billy's?"

"Yes. He insisted on going over my concept drawings before I start painting Monday."

"Really? That's so weird. He was here last night. He must've helicoptered out this morning to meet with you."

I stop walking, and someone bumps into me from behind.

Something makes me scan the street for an electric blue Porsche. "It *is* a little weird, right?" I don't see anything unusual, so I start walking again.

"What is?"

"Him cutting his weekend short to meet with me? About a mural he didn't even want?"

Madi is silent, which throws me off. I expected her to jump right in and validate me.

"What?" I probe.

"Yeah, it's strange. I'm just trying to think what he might be up to."

Goosebumps rise on my arms. "You suspect he's up to something?"

"I don't know. It's hard to trust him after everything. And he doesn't like..." She sucks in a breath.

"He doesn't like *what*?"

She hesitates again. "Uh...well, I just have found him to be sort of... classist."

I try to figure out why she's pussyfooting around. "Do you really mean *racist*?"

Is this about the color of my skin being darker than his?

"No," she says immediately, so I'm sure it's true. "Not that. But he didn't think I was good enough for Brick."

"Right. Because you weren't rich? Or blue-blooded?" I jog down the steps into the subway.

"The latter. But I'm thinking this all through, and I can't imagine he'd be up to anything with you. He suffered a lot when he was out of favor with Brick. Like, he looked like he wasn't sleeping."

That news creates a lump in my throat.

I don't want to think of Billy as someone with a heart so easily punctured. It makes him less torture-able.

"Unless he's really that evil and is still trying to split me and Brick apart," Madi adds.

"Well, he told me that planning the bachelor party was his penance for fucking with your relationship." I find a bench in the subway and drop onto it to wait for the train. After being on my feet all morning, I'm ready to rest.

Madi lets out a soft chuckle. "Ah. That explains it. He's still trying to mend things. So I guess he's sucking up."

"He came to pick me up at Sentience two nights ago." I let that bomb drop to see if it changes her perspective.

"*What?*"

Good. She's appropriately surprised. I'm not the only one who thought it was weird.

"Yeah, and then he wanted to know if there was something between me and the security guard."

Madi gasps. "Holy shit. *He's into you.*"

"Kind of seems like it."

"So into you, he hired you to be in his loft for the next two months." Madi sounds thrilled.

My heart skips a little although I'm not sure if it's over the joy of Madi and me having something to gossip about together again or about a Wall Street suit being into me.

"Yeah. He sent me a contract and wired the down payment the very next day."

"Which allowed him to bully you into meeting him this weekend."

"Uh-uh." That slows my heart rate back down. "No amount of money will allow him to bully me," I say firmly. "Weekends are actually better for me with school, or I wouldn't do it."

"Good for you. Yeah, never show fear with Billy. He can smell it, and he'll work any advantage he can find."

I recall the feel of his large hand steadying mine as he handed me into the car. Is he working an angle with me?

He might be. But I suspect the angle is only about getting in my panties. Like Madi said, he's too much of a stuck-up society douche to be interested in anything real.

He probably just wants to know what it's like to fuck a lowly barista. What does he call me? *Cafe Girl??*

But whatever. I'm not entirely opposed to a hot round or two in the sheets with him.

Call me curious. Maybe I just want to know what it's like to screw a billionaire.

My train pulls into the station, and I press my earbud to my ear to finish the conversation as I stand. "He won't be working me. I intend to make him suffer."

Madi laughs. "Good. How?"

"Well, I already decided that if the bachelor party is his penance, I won't make it easy for him."

"And now?"

"And now, I guess I'm not above a good cock tease. If he wants between my legs, he's going to have to work for it."

Madi lets out an exaggerated, scandalized gasp. "Are you into him?"

"Mmm..." I deliberate.

"You *are!*" She sounds thrilled.

"Of course not."

"But?"

I laugh. "You heard a *but?*"

"I mean, you implied he *would* be getting between your legs."

"Okay, I'm a *little bit* interested," I admit as I step onto the train and find a handle to hang onto. The train takes off, and my weight falls backward.

"Yeah, I don't know," Madi says. "Part of me thinks sex

with Billy would be horrible. Like it would be all about him."

"Why in the fuck are you talking about sex with *Billy*?" I hear Brick demand in the background, as if he just walked into the room.

Madi laughs. "I'm talking to Aubrey," she tells him. To me, she says, "But he's also very good at knowing what people want. That's what makes him a brilliant strategist. So maybe he'd be a decent lay."

"You're going to stop that conjecture right now," Brick growls, and Madi shrieks, like he just picked her up or tickled her or something.

"Uh oh. Mr. Possessive is getting jealous." I don't mean to sound as judgey as it comes out.

Honestly, I'm the one who's jealous.

Shame tightens my chest. I hate that I resent Brick for stealing Madi's attention. What am I, twelve years old? I should be able to share my best friend with the man who loves her.

"He knows I don't want Billy." Madi's voice is breathy, and I'm certain she's talking to Brick not me. They're probably staring into each other's eyes about to get naked again, if they aren't already.

"Okay, I'm gonna let you get on with whatever is about to happen over there." I try to make my voice lighter this time. "Can't wait to hang out Thursday night!"

"Me neither!" she sing-songs and ends the call.

I drop into a seat that opens up at the next stop. I'm not sure why I suddenly wish I'd worn something a little more tempting. I'm in my standard first nice day of spring wear–a tight-fitting crop sweater, short-shorts, and Doc Martens on my feet.

But I don't know what I'd rather be wearing to torture a

guy like Billy–certainly not a pair of heels. He's already attracted to what he's seen. I don't need to go changing into something I'm not. But I could push the bounds here.

My imagination starts churning out all the ways I could tempt Billy White.

That's right, Big Bad Bully.

I'm going to make you sorry you hurt my bestie. Sorry for every uppity judgment you've made about young women from working-class families in Jersey.

I'm going to flip your world around and serve it to you backwards, and in the end, we'll see who is bullying whom.

* * *

Billy

I unlatch the door when Grayson, one of our pack security guys, tells me Aubrey's on her way up. Then I return to my glass breakfast table by the floor-to-ceiling windows overlooking Central Park reading the *Times*. She can see herself in. She's not a guest in my home. She's here to work.

But I'm sniffing the air in anticipation of her nutmeg and honey scent. Sweetness and spice from the coffee shop where she works. I never thought it would become one of my favorite scents. After my showdown with my father, I've been looking forward to seeing her.

My father would fucking hate her. She's a human and proud of it.

Good. Going against my father's wishes is a win these days. And it'll prove to Madi I'm not controlled by prejudice. I might even gain some leverage over Madi by getting closer to her best friend. And I get to play Aubrey's boss. So many birds killed with one stone.

She struts into my place in a swirl of colorful chaos.

She's mayhem to my order. Pattern and color to my straight lines and monochromatic palette.

I would swear a warm breeze follows her in–the kind that promises pleasant weather after the nip and chill of winter.

My lip curls as I give her a cool glance from over my newspaper and take in her outfit. "You look like..." I break off.

It's in the high sixties today–a warm spring day but not hot by any means. Why in the fuck is she wearing those short jean shorts?

And her midriff is bare. Fate, does she have a pierced navel? A silver ring. Sexy as hell but would burn the fuck out of me if I railed her from the front. She'd better not have a clit piercing, too.

"*What?*" There's a challenge in her posture and her gaze. She didn't come here as some eager-to-please contractor.

She's here to fuck with me.

This mural idea is probably my most ill-conceived idea yet.

I need to take control back in this conversation. I give her a grim, assessing look, noting the sketchpad tucked under her arm.

"Did you bring your concepts?"

"I look like *what?*" She strides over her in clompy boots and stops in front of me, cocking a sassy hip.

I want to bend her over the table and teach her a lesson in subordination. I'd unbutton those jean shorts and shimmy them down to her upper thighs. Maybe caress that plump ass a few times before I spanked it.

"Like summer," I mutter.

She raises her brows. They're sculpted into perfect

arches. I have the urge to trace one with my fingertip, which is...disturbing.

But I want to touch some part of her. To put my hands on that bare waist and feel the texture of her smooth skin. To pick her up again and measure her weight. How would she feel straddling my hips and riding my cock?

Whoa. I just went way too far with that thought. My dick engorges with blood.

"Have a seat," I say because there's no way I can stand now without showing her effect on me. Not that I was going to stand, anyway. I need to establish some ground rules with her today.

I'm the boss.

She's working for me.

She slides into the chair opposite me with more grace than you'd expect from a girl stomping around in a pair of military boots, looking like she wants to kick someone's ass.

And she is just a girl. Twenty-three years old. A full decade younger than I am. I'm basically dealing with an insolent teenager here.

"Show me your concepts."

"Good to see you, too." Her smile tells me she's unfazed by my rudeness. "Thank you for the food delivery the other night. I have enough leftovers in my freezer for the month now."

I don't answer. I still don't know why I did it. Something about hearing her stomach growl had made my wolf antsy, and he couldn't stand me driving away without being sure she had enough to eat.

Which was stupid. She is a grown woman who feeds herself every day.

She flips open her sketchbook on the table and pushes it across to me.

The page has a neat rectangle marked out to designate the edges of the mural. Within the lines, she's sketched a cacophony of blooms. The perspective is close up, a la Georgia O-Keefe, but the canvas is packed with them, like they're pressing forward and tumbling off the page.

"This is for the color one," I say.

Aubrey smirks. "No."

There's challenge and innuendo in the syllable. She's testing me.

I stare at the sketch again. "You want to paint black and white flowers." I make my voice flat instead of lifting it in question.

She nods.

"And what design did you come up with for the color mural?"

She sits back in the chair. "I haven't decided yet. I want some time in your space for inspiration."

Oh, I'll inspire her.

I'll inspire her to take her clothes off. To spread those gorgeous thighs and scream my name at the top of her lungs when she comes.

To distract myself from that mental image, I pretend to examine the sketch. "Have you ever seen gray flowers?"

Her pouty lips spread into a wide smile. "Never." Her eyes are lit with challenge. "Have you?"

She's trying to prove that a colorless mural doesn't make sense.

With this tigress in my space, it feels true. Before she walked in, I found the palette soothing. It's also true that I find her disruptive, chaotic, and agitating.

I *really* need to fuck this female out of my system.

"Use this design for the other mural," I instruct.

"This is for the black and white one," she counters firmly.

She's fucking with me. Issuing a challenge. Trying to show me the folly of my ways.

One part of me–the most familiar part–wants to tear her to shreds. Give her a verbal dress-down, fire her from the project, and send her marching back to Brooklyn in those white patent-leather boots.

But then she wouldn't come back on Monday.

And I'd still have to deal with her for this bachelor / bachelorette party. And the wedding. Brick would be pissed at me for causing any ripples or discomfort for my luna.

Fuck.

The other part of me refuses to be taught a lesson by this she-devil. She wants to show me that a palette of grey is wrong?

Fuck that. I gave the constraint for this mural. She's the one who will have to make the mural beautiful within the constraint.

"Approved," I say flatly. "You'll start Monday?"

She quickly hides her flicker of surprise. "Yes. I can be here in the morning. How will I get in?"

The normal thing would be to give her a key. I'll be at work, after all. Or Grayson could escort her up and let her in.

"I'll be here," I say before I even realize I made up my mind.

Her brows rise. "You don't trust me in your place? What, do you think I'll steal the silver or something?"

"I think you require supervision."

Her lips part with indignation, but then she lets out a puff of laughter. "I think you have control issues."

I lock gazes with her. "Definitely."

She gives me that cat-that-ate-the-canary grin again. "Good luck managing *me*."

My dick gets hard. I have a half-dozen ideas of how I'd like to manage her. The punishments I'd issue when she misbehaved:

Clothing restrictions.

Spankings.

A ball gag.

Edging.

Tying her to the bed.

"Good luck *working under* me." I might have put a touch of innuendo in my retort.

She lets out another surprised chuff. Her eyes dilate like she's turned on. I catch the scent of her arousal over her nutmeg scent. Her swallow is audible.

This is the way I want her. Off-balance. Aroused. At my whim.

Now, I act the host. "May I get you something to drink?"

"Nope." She pops out of her chair, and I instantly regret giving her an escape. "I'll be on my way. I need to pick up supplies for the job."

I pull out my gold Amex and hand it to her.

Her thick lashes pop open when she reaches to take it. I don't relinquish the card, and she's trapped in my gaze.

"For your expenses. Or for any you incur for the bachelor party."

"I thought you didn't trust me with your things."

"Oh, I'd trust you with my thing." This time, the innuendo is clear. I release the credit card, and she flips it up to flag between us.

"Careful, Suit. You have no idea what you just unleashed."

Chapter Eleven

Billy

B After Aubrey leaves my apartment, I'm on edge.

I should go back to the Adirondacks to run off this aggression. Having Aubrey scantily clad in my penthouse made me cranky as fuck. The image of her bare legs and midriff keeps flickering in my mind. Her scent has me all keyed up, and now the need to jerk off is almost overwhelming.

But I have more control than that.

Besides, she'll be back Monday. I can exact my revenge for her ruining my weekend then.

Right now, I need to deal with my dear old dad.

He's still in town, and Boudicca was able to get a Maine pack member to tell her where he's staying. The residences at the Four Seasons are lovely, but out of my father's price range. His small Maine pack doesn't have the resources that we in the Blackthroat pack do. He's either abusing the pack's credit card–running it up for his own personal gain–

Renee Rose & Lee Savino

or someone like Aiden Adalwulf is bankrolling him. My dad's a piece of shit, so it's probably both.

It ends now.

I enter the lobby of the Four Seasons and head to the help desk. "I'm staying in the residences, but I've left my key card upstairs. William White," I flash my ID, and turn on the charm, so they won't notice that I'm not the William White they checked in.

With my new keycard, I stroll down the hallway of the fancy hotel like I own the place. When I get to my father's residence, I knock, and when someone comes to the door, I kick it in before they can open it fully.

The wolf behind the door grunts, knocked backwards as I rush him. It's one of my dad's enforcers, probably here acting as a bodyguard. "Hiya, Chip." I hit him hard enough to send him crashing to the floor. "Where's Dale?"

Dale rounds the corner, sees his fallen partner, and rushes me. With a swift jab to the throat, I take him out, too. A crushed windpipe won't kill a shifter, but it'll incapacitate him for a while.

My attack was brutal and efficient, just the way my father taught me.

My father peers around the corner and sees his enforcers laid out on the ground, groaning.

"What is the meaning of this?" He wasn't expecting a surprise attack from his favored son.

"You brought Chip and Dale," I jerk my thumb towards the half conscious enforcers.

"Their names aren't–"

"I don't care. Why did you bring them? Expecting trouble? From the Adalwulfs perhaps? I know you're probably trying to do a deal with them, but they're known for stabbing their business partners in the back."

104

He recoils, and I add, "Oh yes. I know you met with the Adalwulfs. Now you're going to tell me why?"

"Are you questioning me?" His nostrils flare, and he leans forward, transforming into a disapproving father figure before my very eyes.

But he lost the right to parent me a long time ago. "I am. On behalf of my pack. Tell me why you met with the Adalwulfs." He hesitates, and I bark, "Now, goddammit."

"I wanted to make a deal," my father speaks through gritted teeth, as if my order forced him to talk. "I tried to trade information about you to Aiden."

I thought I'd reached the depths of disappointment with my dad, but we're reaching a new lower limit. "In exchange for what?"

"A partnership. Investment into our pack—"

"You tried to sell my pack out for money. Let me guess, Aiden refused to deal." My dad presses his lips together, remaining silent, which tells me all I need to know. "You gave him all the information you had, which is not much, and then he said it wasn't enough and asked for more. Keeping you on the hook, seeing how far you're willing to go in betraying your own son. That's why you came to me asking for a wedding invite." I don't need him to confirm or deny. I know that's the play Aiden made. It's what I'd do. I don't blame the Adalwulfs for being snakes. The real traitor is my father.

As a pup, I almost killed myself trying to earn his approval. Be strong like him. But now, I see him clearly. He's weak. That's why he hates humans so much—he can't stand up to other wolves, so he punches down.

For some reason, Aubrey's face flashes in my mind. The thought of him ever turning his abusive gaze on her makes my wolf bristle. I don't even want him to know she exists in the world.

"You disgust me."

My dad's eyes flare bright. His wolf is showing. He wants to fight me, but he knows he can't. He's not strong enough to fight me and win. It's time I remembered that.

Still he blusters, "You dare come here–"

"No, I'm talking now." My father would love the story of how I breached my opponent's safe house and gained the upper hand even when outnumbered, except that in this case, he's the opponent. I'm using his own tactics against him. Not only that, but I'm doing it better than he ever did. The student has become the teacher, and it's time my dad learned this lesson. "You came to my city and met with my pack's enemies before knocking on my door. You're a weak alpha, leading an unimportant pack. You can't do much more than sniff around under our table for scraps, but I don't appreciate you trying to forge an alliance with the Adalwulfs before coming to me with your hand out."

"Unbelievable." Spittle flies from my father's mouth. "You cannot talk to me that way."

"I just did." It was a long time coming too. I feel fucking fantastic. "And now I'm telling you to pack your things and go back to Maine. Leave the underhanded deals to the pros."

William White II sputters. He's in full charlatan mode, shaking his finger at me while he stands on an imaginary soap box. I'm old enough to see him for what he truly is: a bullshitter to the end. He's got nothing: a pack he weakened with his own tyranny, a bunch of sycophants who can't even hold a hotel room against an intruder. All he can do is bluster. "The day is coming when you're going to need to choose a side."

"I've chosen my side. So it's up to you to decide whose side you're on. And I advise you to choose carefully."

I turn on my heel and stride back to the door, stepping over the writhing bodies on the way.

My father follows at a distance. He doesn't dare get close to me, and he's not going to lift a paw to help his pack-mates, either. "Blood is thicker than water," he calls from the end of the hall.

I stop short a foot away from the door. I can't stand it when people misquote things. "That's not the saying. The real phrase is: 'The blood of the covenant is thicker than water of the womb.' Which is the opposite of what people think the saying means. Thank you for coming to my Ted Talk."

"You'd side with Brick against your own father?"

I put my hand on the door, not bothering to turn around to answer. "That's what I'm telling you. If you don't believe me, then...feel free to fuck around and find out."

Chapter Twelve

ubrey

Monday morning, I show up at Billy's in an outfit that I deem *sexy-functional* for both painting and male torture. I'm in a pair of purple overalls with a white string bikini top underneath that looks great against my dark skin. My hair is pulled up on the top of my head, giving him a view of my long neck. I took the time to refresh my lip gloss in the elevator on the way up.

Yesterday, I went crazy with Billy's gold card, just to fuck with him. I was hoping he'd receive notifications because I made five separate purchases. I can't tell if he knows yet—I didn't get any protests, even after I bought and paid for delivery of everything new—drop cloths, paint brushes, and trays, a can of literally every color of paint, even though I'm starting with the black and white mural—ha! None of it was needed. He already has my drop cloths and paint supplies. All I really needed was a can of black paint and a can of white. Maybe some grays with warm undertones.

I try the knob without knocking and, like before, find it's open.

I pop my earbuds out. "Honey, I'm home!" It was a dumb joke the first time, and it's even dumber now, but my goal is to drive Billy nuts.

He's moved the furniture away from the wall I'm supposed to paint, and all the stuff I ordered is neatly stacked beside it. A stepladder leans against the wall. He even removed the sconce light fixture that I was planning on painting around. Or did he hire a handyman to do it?

I spot him sitting at the breakfast bar in the kitchen, sipping from a one-shot espresso cup while he works on his laptop. The cup looks miniscule in his large hands.

Damn, he has hot hands for a Wall Street billionaire. They're not manicured and pale; they're large, and they look strong. I've never thought about a man's hands before, but something about Billy's makes me wonder how they'd feel on my body. I remember how strong he was when he picked me up by the waist. Those fingers could close around my throat and probably choke the life out of me. I imagine the feel of his huge hand spanking my ass.

He barely spares me a glance.

Like last time, he's setting the tone. The message is that we're not friends. I work for him. Under him.

Oops. I shouldn't have had that thought, especially not after perving on his ham-hands. My nipples tighten under the bikini top. Moisture gathers between my legs.

His nostrils flare, and his head jerks up from his screen. He's suddenly up and moving toward me before I can plan my attack.

My strategy against his attempts to put me in my place is to keep playing it over-familiar. To spread my stuff everywhere. Take over the energy of his space.

Drive him out.

Except that thought doesn't land right. I don't actually want to make him crazy enough to leave. I rather enjoy the idea of him being here where I can torture him.

I rather enjoy the idea of being near him all day.

Maybe I should scratch this itch with him.

He arrives in front of me, and some of my breath leaks away. He stands too close. His position is too dominant. The way he looks down with that glower makes me lift my head and stare defiantly back. I wait for some reprimand about how much I've spent, but instead he asks gruffly, "What do you need?"

Your hand in my hair.

A hard fuck against the wall.

Whoops. I'm losing focus. Time to put him in *his* place.

I pop my earbuds back in my ears. My 80's Monday playlist is still rolling. "Nothing from you," I say airily and ignore him, spreading the dropcloth.

I feel the laser focus of his stare on my ass as I bend over and pull the cloth long.

He doesn't offer to help.

I just have to ask. "Did you remove the light fixture yourself?"

He frowns. "Of course."

"Wow."

He lifts his brows. "You find that impressive?"

"Well, you don't strike me as the handyman type."

He gives a faint shrug. "My father was the definition of toxic masculinity," he says. "There is no man-job I wasn't forced to learn by the time I was twelve. Removing a sconce took me thirty seconds."

Hmm. I find that surprising. I assumed he was spoon fed with silver and never forced to do a moment of manual labor. I file this new tidbit about him away to chew on later.

I keep working while he looks until he finally has had enough of being ignored and walks away, down the hall to what I presume is his bedroom.

Don't think about his bed. Or what it would be like to be tied to it.

I wonder if he's kinky like that. He's beyond dominant—he's domineering. But, as Madi and I conjectured, it could mean it's all about him. To tie me to the bed would be more about me.

Oh God. I need to stop this train of thought because I am getting more turned on by the minute.

I pull out a measuring tape and measure the wall, then set the ladder up against it, and make a light grid line of pencil marks.

This is the first thing I learned when I started painting murals. It's hard to get the full perspective on your work when you're working up close but creating something large-scale to be viewed at a distance. If you divide your initial sketch into grids, then make the same number of grids on the wall, you can easily blow up your vision. It's like creating pixels in digital images.

Once I have my grid lines set up, I take out my charcoal pencil and start sketching the outline of the largest flower on the wall.

The Boomtown Rats song "I don't like Mondays" plays in my ears, and I hum absently as I fall into the groove.

As the flower takes form, I get lost in the work, forgetting where I am. Forgetting I'm not alone. I don't realize I'm singing out loud until I hear what sounds like a groan from the bedroom.

* * *

Billy

She's *singing*.

Fucking singing.

And fuck me, she has the voice of a damn *angel*.

Except rather than lifting me, rather than transporting me, the beauty of her voice produces a ferocious wave of lust.

Add to that, the fact that she's wearing the exact white string bikini I pictured her in when I was imagining her on the beaches of Monaco, and my pants are way too tight at the crotch.

My canines sink into my lower lip as I stifle a groan.

I shouldn't have stayed home today. Her nutmeg scent filters everywhere in my penthouse—and more than that—I swear I caught the scent of her arousal when she arrived.

I walk into the en suite bathroom and turn on the faucet to cover any more groans. I can't take it. Either I blow off some steam, or I'm going to do something inadvisable to that human.

Something that involves slicing those overalls to shreds and pulling her miniscule bikini triangles to the sides to get at those luscious breasts.

I unzip my trousers and shove my hand into my boxer briefs to grip the base of my cock.

She got aroused the moment she walked into my penthouse. I had planned to ignore her, and then I caught the scent, and my wolf nearly pounced.

I squeeze my dick tight and slide my fist down to the head and back.

She wore that bikini top for me. I pump my fist faster.

Fuck, she definitely wore that top for me. And her nipples were hard when I prowled close.

So she's as physically attracted to me as I am to her.

That shouldn't be a surprise. She gave me shit from the first time I met her, but it always had a sensual edge to it. It wasn't the type of cold disdain I might have expected considering I had hurt her best friend. There was heat coming off her, but not the rage-filled kind.

The smoldering kind.

Like she knew she was a smoking hot goddess and wanted me to recognize it at the same time she showed me how little she thought of me.

My dick is rail-hard, balls heavy with cum. I beat off, letting myself go to my dirtiest thoughts.

Aubrey, naked and on her knees, her pillowy lips spanning the width of my cock.

Me feeding it into her wet mouth as she plays with my balls.

Fuck. Yeah...fate. Fuck.

My balls draw up tight and contract. I'd come on her face. No, on those breasts she taunted me with this morning.

Blood seeps in my mouth from the gashes in my lip, and I relish the pain. The moment of focus it gives me to...

I aim for the sink. Ribbons of cum spurt onto the counter, the floor. A tribute to that she-devil in my living room.

No, not a devil.

I have a moment of clarity following my release. My resistance to Aubrey drops away.

Of course she's not suitable. Not mate material.

She's human. She hates me.

But some part of me already thinks of her as mine. She's here in my penthouse. Doing my bidding.

She may be putting on a show about not doing my bidding, but the fact is, she's here because she wants to be here. She feels the chemistry between us, same as I do.

She's mine.

Chapter Thirteen

ubrey

I'm fully absorbed in my work when a heavy knock sounds at the door.

Startled, I shriek and teeter on the step of the ladder.

Strong hands grip my hips from behind, and I'm suddenly balanced and held perfectly still over my feet by Billy.

"Whoa." My hand flies to cover his. "Okay. I guess you got me."

His face is that blank mask, but he seems reluctant to let me go.

I can't say I mind.

After a moment, his grip eases, and he strides to the door without another word.

A delivery guy stands there with three large bags. Must be lunch–it smells heavenly. Like Thai food. He takes bags and tips the guy cash.

"Are you hosting a lunch meeting?"

He turns and frowns at me. "Why do you say that?"

"Are you going to eat all that food?"

"I wasn't sure what you wanted, so I got one of everything." His voice is grumpy, like he's pissed off he had to order one of everything for me.

Like he couldn't have just *asked* me what I wanted.

One of everything is what he sent to my door the night he drove me home from Sentience.

"Who in the world is going to eat all this?"

He doesn't answer, ignoring me and walking the food to the kitchen.

Suddenly aware that I'm starving, I trail behind him. I check my phone–it's already one-thirty. I worked straight through my usual lunch time. "Thank you. I didn't realize it was past lunchtime."

"I heard your stomach growling from in here." Billy plops the giant bags of food on the counter and starts taking out and opening containers.

Seriously, there's enough food for ten people here.

"That is when I could hear it over your singing."

Oh God. I was singing out loud. I feel my face get warm, but I quickly force the embarrassment down.

I lift my chin. "Singing is part of my process. If you don't like it, you might need to find another place to work."

Yeah, I definitely crossed the line now.

Billy's eyes glint in the light. He shows no irritation or trace of emotion on his face. "Did you sing at Sentience?"

I'm blushing again.

"Well, I don't know. I wasn't aware I was singing out loud until you pointed it out."

He arches a brow like he doesn't believe me. "I think you just want the attention." He cocks his head. With that sculpted jaw and sharp gray eyes, he's sexy as fuck, and I wish I weren't acutely aware of that fact. His voice drops to a low purr, and his lids droop slightly. "Do you want my attention, Aubrey?"

What a bastard.

I want to slap that smug expression right off his face even as my nipples harden into stiff points.

"Oh, trust me, Suit. When I want your attention, you'll know it."

His gaze trails from my face, down my heated neck. He angles his head to peer at my side-boob in the gap between the bib of my overalls. I purposely wore the bikini top because it highlights the swell of my breasts when you look at me from that angle.

He's pointing out that he's aware of that fact.

He knows I dressed for him.

Gah–that I wanted his attention.

Dammit!

He makes a show of lifting his head and meeting my gaze. "You sure about that?" He flicks his brows.

He brings his fingertip to the buckle on my overalls. "If I unhooked this, what would I find, Silver?"

"Silver?" I try to catch up, confused. First it was Cafe Girl. Now Silver.

"Silver. For the ring in your nose. And navel. You call me Suit. I call you Silver."

His fingertip caresses the button. I want him touching *me*, rather than the metal. My skin. My nipple.

He noticed my belly button ring. He has a pet name for me. I wasn't wrong that he's into me.

"Are your nipples hard for me, Aubrey?"

My pussy clenches. "No."

The corners of his lips lift in a ghost of a smile. "Liar."

He brings his other hand to the buckle. "I'm going to

119

unbuckle just one side of your overalls to find out. If I'm right, you leave it unbuckled the rest of the day."

Of course, the ruthless businessman likes to strike bargains. God, I want him to. I want to take this thing between us another step. What would be the harm?

Except my pride is at stake. I don't like letting him win at anything. He's a white cis male billionaire who works on Wall Street. He already owns the world. He could have any woman.

But I'm not any woman.

And I'm not going to let him seduce me so easily.

I bat his hand away. "No deal." Then I cross the line by reaching out and pinching his nipple. Beneath the crisp, thousand dollar button down and the undershirt, I feel the thick stub of his man-nipple, and it's hard, like mine.

"Looks like *you're* the one who's hard," I taunt.

He grabs my wrist, moving lightning fast. "Now who's touching without consent?" His voice is low and dangerous.

The hairs on the back of my neck stand up at the threat, even though I'm 99 percent sure it's all sexual.

Oh God.

Something crazy happens to me while he's holding my wrist. The flesh between my legs doesn't just squeeze. It spasms. I'm having a mini-orgasm just from having my wrist clamped by Billy Billions.

His nostrils flare, and he lowers his head and inhales, as if he's breathing in my scent.

Before I know it, my back hits the kitchen cabinets. "Do you like a dominant touch, Aubrey?" His voice is pure sin. I didn't know you could pack that much sex, lust, and innu-endo into a few words.

Another orgasm drives up to the cusp.

"N-no." The backs of my knees tremble. Heat flushes down my arms and legs. Between my breasts.

I have a hard time catching my breath.

"Another lie. I just made you come when I grabbed your wrist. You're about to come again now, aren't you?"

Oh God.

I *am*.

My inner thighs shiver. Everything in me coils, like a mousetrap set to spring.

I'm pissed as hell at myself when a little whine of submission comes out of my throat. No. I'm not going to lose this battle. I'm not going to–

"I won't move another muscle." He's so close, his breath is warm on my face. His blue eyes have a strange, silvery glint to them. "But I'll bet if I just moved my knee between those sweet thighs and give you something to press against, you'll give me another one."

"I...won't." My voice sounds strangled. I'm too mesmerized by my body's reaction to him to throw it back in his face–something I'm normally adept at.

"Should we test it?" he murmurs.

I don't want him to.

Wait–yes, I do.

Do I?

I never want to give him the upper hand–I know that much. But damn, if I don't want to let this moment play out. I know he's right. I could grind down on his thigh and come–*hard*.

Harder than a moment ago.

I try and fail to swallow. Then I manage to croak, "On your knees."

The only way I will come again is if I get to take back the upper hand, and he services me.

Again, he moves faster than I would've thought possible. Like a gun already loaded and cocked, he yanks my overalls down on his way to the floor. His thumb catches my clit even before he's ripped my panties to the side with his other hand.

I brace my hands on his broad shoulders, pushing away even though I want him closer. The moment he presses my nubbin with the pad of his thumb, I come, but he doesn't wait for me to finish. He goes in for the kill.

His tongue slides between my exposed labia, and he penetrates me with his middle finger.

"Jesus!" I gasp. My orgasm pulses around his finger, every muscle below my waist shaking and clenching.

He pushes the hood of my clit up and gets his lips around it, managing to suction them over the tiny bundle of nerves. He slides a second finger inside me, curling them to stroke my inner wall.

I cry out, squeezing more.

I can't believe I'm still orgasming. We didn't even have sex. Well, I guess this is sex, but I usually need penetration to come.

"Billy..."

He pauses and looks up at me. His lips shine glossy with my juices, and his eyes have a weird silvery glow to them— the way a cat's catch the light at night.

His expression is feral, but some of the wildness fades as he looks at me, and then smugness sets in.

Damn him.

My stomach growls.

His brows lower, and he eases his fingers from my sopping channel and puts them in his mouth to suck my juices off.

I thought he was going to pick me up and carry me to

the bedroom. I mean, this was foreplay. Now we could've scratched the itch we both had and gotten it over with. Maybe even call this whole mural farce thing off afterward. Although I already used the fifty percent retainer he sent me to pay down my student loans, so maybe I wouldn't push for that.

But apparently, he thinks we're done. He pulls my white lace panties up–the ones I wore to match the white bikini top–then slides my overalls back on.

My belly flutters as he does. It's weird to let him take care of me this way.

Not weird because I don't usually let guys take care of me–I do. But weird because I wouldn't have thought he was capable of it.

I wouldn't have thought he knew how to be intimate. Or tender.

I remember what Madi said–that he's very good at knowing what people want.

But I gave him no reason to believe I want anything from him besides ripping him a new one every time he walks in the room.

He slides one of the straps over my shoulder but unbuckles the other one, letting the front bib fold on the diagonal to expose my breast. Then he brushes the back of his knuckle over my peaked nipple. "I was right."

* * *

Billy

Aubrey tastes like heaven. Like something foreign and familiar at the same time.

Like mine.

It's a damn good thing I jacked off earlier, or I wouldn't

have been able to hold myself back. I would've yanked her down to the floor and fucked her into oblivion.

But as it is, I won this round. I gave her a hint of the pleasure she could have with me.

Now she'll want more.

The first taste is free.

The next time, you'll pay for it, darling.

She'll pay with her submission. I want her body and soul. Fully surrendered to me. Mine for the ravishing.

Right now, she can't decide if she's pissed or pleased with me. She's weighing whether I have the upper hand.

If she needs to fight back.

I let her regain her dignity by turning to the cabinet and pulling out two plates. "What would you like to eat?" My voice is almost friendly. My usual clipped tones have softened into something warmer.

I can't deny the buoyancy in my body. My wolf celebrates getting hands on the lush human.

It's satisfying despite the fact that she's everything I don't want in my life. I may love the way she tastes, but I definitely don't need anything more from her. My life is complete without a chaotic artist who shatters my sense of order and structure.

Who invades my sanctuary and makes it into her personal playground.

I hand her a plate, and we make eye contact for a moment as she accepts it.

I swear I see the exact moment she decides to just relax and let me take care of her. The oxytocin from the orgasm is probably flooding her body with feel-good, bonding sensations.

That's right, Silver. No sense in fighting me.

I always win.

It's just a matter of how you want to feel as you go down.

She could enjoy having my dick down her throat. Or she could choke on it. Either way, it was going to happen.

That was a crass metaphor only, of course. I never take a female without full consent.

I watch her pile food on her plate, and my wolf preens at having satisfied her in two ways today.

But she hasn't satisfied me yet, the ruthless businessman in me protests, examining whether the trade was fair.

Not true. I am satisfied. I have her exactly where I want her. In my penthouse, beholden to me. Working for me. I have her juices on my tongue, and she just gave me two beautiful orgasms.

My wolf is satisfied.

I am satisfied.

I can't fucking wait to see how she looks when she begs for more. Or how she looks when I give her a ride on my dick.

I'm suddenly harder than marble.

Fuck, I wait until my erection lowers before I take my food to the table by the window where she's already invited herself to sit.

No sense in giving her any sense of power.

My goal is to completely strip her of it and leave her breathless and begging for more.

She may not know this, but there's no negotiation I haven't won.

She pops her earbuds in when I sit down, her version of giving me the middle finger. I hear the cheesy strains of 80's pop coming through them.

She eats quickly, then stands, and waltzes to the kitchen, where she rinses her plate and drops it in the dish washer. I half expected her to leave it in the sink as another message to me, but doing her fair share is likely too ingrained in her.

She wasn't born into pack royalty like me or Brick. She works hard for her money.

She starts singing "Manic Monday" loudly as she sashays back to the living room.

Now she's just fucking with me. I have virtual meetings this afternoon with my team members. I can't have her voice be heard in the background, no matter how gorgeous it is.

Especially because of how gorgeous it is.

My wolf hackles suddenly rise in possessiveness. *Mine.*

No one else gets to hear her.

See her.

Touch her.

Because he sends a rush of aggression to the fore, I snap, "No singing."

Aubrey stops and slowly turns to look over her shoulder. "I require music to work."

"I have meetings this afternoon. I require perfect silence."

Her chin tucks down, a smile spreading across her lovely face. That smile is a warning. If she was a wolf, she'd be ready to pounce.

Her eighties music obsession must be rubbing off on me because the first riff of *Running with the Devil* starts to play in my head.

Fuck. This human doesn't know she's dealing with a big bad bully.

This should be fun.

Chapter Fourteen

ubrey

A I find a bench at Penn Station and sink into it.

I wrapped things up late this afternoon and slipped out while Billy was on a video call. The last thing I needed was him insisting on driving me home today.

Or following me.

Because I'm meeting with Jamie and Jan here to talk about where we are on the Sentience case.

Jamie's been super paranoid–I can't tell if it's legit, or she's just scared, but she didn't want to meet us at La Résistance this time.

A guy with weird energy slides onto the bench next to me, and I scoot over to put space between us. He's wearing a baseball cap and a surgical face mask–the type a Covid-cautious person would wear–and his head is down.

"It's me."

My head jerks up sharply to identify Jamie under the cloak and dagger clothes.

"Don't look."

I lean to the side to look past her, like I'm checking out a sign.

"Everything okay?" I ask.

"No. I'm still being watched. How about you?"

Cold tendrils of fear filter into my chest at that question. But no, I'm not being watched by anyone except for Billy White.

Who I'm not going to think about right now.

Definitely not thinking of how it felt to have his tongue between my legs.

"No, all clear."

Jan arrives, looking slightly annoyed about this meeting place. "This is where you wanted to meet?" she snaps.

"Shh," Jamie warns, jumping to her feet and putting her back to us.

Jan slides onto the bench next to me.

Jamie angles her body toward ours, but folds her arms over her chest and looks over our heads. "Did you get a security keycard?"

"A security card?" Jan frowns. "Why does she need that?"

"The hard drive wasn't enough," I say, looking to Jamie for confirmation. "We need access to the servers."

Jan is already shaking her head. "This is going too far."

"Jan–"

"No, Aubrey, this is too much. Too risky. And I can't use anything obtained illegally."

"Can't you subpoena it?" I ask, remembering our last conversation.

"We don't have enough to file a suit, yet."

"But we will, if we can get the email server," Jamie murmurs.

"Again–" Jan is totally impatient with the conversation now, but I can see both sides.

"If we had the email server contents, they wouldn't be admissible in court, but they could be leaked to the *New York Times*, like you said at our last meeting. Then the District Attorney might pick up the case and subpoena everything."

Jan takes a deep breath and sighs. "I'm not behind any plan that involves breaking and entering."

"It's already done," I say. "I have the keycard already. That's what you need, right, Jamie?"

"It's step one," Jamie says. "I need you to break into the server room, too."

"What?" Jan and I say at the same time.

"I thought I had someone who would do it for me. But he changed his mind."

Jan and I exchange looks. We both feel uneasy with Jamie including another person in our conspiracy.

Jamie doesn't seem to notice our worried faces. "And it can't be me–I can't be on the premises. But you, Aubrey–"

"Absolutely not," Jan says. "I don't want you in there."

I gnaw on my lower lip.

I don't want to do it, either, but who else can? Jamie's already being watched. I have a semi-excuse to be in the building. Or at least I could claim one.

"I'll get back in there. There's a gala to unveil the mural, and I'm invited. If it's easy to slip away from the party and get down to the server room, I'll do it. If not, I'll abort."

"I'm not going to answer to your parents about why I let something happen to you," Jan says. "If you do this, I won't represent either of you."

I stare at Jan in surprise. *Damn.* Tough love.

Jamie's watching my face with a worried expression. She's counting on me to make this right. She risked and lost her job over her ideals. Ideals that I share. She would do more, but she thinks she's being watched.

I rise to my feet. "I'll see what I can do. No promises," I say.

"Aubrey–" Jan sounds upset.

I wave my hand. "Don't worry. I've got this. I won't take unnecessary risks."

She frowns and shakes her head. "I don't want you in there again."

"Understood." I raise my brows to punctuate the firmness in my voice. She doesn't want it. I do. I'm an adult who can make my own choices.

Her shoulders sag, and she shakes her head. "We'll talk more later," she says as she moves away.

I glance at Jamie. "If I can pull this off, what do you need me to do?"

"There's a jump drive in my coffee cup," she nods to the paper cup she left beside the bench. I didn't even notice it. "Once you're in, you'll insert that into any server. It'll give me a back door window into their entire network."

My mouth goes dry as I process what she's telling me. I'm basically helping her hack into a billion-dollar company. "Are you sure?"

"You got this," she says.

I nod and pick up the cup. It rattles a little—there's no liquid inside, just the jump drive.

Yeah.

I've got this.

I owe it to artists around the world. It's not right for a big corporation to steal their work and then stalk its former employees to intimidate them out of whistle-blowing. It's not right, and someone has to stand up to them.

I have an in there.

It has to be me.

Chapter Fifteen

illy
B   I take the elevator up to the rooftop helipad at six p.m.

I missed Aubrey leaving my place, but I put a tracker in her phone.

What? I'm not obsessed. I just have trust issues, and I'm controlling as fuck. Aubrey works for me now, which means I need to know what she's up to. Whether she can be trusted.

By the time I got off my afternoon video call, she was at Penn Station. She didn't take a train, though. Judging by the way her tracker stayed in one place for twenty minutes then exited the station, it looks like she had a meeting with someone.

In the busiest train station in the city.

If that's not highly suspicious, I don't know what is.

I also didn't buy her story about painting a mural for Sentience. A woman like her–a social justice warrior / artist–wouldn't take a job for them out of principle.

They are the devil to the lefties. They exploit child

labor in third world countries to scan and upload the information they feed their artificial intelligence, and everyone knows they don't compensate the original creators of that content.

She, as an artist, would take exception to their blatant thievery.

So that makes me think she's there for subterfuge. I searched her bag this morning while she was using the bathroom and found one very interesting item—a keycard to Sentience with the photo of the bastard she'd given a hug to the night I picked her up.

I still want to stomp him into the ground, but my wolf nearly did a backflip when I realized she might have hugged him to steal the card.

The alternative thought is that they're screwing, and he left it at her place.

Maybe she went to Penn Station to meet him to return it.

Fuck!

If that's the case, I will throw him off the roof of the Sentience building and watch him scream.

Right now, the tension of it all has me nearly feral, which is why I have to get to the woods. My wolf needs to be off-leash.

The helicopter touches down on the roof helipad. We have one here and one on the top of Moon Co. When I called the company pilot, John Acker, to pick me up, he said he was already scheduled for a trip out to the Adirondacks, but there was room for one more.

Sure enough, Jake, Vance, and Sully are sitting in the back of the helicopter. I climb into the front passenger seat and put on the headset.

I twist and give them a salute. "Going for a run?"

"Hell, yeah." Jake rolls his stacked shoulders. "There's only so much tension you can work out in the gym."

Sully nods his agreement.

"Where the fuck were you all day?" Vance demands.

I turn back to face front to give them my back and end the conversation. "Working from home."

"Why?" Vance won't let it drop.

I don't answer.

"Are you fucking her?" Sully's voice is flat.

I want to kill him. As our pack enforcer, he makes everyone's business his business. He's not just the muscle, he's a full security firm packed into one guy.

"You sure you want to go there? I doubt you want me to dig into your sex life."

Sully is a sadist who frequents BDSM clubs. If he weren't our enforcer, I would consider his sex habits a pack vulnerability considering how many different females he's played with over the years. But he's careful, and he understands his job is to eliminate all liabilities from the pack and Moon Co.

He chuckles at my rejoinder. "So you *are*. I was just taking a wild guess when I saw her in the elevator, and you didn't come in."

I remember the taste of her on my tongue. The way she threw her head back and gasped as she came. She's the reason I need to shift to wolf form and run tonight. There's too much power and potency vibrating through my cells right now. I need to tear something apart. Run until my paws ache. Fuck.

I can't do the latter tonight, but tomorrow she'll be back in my penthouse. I can't fucking wait.

"Brick ordered me to liaise with Madi's human contingent for the wedding. That's what I'm doing."

"What kind of *liaising* are we talking about?" Jake joked.

"I'm serving my alpha," I growl.

All three of them chuckle, and I want to throw them out of the helicopter one by one.

"Sounds to me like you're serving a human. Or is she serving you?" Vance pokes.

My wolf tears to the surface. I lunge through the seats to punch Vance in the nose. I'm too fast for him to block, and he roars in protest as the bones crack.

The pilot shouts, "Hey!" but something in my face must tell him to mind his own fucking business because he turns his attention back to the windshield.

Vance straightens his nose. He's a healthy shifter–it will heal by morning. I made a point, no more.

"Fuck," Jake mutters. "There's really something going on here."

I want to snarl, "No, there's not!" but I know it would just make me sound weak.

Make it seem true.

It's not true.

Of course, it's not fucking true.

She's a human. A nobody. She hates my kind. I have no use for her kind. We're incompatible in every way.

Okay, I need to put this to bed right now.

I suddenly realize how wrong I played this. I should've made her seem like a toy.

"She's nothing," I mutter, turning around because I know my eyes are still glowing the pale grey shade of my wolf's, and I don't want the guys to see. "Just a piece of pretty ass and a duty to my alpha."

"Dude, there's nothing wrong with screwing a human," Sully says.

"Yeah, he does it all the time." Jake hooks a thumb in Sully's direction.

"I know your dad is kind of a Nazi about them, but you gotta get over that. Especially with Madi as our luna," Sully continues.

Great. Now they're therap-izing me. This is the last fucking thing I need.

But I have to stop reacting. I showed too much already.

"She's not my first human," I lie.

I'm a good liar. I had to be growing up with a psychopathic father. Shifters can smell lies, so I learned to shut off all emotional responses when in tricky conversations. It's what makes me the best deal-maker and fixer for Brick.

For some reason, I've lost all control of my ability tonight.

Still, I think they've bought it until I hear Vance mutter something that sounds like a dubious, "Uh huh."

Chapter Sixteen

ubrey

A Just to fuck with Billy, I charge my scone and morning coffee to his Gold Card on the way to Central Park. I can't decide if he's the kind of guy who is so rich he won't even notice or enough of a control freak that he'll try to nail my ass to the wall for it. I strut down the sidewalk in a pair of paint-splattered ripped jean cut-offs with fishnets under them and a push-up bralette under a button-down paint shirt that I took from my dad's discard pile years ago.

My mom saves all cast-offs for me to use as paint clothes or rags.

I'm walking along the sidewalk in front of Billy's building when a blue Toyota pulls up to the curb. The back door opens and someone chucks a cardboard box onto the sidewalk before the car drives away.

Everyone on the sidewalk freezes, giving it the side eye. I guess we're expecting a bomb. Or poisoned gas or something, but a little yip sounds from within the container.

Oh shit.

"Hey!" I yell at the departing car and march over.

Some assholes just abandoned their dog.

"What dicks," I mutter to myself as I pry open the top flaps of the box. Inside is the cutest little salt and pepper puppy. He's some kind of mutt, I'm guessing, with long matted hair covering its big brown eyes.

"Oh, baby!" I croon, picking him up.

He promptly pees a little on me. "Shit!" I mutter and hold him away from my body, angled away.

"What's up, cute thing?"

He tries to lick my face. "Don't you have the sweetest little floppy ears?" I use my baby-talk voice. "Did someone throw you out?"

His hind end wiggles with the force of wagging his tail.

"You're a sweet thing. Who would want to give you up?"

I look up and down the street. His owners are long gone, not that they deserve to be pet owners. What am I going to do? I'm not taking this puppy to a shelter, and I need to find a good home for him.

My apartment doesn't allow pets.

I'm also supposed to be at Billy's in two minutes.

A loose plan takes shape in my head, and my lips kick up a notch.

Yes. Showing up with a puppy will make Billy White the Third flip his proverbial lid. And I definitely want to see his reaction.

I lift the pup to my shoulder and carry him with one arm, gripping my coffee with the other hand.

Let the fireworks begin.

The doorman holds the door open for me as I approach.

"Hi, Grayson." I made a point of learning the giant

burly guard's name yesterday. I'm trying to get him past the formal phase, but he resists.

"Ms. Cook." He gives the puppy a slightly alarmed look. "Does Mr. White know you're bringing a dog to his premises?"

"It couldn't be helped." I breeze by him, straight to the elevators, even though I know he has to use his keycard for me to access Billy's floor.

The puppy barks at Grayson, squirming in my arms to be let down.

"Nuh uh." I turn the pup to look at me and give him a stern look. He attempts to lick me.

Grayson steps into the elevator, presses his keycard to the sensor, then hits the button for Billy's floor.

The puppy barks at him again.

"Good luck with that." He sounds dry, which makes me think we are actually becoming friends after all.

I flash him a broad smile. "I'm expecting the worst."

As the doors close, I catch his brows pop in surprise, and I hear him mutter, "Oh, boy," as the elevator ascends.

When I arrive on the upper floor, Billy's door is open, and I waltz in, ready for him to freak out.

He's in the kitchen, making an espresso. His hair is still wet from a shower, his pinstriped button-down shirt gaps open at the throat. A tie with black and gray stripes lies beside him on the kitchen counter.

Oh...damn. I'm unprepared for how hot this not-quite-dressed look is on him. I wonder what he'd look like stepping out of the shower. Is there hair on his chest? Or is he the kind of guy who waxes his back and chest?

I wonder what it would be like to be tied up with that tie of his...

So many unanswered questions.

The biggest one is, will I find out the answers to all of them? I know I could. The better question is, should I?

Billy's nostrils flare as he whirls to look at me.

"What. Is. *That*?" He metes his words out like punishment.

"This little guy just got thrown out of a car." I lift the pup's face to mine to give his head a kiss.

"And you brought it here, why?"

To torment you.

"Where else was I going to bring it?" I ask with mock innocence.

"To the pound. Where abandoned mutts belong."

As if the little dog senses his disapproval, it tucks its little tail and whimpers.

He strides toward us, and the dog whimpers louder. "Did it pee on you?"

"What? You can smell it?" I hold the dog away to survey where the pee dribbled. It wasn't that much—I can't believe he can smell it.

He reaches for the dog, and I pull the little guy away to protect him.

Billy's mask is his usual cruel visage, but he doesn't appear any more annoyed than other times. "Give me the mutt. You go clean up."

I hesitate. I seriously don't trust this guy not to throw the dog off his balcony.

Well, maybe that's too ungenerous. I hold the dog out doubtfully, and he takes it, lifting the pup eye to eye with him. "Be nice to Pepper."

"You *named* him already?"

I give him a flippant *why wouldn't I?* shrug.

Pepper whimpers and tries to lick Billy.

He stares at Pepper for a moment. I don't know what in

the hell he's doing—but then he says, "that's right," like they've come to some understanding.

Since I was going for a sexy vibe and smelling like dog pee isn't, I take his advice and head to the bathroom to get cleaned up.

When I return, I find him with his shirt sleeves rolled up, his watch on the counter by the tie. The corded muscles of his forearms flex as he washes the dog in his kitchen sink.

Oh, damn.

My ovaries just dropped an egg. Maybe two.

That should not be so sexy, but for some reason, it winds my crank. I'm not sure if it's the view of his forearms, the semi-domestic sight of him at the sink, or seeing the normally cold, stiff asshole doing something generous for another being.

Even if that being is a little dog.

The drenched waif shivers, tail wagging, big brown eyes staring adoringly up at Billy.

He looks over at me. "What do you intend to do with this thing?"

I set my paper cup down on his glass coffee table and kick off my boots. "Honestly? I haven't developed a plan beyond annoying you by bringing him here."

Billy's eyes shine in that strange silver-blue sheen they sometimes take on. "Was that your plan with the credit card, too?"

Something about being called out makes my nipples tighten. Like I want him to punish me over this. Want to see what happens when the mighty Billy Billions attempts to flex his power over me.

Which doesn't make sense, since I spend all of my waking hours scheming about how to keep my power over him.

I cock a hip. "Is it working?"

"No."

"Good. Because I plan to use it to buy stuff for Pepper."

He turns off the water and grabs a kitchen towel to dry off the dog. When he finishes, he sets the sweet pup down on the floor and strides over to me. The little dog follows right at his heels, his whole butt wagging with the force of his tail.

"Good boy, Pepper!" I croon. "Are you all clean?" Yes, I'm talking to the dog to distract myself from the approaching danger.

I try not to look at Billy's bare forearms. They're not that sexy. They're not sexy. Oh God—*why are they so damn sexy?*

Billy comes right up to me, crowding into my space. "What reaction were you looking for?" If I didn't feel the electric magnetism pulling my body toward his, I might find him intimidating. I'm sure his employees cower when he brings this forbidding expression.

I put a hand on his chest to push him back, and he catches my wrist and twists it, spinning me until it's pinned behind my back. It doesn't hurt, but the agility of the move shocks me. Like this guy is some kind of Taekwondo expert or something.

He uses his grip on my wrist to pull me flush against his body. "Are you waiting for me to punish you?" His voice is a low rumble. So sexy. He's so close I can smell his minty fresh breath. I'm acutely aware that mine probably smells like coffee. I close my lips.

His eyes track the movement.

"I had a feeling that's what you were into," I accuse, trying to turn it back on him. I hate how breathless I sound.

A feral smile creeps onto his face. I'm not sure I've ever

seen him smile before. It changes his entire face. Makes him twenty times more handsome. "Oh, I'm definitely that guy."

Everything in me ignites, turning my insides to molten lava. My pussy gets wet–dripping wet. I'm close enough to examine his perfectly shaven square jaw. The divet in his chin. The patrician nose.

"I had a feeling you crave being overpowered." The velvet bass of his voice seems to lick between my legs.

I get dizzy with the impact of his observation. It's not something I ever identified in myself, but the words ring some internal bell so soundly it's like every nerve ending in my body reacts.

I don't like how out of control I feel. How exposed. "You wish." I throw as much scorn into the words as I can.

The ghost of a smile reappears around the corners of Billy's lips. I find it alarmingly enticing. "Silver," he rumbles, "I watched you come in the middle of my kitchen just from me *grabbing your wrist.*"

A puff of breath leaves my lips. He has me off balance right now, and I hate it. God, I still can't believe he saw that!

"I could make you come again in less than sixty seconds right now. Just say the word."

My pulse picks up speed. Word. *Word!* Yes, please. Except no. I can't give him the satisfaction.

I draw scorn around me like a cloak. "Full of yourself much?"

He gives me a cool look. I'm burning up, and he's all calm containment. "I'm just stating facts. I think you want to know what it's like to have all control wrested from you."

Something squirmy happens in my belly–a mixture of excitement and tension. I deny it all. "You don't know anything about me."

He tilts his head, still cool as a summer popsicle. "I

know a bit. For the rest, I have some guesses. You want to hear them?" I'm still his captive, my arm twisted behind my back, my front pulled against his body. I'd fight for my freedom, but he's right—I love feeling his strength and power. And I want to know what happens next.

I lift my free hand and make a beckoning motion— the kind you see in martial arts movies. *Show me what you've got, Suit.*

"Let's hear it."

"You're attracted to me, but you also actively dislike me. Which is why you don't want to give me anything, including your smoking hot body. You think you can't trust me. Understandable. For one thing, I screwed over your best friend—an act I partially regret."

I open my mouth to demand why only partially, but he's on a roll.

"For another, you have a hang-up with Wall Street guys in general. Or maybe just the broad swatch of the wealthy. You assume I'm conservative, politically, because I love money, and you're so far left, you're coming around the bend to the right. Regardless, I'm about as far from your type as they come." He tilts his head to the side. His gray gaze bores into me. "Maybe that's part of the attraction."

Now I interrupt because I can't let my anger go unregistered. "Why do you only *partially* regret screwing over Madi?" I demand.

"Protecting Brick from any and all threats to his company is my job. Especially if he's lost perspective because he's thinking with his dick—or his heart as the case turned out to be."

It's weird to hear Billy Billions speak of anyone's heart. I wouldn't think he even knew the organ exists.

"So I don't regret my impulse to expose any threats. But

146

I do regret that I was mistaken about the direction of the threat, and I hurt them both."

Hmm. That implies he cares about Madi's feelings now. That would be a change. Madi still doesn't trust him, but I believe him.

"But back to you." He starts to massage the heel of my hand—the one he has bent behind my back. His thumb kneads the aching muscles in my palm. Wow. Who knew my fingers were so achy from painting yesterday?

"Go on." I'm not sure if I'm encouraging his observations or his touch.

"I think you suspect—and you'd be right—" he arches a sexy brow– "that I can deliver on every fantasy you've ever had about giving up control. You want to know what it's like to be tied up by me."

He abandons massaging my hand and slides his large palm lightly over my butt cheek. The heat of his skin registers through my shorts and fishnets. "Blindfolded in my bed." He squeezes my ass. "Cuffed to my ceiling." His touch lightens again, and I sense one finger trace the seam of my ass cheeks. Somehow, he hooks one finger to burrow between them, exactly over my anus.

The sensitive nerve endings there respond to the stimulation. Tension coils in my core.

"You want me to pull you across my lap and spank this gorgeous ass until it's hot to the touch."

Oh dear lord. I'm going to come again.

He must sense it because I note the smugness creeping into his expression. He goes on, mercilessly. "You want to know what it's like to be held down while I fuck you hard."

I find myself breathless, staring into his pale gray eyes. So far, he's dead on.

He brings his other hand to the front of my hips,

between our bodies. The moment he cups me from the front, stimulating both my anus and clit at the same time, I go off.

My hips buck, and I gasp. I'd lose my balance except I'm sandwiched between his strong arms. It's hardly anything–he's not moving his fingers. Not rubbing or circling. He's just applying pressure to both places and making me come like I've never been touched before.

He leans his head forward and bites my neck, a little too hard.

I jerk at the sensation.

The bulge of his cock tents his trousers and presses against my belly. I'm about to reach for it and give him pleasure in return, but the smug bastard gloats, "A little over sixty seconds, but still, here we are again."

I'd push away, but I don't want it to stop.

Now he starts to slowly slide the fingers cupping my pussy up and down, stroking over my clothes. An aftershock rolls through me like a wave of pleasure washing up on the beach.

"I think you want to have control taken from you so you don't have to be in charge for a change. You're a highly capable, intelligent, and creative powerhouse who has been moving mountains all by herself, probably from a young age. You want someone else to take the lead for a change."

That makes my eyes sting. Maybe he does really see me. Until this moment, I believed he only saw what I wanted him to see. The bad-ass best friend of the girl he screwed over. The one who was going to make him pay for his sins.

Now I'm suddenly exposed. Wondering how and when he peeked past my fortress of defenses to see a real person, not a caricature.

The finger between my ass cheeks presses in with a slow pulse. I grind against his hand in front.

"You want to pretend you're at my mercy while knowing you're safe." He lifts his head and catches my gaze. I suspect my eyes are glassy because it's hard to focus on his handsome face. "Aubrey, you can trust if you say no at any point, I'll respect it."

Now he's not observing me, he's offering something.

"I propose a mutually beneficial arrangement. You retain your right to all your scorn and disdain for me while still submitting to pleasure at my hands." He gives another delicious rub of his fingers between my legs and another ripple of pleasure releases. "I guarantee your sexual satisfaction, your physical and emotional safety, and an absence of any commitment or a relationship."

* * *

Billy

Something in Aubrey's scent turns sour. I catch a flash of anger in her brown eyes.

I immediately release her, and she stumbles back.

As I watch her expression shutter, my wolf surges to the fore. I almost had her. He's furious I let the opportunity slip by.

"I sense I missed something that is important to you," I say.

The more we get out in the open, the better I can negotiate. I need to know what her pain points are. What she wants from me. What she won't stand for.

What did I leave out? She can't possibly want a relationship. She would never want to be associated with a man like me. Just like I wouldn't want to be associated with a female like her. A human. A hippie artist who leaves a wake of chaos and trouble behind her.

I shrug my shoulders in the most casual way I can manage. "This is a negotiation. Feel free to submit your counteroffer."

The mutt she brought to annoy me chooses this moment to bark. He's some kind of Shih-poo mutt–still a puppy. Probably the runt of the litter. We have that in common.

"Uh-uh." I make the reprimand sharp, and he instantly responds, lowering his head and rolling to his back to show his belly. At least he's smart.

Mastering a dog is easy for a shifter. The pup recognizes my alpha dominance, and we share low-level telepathy as fellow pack animals.

Aubrey's face is flushed, giving her brown skin a glorious glow. She lifts her chin at me. "I'm the one in charge. *You* submit."

Ha. She's fucking adorable. A hundred times cuter than the little rat of a puppy at our feet gazing up at me with his big brown eyes. Aubrey wants on top. I love it.

I'm reminded of last Christmas when Brick's four-year-old niece, April, put us all in her "jail" and then served us tea with her new china tea set. She was intoxicated by the power gifted to her by six hulking adult male shifters willing to pretend to be at her will for a half an hour.

So, sure. Like with Ruby's pup that afternoon, I'll play along. If Aubrey wants to call the shots in bed, I'll let her ride on top. Or sit on my face. Or whatever her wild and weird imagination can conjure. I'm happy to give her the illusion of control, so long as my wolf gets to taste her. Nevermind that I could physically overpower her with the twitch of a finger.

Her pillowy lips press together. The silver nose ring

winks at me. I can tell she expects me to reject her counter-offer. In fact, she thinks there's no way in hell I would ever submit to her in bed.

But she underestimates my masculine security. She couldn't possibly know I was raised by an alpha who was the definition of toxic masculinity. His paranoia that my small size as a youth would mean I wouldn't grow to alpha size and take his place made him relentless in indoctrinating me in all things he considered masculine.

By the time I was ten, I could fight and win any match against sixteen and seventeen-year-olds in my pack. I fought with claws and teeth to win my battles. I was vicious. Unrelenting. And always on the offense. By the time I was a teen and still hadn't hit the growth curve, I could outwit, outmaneuver, or outrace any adult in the pack.

I didn't complete my growth spurt until well into college, when my father had already written me off, and I'd won the position as Brick's second in command. Brick found in me a ferociously loyal pack brother. And beyond that, with him or any of my new pack members, I had nothing to prove.

I don't need glory. I don't have to save face. I'll play the bad guy or take the fall for any of my brothers.

I open my hands and spread them. "I'm yours to command."

* * *

Aubrey

I stare at Billy, shocked.

I would not have seen this coming from any direction. He just...doesn't strike me as the kind of guy who would ever abase himself. Especially not to someone like me.

I mean, Madi said he's a classist fuck.

Why would he ever agree to submit to me?

The logic eludes me, but it doesn't matter.

I was pissed off when he said no commitment or relationship because I took it to mean I'm not worthy of being his girlfriend. But whatevs. He's not worthy of being my boyfriend, either.

That doesn't mean we can't have a little fun.

Right now, all I can think is that he's *mine*. Those muscular forearms are mine to command. I could strip him naked and—

Billy disproves his pledge to submit by taking charge. Moving faster than I can track, he grips my waist and boosts me up to straddle his waist.

Pepper gives a yip of excitement, noting that it's playtime.

One growl from Billy quells the little dog's enthusiasm.

"Oh...okay. Yes, lift me up." I can't keep the laughter out of my voice as I pretend I ordered it first.

The fact that I *love* being picked up by this man pretty much proves his entire case against me. Billy isn't Incredible Hulk-big like Grayson, the door guy downstairs. He's muscled but on the wiry side. Still, he makes me feel as light as a child the way he easily holds me, his forearm propped under my ass.

"Carry me to your bedroom."

His answer is a dark rumble, but he swiftly strides down the hall. My breasts thrust in his face, and he bites one boob through my thin shirt.

I cry out, clamping my inner thighs more tightly around his waist, my pussy contracting.

I suddenly can't remember why I was resisting sex with him. Oh, yeah, because I didn't want him to win. But clearly I'm the one winning here. I'm being charioted to a bedroom by a tall, strong, billionaire who apparently is willing to do my bidding when it comes to bed-related activities.

Plus, no commitment or relationship. Just sex.

Now that I'm over being offended, I can realize that it's a perfect scenario. The idea that men only want sex and women have to use that bargaining chip to get them into relationships is just an old philosophy stemming from times when women had no agency or rights to property. As if we're not supposed to love sex, too. As if we can't just be in it for pleasure alone.

So yeah. I'm burning down the patriarchy right now. Starting with ordering Billy Billions around in his own bedroom.

The bedroom is like the rest of Billy's penthouse–decorated in glass and metal and devoid of any color except black, white, and gray. White walls. Dark grey rug. An enormous California King four post bed in lacquered black stands in the center of the room. Floor-to-ceiling windows overlooking Central Park shape one wall. On the wall opposite the bed hang a series of three framed black and white prints of sweeping mountain and forest landscapes. They look like Ansel Adams' prints of Yosemite. I make a mental note to examine them later.

Apparently, Billy doesn't know how to not be in charge because he drops me in the center of the bed and unbuttons my shorts.

"Whoa, whoa, whoa." I hold up my hand. "Take off your own clothes."

Let's see if he's truly capable of following my orders.

He holds my gaze, that small smile playing around his lips as he swiftly unbuttons his dress shirt. I hold my breath, waiting for him to take off the undershirt. I'm dying to see his chest to find out–

Hairy. Not waxed.

Yum. I do love a hairy chest.

I scramble off the bed.

Billy's hands move to unbuckle his belt.

"Wait!" I hold up a finger. I'm making this up as I go.

Billy holds still, his fingers still on the buckle. It's a sexy look. I don't know why I'm imagining him using that belt on me. Buckling my wrists together. My thighs. Spanking my ass with it.

I've never played that kinky, but something about Billy and the things he just said about me inspires these crazy thoughts.

I walk around behind him and take over, slowly sliding his belt out of the loops. I drop it on the floor and then slide my palm over the hard ridge of his cock in his trousers. Damn, he's big. I unbutton his pants and tug the zipper down.

"Kick off your shoes."

He toes off his expensive Italian leather loafers.

"Sit on the edge of the bed."

He turns and sits. He's relaxed, his gaze half-mast, like he's drunk with lust. If I were truly evil, I would order him to strip, tie him to the bed, and then leave to paint the mural.

That might serve him right, but I'm not sure I could handle the blow-back. Maybe I'm starting to care about this pseudo-relationship Billy and I are developing.

Besides, that's not what I want. I want to taste him, like he's tasted me.

I kneel on the plush rug that probably costs more than I've made in my entire lifetime and free his erection.

He groans, and his hands clench into fists by his side, but he keeps them there, like he's at a strip club, and I'm a dancer on his lap. I can touch him, but he can't touch me. I fist his cock and slide my hand up and down his length.

A low rumble sounds in his chest.

Wow. He's more of an animal than I would've thought. Before this week, I imagined sex with him could be a cold, manicured endeavor, but he's off-the-hook hot.

I show him my tongue as I slowly lean forward, creating anticipation. His thighs tense.

"Do you want me to put your cock in my mouth?" I ask.

"Don't tease." His voice is even. Maybe there's even a slight challenge to the words.

I get the message loud and clear. He might obey, but he won't beg.

And any illusion I had that I'm actually in control just slipped away. He's toying with me–letting me have my turn, so to speak, before he takes back over.

I slide the tip of my tongue along his weeping slit. "What if I do?" I ask.

I see a wicked glimmer in his eyes. "There are punishments for girls who tease."

A zap of lightning goes straight to my clit, and the inner walls of my core contract. Yep. He's got my number. Apparently he understands me better than I do. Maybe this whole time I have subconsciously been daring him to punish me.

I exhale on the head of his cock, but still don't take it into my mouth. It surges in my hand, thickening to an alarming width, veins popping.

"Ask me nicely," I purr.

"Show me, Silver."

"Show you what?" I smile up at him. I've definitely got him where I want him now.

"Show me heaven."

Well, all right, then. He's not begging, but he did ask nicely. I slide my tongue under his cock as I engulf it in my mouth.

Billy jerks and sucks in a sharp breath at the sensation. I take him deep, going slowly, so I can relax my throat.

"Oh, fuck," he mutters when the head of his cock hits the back of my throat and keeps going.

I cup his balls. He lets out a pained exhale. "Aubrey..."

I like hearing my name in those pained tones. Knowing I'm the one who made the manicured billionaire lose his cool.

I hollow my cheeks to suck him hard as I pull back, and his hand tangles in my hair. He closes his fingers in a fist and uses my hair to guide me in and out.

I pop off and run my tongue around my lips. "Did I say you could touch?"

He releases my hair, but his fingers drift to my throat. He gives me a hand necklace—not squeezing, just cradling the column of my neck. "May I touch you here?" His voice is deep and raspy.

I swallow under his hold. My brain skids around in my skull for an answer. Half of me wants to tell him no. Reestablish control. Refuse to let him dominate me. But I soaked my panties the moment he put his fingers there.

So I settle for a non-answer and take his cock back in my mouth. He keeps his fingers around my throat, but his thumb lightly strokes up to my chin, as if he's tracing the location I'm taking his dick.

His fingers tighten when he gets excited, but the moment I stiffen, he releases, moving his hand to massage my nape, then traveling back up into my hair where he fists it again. He guides me faster, and I let him for a moment because it's hot as hell, but then I pop off again.

This time, he instantly releases my hair.

I lift his cock with my hand and lower my face to his balls, licking, then sucking them.

Billy's breath grows harsh. When my nose brushes his dick, he chokes on a sound and stiffens.

Chapter Seventeen

illy

B The scent of my seared flesh momentarily clouds Aubrey's delicious nutmeg and honey aroma, and I rub my nose to clear it. Her silver nose ring burns my dick, but nothing in the world would make me stop her. For one thing, I'm immune to pain—I took too many beatings as a child to even register physical discomfort anymore.

But more than that, I'm in fucking heaven.

I've had at least a thousand blowjobs in my lifetime, but none have ever felt like this. I can't decide if it's her scent or the fact that she hates me that turns me on so much. Maybe I like that she insists on maintaining her alpha nature, even while on her knees pleasing me.

I haven't had a female like her before. I haven't had this sense of craving that goes beyond the physical, straight to my core. Like the very *essence* of me craves Aubrey.

Her impossibly long, thick curls cascade around her shoulders and down her back.

She moves my cock to the other side of her face and

continues sucking my balls and the burning stops. The flesh will blister, but it will heal by tomorrow.

I watch as the lovely human extends her tongue to lick a long line from my balls up the underside of my dick, all the way to the head. I see her gaze snag on the red welts at the base of my cock, so I move quickly to distract her.

I catch both her wrists, hold them together and tug them upward as I stand, pulling her off her knees with her arms stretched above her head. "Do you want my tongue or my cock in that ripe pussy of yours?"

Her pupils dilate, and she sways on her feet. A fresh hit of lust rockets through me at the scent of her arousal. "Both."

"Greedy. I like that." I rip her shirt off over her head. She's wearing a pale pink lace bra beneath it that makes my mouth water.

She shoves her shorts and fishnets down her hips. "You would."

Holding her gaze, I slowly shake my head. "There's that mouth again."

She looks right back at me. Is she daring me to take her in hand? I know by the scent of her arousal that the idea turns her on, but it's a big leap when I don't have verbal consent. I suspect she simultaneously wants my dominance and to maintain control. Or she wants me to take her in hand, but to let her save face at the same time. I'll have to tread carefully.

If this goes wrong, and she tells Madi, Brick will cut off my dick.

I spin her around and press her upper back down over the side of the bed. She tenses and holds her breath but doesn't fight me or protest. I unhook her bra from the back. Anticipation sparks everywhere in my body. My need to consume her flames hotter. I want to dominate the hell out of her. To own that hot body. To show her everything I make her feel.

I want to hear her moan. Scream. Beg.

I want Aubrey Cook. The chaos-inducing, puppy toting, disrespectful human who, for some inexplicable reason, makes my cock harder than steel.

I slap her ass, then slide both of my hands over her hips and down her outer thighs to finish removing her shorts and fishnets.

Since she didn't complain about the spank, I'm torn between giving her a proper punishment and getting my mouth on that wet cunt of hers.

Before I remember not to show her my strength, I've lifted her hips in the air and placed her knees on the mattress. She balances on her hands and knees, but I push between her shoulder blades, forcing her beautiful breasts to my gray silk bedcover.

Dew glistens on her labia. I give her other butt cheek a slap, hard enough to make a loud smacking sound. I lean over and bite her ass. "You're so fucking delectable."

It's not like me to dish out praise, even to a sex partner, but the honesty just tumbles out of my mouth. I part her ass cheeks and lick her pussy. "Push that ass out," I order, making my voice a bark.

Pepper whimpers at the sound from outside the door. I sent him a mental image of waiting for me in the hall earlier, and he wisely obeyed.

I slide my thumb in Aubrey's wet channel, splaying my fingers over her sacrum, and pump in and out. She's juicier than a peach, ripe for plucking. "I'm going to show you what happens when you've earned a punishment from me."

Her walls squeeze around my thumb, proving my notion that she's *more* than into this scenario.

I remove my thumb from her channel and use the moisture gathered to rub over her asshole.

She squeezes against the sensation.

I spank her–just one slap–but when she moans in pleasure, I decide it's time for a proper punishment.

I deliver a flurry of light spanks, warming her ass without challenging her, then I stop and circle her ass with my palm, rubbing and squeezing. "Stay right there," I command.

I have no idea if she'll obey.

Or if she'll obey but give me lip about it.

She doesn't. She appears to have entered the mental zone of surrender.

I kiss one red cheek before I swiftly go to retrieve a bottle of lube from my ensuite bathroom.

Pepper sticks his nose through the bedroom door and wags his tail, but I ignore him. He retreats again.

Returning with the open lube bottle, I dribble a dollop over her anus.

She jerks, so I hold her hip to steady and reassure her. Like the puppy who simply requires an alpha, her body needs the security of being owned, so she can let go and experience deep pleasure. If she feels unsafe, her brain will stay on line, parsing the situation, trying to decide what to do next, or how to respond. She will be in performance or protection mode.

I want her in receiving mode. I need her to feel my control deeply. To know that I'm in charge now–she doesn't have to worry about anything but obeying my directions.

A blindfold would help. Tying her up would add to the sensory experience as well.

I need to slow down and deliver a scene she'll want to repeat. My wolf has me on edge, dying to fuck her into oblivion, but now is not the time for me to take. Now is the time to give.

I marshal my self-control, putting my wolf on lock. I walk to my closet and grab two ties. When I return, I slide one around Aubrey's head to cover her eyes. She shifts and turns her head to let me tie it in the back, then lowers her cheek back to my bedspread.

I grab a pillow from the pile at the headboard and lift her torso to slide one under her chest to take some of the pressure off her neck and make her more comfortable when her hands are tied behind her back.

I pick up one wrist, twist it behind her back, and then twist back the other. I take my time looping the silk tie around her wrists, but I tie it snugly. If she wants out, she'll have to ask. I sense the anticipation building in Aubrey. Her scent has a warmth, like she's in the throes of pleasure already.

"Now you can focus, Silver," I tell her. "I'm going to give you my tongue and my cock, as requested. But first there's the matter of your punishment."

Aubrey's only response is a soft sigh.

She's fully on board.

To keep her off-balance, I don't spank her yet. I pry her upper thighs open with my thumbs and lick into her. I tongue her swollen clit, then suck on her labia. She's freshly shaven from front to back, making her skin smooth and easy to devour.

A strange sensation comes over me as I taste her. A wash of pleasure–not physical. More ethereal. Metaphysical. I work and wiggle my tongue in her folds, and lap her juices and the pleasure increases. It's a sense of rightness mingled with excitement—like the thrill my wolf gets when he's caught the fresh scent of wild game and knows the kill is nigh.

I try to tell myself it's my dick talking.

I've been hard for this human since Brick and Madi's engagement party. Actually, since I first met her at La Résistance. My dick's just happy I'm finally going to get to fuck her out of my system.

It's definitely not fate talking. That would mean...

No.

Absolutely not.

I'm not fated to a human.

The idea irritates me enough that I spank Aubrey as I lick her.

She moans. I spank her again, staying busy with my tongue as I smart her soft ass with the flat of my palm.

No fucking way I'm fated to a human.

I change hands and slap her other cheek, delivering several stinging blows as I lave her entire pussy with my tongue.

I find her asshole with my right thumb. The lube I dribbled there earlier has warmed to her body temperature now, and it's easy to work my digit into her opening.

Her moans grow more guttural.

I don't fuck her ass with my thumb, I just leave it inside her. Then I lift my head and start spanking her in earnest—hard slaps where ass meets thigh, first one side, then the other.

She whimpers, but takes it well, staying perfectly still. Her thighs begin to tremble. Her cunt drips arousal onto my bedspread.

I'm normally OCD neat, but I already know I'm not

washing anything when we're done. I want to sleep with her scent in my bed tonight.

Every night, my wolf insists.

I shut him up by spanking Aubrey harder. The pitch of her cries takes on a note of intensity, so I stop and rub her heated flesh as I slowly fuck her ass with my thumb.

Realizing she's about to come, I rub her clit with the fingers of my other hand.

"Oh God!" she cries.

"Did that spanking get you hot, Aubrey?" I rumble. "Are you going to come before I even put my cock inside you?"

Two fingers slip inside her without me even meaning to penetrate–her flesh is that swollen, slick and open.

"Oh fuck."

I pump my thumb and fingers.

"Oh my God. Fuuuuuuuuuuck!" She immediately clamps down on them, as if waiting for something to come around. Her juices soak my fingers as she orgasms.

My wolf howls with satisfaction.

That sense of metaphysical satisfaction also loops through me.

I pump until Aubrey's done, then I say, "Bad girl. I didn't say you could come."

* * *

Aubrey

Now that I've had my funishment–and it *was* searing hot–I wrest back control.

"I'm the one giving orders," I assert although considering I'm breathless and mumbling, I might lose some of the oomph to my statement.

Billy bites, then kisses my smarting ass, then unties my wrists. I groan as the blood rushes to my shoulders, which had gone a little stiff.

Billy seems to understand exactly what I'm experiencing because he squeezes them, helping massage the life back into them. Well, now I know. Billy White the III is an *animal* in bed. Madi's conjecture that he might be decent because he pays attention to people's desires was right. He's smooth. Experienced. Dominant in a delicious way.

I want more.

He pushes me onto my back with his body on top. His gaze is on the silver ring in my navel. He must think it's hot.

I push him away, and he yields. His normally closed expression is still inscrutable, but I detect a softness in it that wasn't there before. An appreciation?

You'd think he'd be ragey with blue balls by now because I've come twice, and he hasn't come at all, but he seems patient.

The man has self-control, I give him that.

I straddle his waist, and his lids droop as his large, talented man-hands come to my hips.

A phone rings, and his eyes slide toward the floor where his trousers are.

"Do you need to get that?"

He grinds his teeth. "Fuck."

I take that as a *yes* and climb off.

Billy springs from the bed and grabs the phone out of his pants pocket. "Brick."

Ah. His boss and best friend. I wonder which role of the relationship comes first? It almost seems like boss since he was so in the dog house with Brick over harming his relationship with Madi. It's weird, though, because I thought Madi said they were college friends before he was a boss.

166

"Where are you?" Brick's voice is so loud I can hear it all the way over here on the bed.

"I'm working from home today."

"Since when do you *work from home*? What the fuck are you doing there?"

Billy's face goes as blank as a slab of marble, not that he was showing much before.

Uh oh. I have a feeling playtime is over. I scoot off the bed and search for my clothes.

"I'm trying to have a meeting with my exec team, and they tell me you're not here. I need you in the office. Now."

"I'll be there in thirty." The call ends without any good-byes. When Billy looks my way, I expect to see that flat businesslike gaze, but there's a flicker of something else. Disappointment? Longing?

Seeing that glimpse of a real human beneath the slick exterior does something strange to my heart.

Am I feeling sympathy? For a billionaire?

That's absurd. He chose this high-powered life. He chose Brick as a best friend.

He walks over to me where I'm standing in the matching bra and panty set that I may have chosen precisely for a moment like this. "I'm sorry." He catches my nape and pulls my face up toward his. "I have to go. Please tell me we can do this again."

Wow. He said *please*. And *I'm sorry*.

"We'll see."

He lowers his face toward mine, but stops halfway there. "May I kiss you?"

It seems hilarious that he's asking permission to kiss me after he had his thumb in my ass a short time ago, but I'm still not in the mood to give him any inches.

"No." I say but then take control, grasping his face and

pulling his lips down to mine. I kiss the hell out of him, infusing all the built up lust I'd hoped to release with sex into his mouth. Our noses rub together. Lips twist. I make it long and passionate to show him what he missed. Not that the flagpole erection pressing into my belly doesn't prove he's already well aware.

When we come apart, his nose appears to have angry red marks. I reach up to touch one. "Did my nose ring scratch you?" It shouldn't be able to scratch—that doesn't make sense, but I can't think of any other explanation.

Billy ignores my question and cradles my cheek in a gesture that seems way too tender for a guy I've been sparring with for months. He gives me one more quick kiss before turning away to pull on his clothes. I beat him in the race to get dressed and sweep out of the room before he does.

Pepper is waiting out in the hallway and—dammit!—he left a little puddle of pee there.

Fuck. Well, at least it was on the hardwood, not a rug I couldn't afford to replace.

"Watch your step—there's dog pee!" I call back to Billy. "I'll clean it up."

I hear Billy growl in the bedroom, and Pepper pees some more.

"Don't be mean to him! He's just a puppy!" I run for paper towels.

Billy catches me on his way out. He kisses me one more time. "I want you," he says and leaves.

Those are his parting words.

I stare at the door he left through, a slow smile creeping over my face. "Noted."

* * *

Billy

I savor Aubrey's scent on my skin as I take the elevator to the garage. My face tingles where her silver nose ring burned me. My balls have to be a dark shade of blue–they ache like a motherfucker, but my wolf is whistling while he walks. I just made Aubrey come.

I had her naked in my bed. Her scent won't just be all over my place, it will be on my sheets.

But as I tear out of the garage in my Porsche, the sound of Brick's rebuke rings louder in my ears.

No one works from home at Moon Co. Twenty-five percent of the employees are wolves. That means no one is sick–ever. Brick runs his business with iron rule. He doesn't demand evenings and weekends unless it's necessary, but you sure as hell better be at your desk when he needs you.

I've always been the guy putting in the sixty hour weeks. I'm there first. Leave last. I make it my job to be on top of every single aspect of the business that might bite us. I work with Eagle–our corporate attorney and Brick's brother-in-law–to problem solve every liability. I run that company as much as Brick does. Maybe more.

So yeah, me fucking around with video meetings yesterday was as far from normal as it gets.

What is happening to me?

I roll down my windows and let the polluted New York air with the stench of the streets slap my face. Aubrey's scent fades, and I pick up the variety of scents on the street– the sweet grease of donuts, the singe of rubber, the exhaust.

As my disgust for the city crawls over my skin, the pleasure from touching Aubrey vanishes.

I'm left only with anger.

Why in the fuck does she have this affect on me? How could I let my need to get into her panties interrupt me doing my job for Brick? I disappointed my alpha–again. And this time under the auspices of making up for last time.

What if...this wasn't about making things up to Brick at all? What if Aubrey is actually my downfall?

The Adalwulf crone predicted Madi would bring about the end of the Blackthroat pack, but that didn't happen. What if she got it wrong? Or what if it wasn't a prediction at all, but a curse? A curse that twisted and found its way to me.

The Adalwulfs had made a pact with witches genera- tions ago, and now every generation produces a wolf-mage– pack seeress to help guide their alpha.

Their old crone died with Odin, their last alpha, but my sources tell me a new young seeress has taken her place– Aster, the virgin mage.

It may be that they sent Madi as a curse to destroy Brick, and when that didn't work, redirected it to me. Why else would I be so entranced with a lowly human? I hate humans.

I care nothing for art. Social justice means nothing to me–I'm a wolf operating in a separate society.

I yank down the visor to look at my reflection in the mirror. Angry red blisters appear along my nostril and upper lip where Aubrey rubbed her silver nose ring.

I *enjoyed* the kiss.

Enjoyed the passion behind it. Enjoyed knowing I inspired that passion.

I allowed myself to be marked by a human.

All the while, my alpha needed me, and I was absent from the pack.

What in the fuck is wrong with me?

I need to get a grip. No more working from home. No more fucking the enemy.

I will pay her for her work on the mural and get through the bachelor / bachelorette party and wedding, but that's it. If we happen to collide in bed a few times while we're at it, I won't complain, but I can't let her distract me.

I can't succumb to whatever strange allure she has.

Aubrey Cook is trouble. Her chaotic beauty is dangerous.

No matter what happens over these next few weeks, I can't let her under my skin.

Chapter Eighteen

ubrey

Well. For a guy whose parting words were "I want you," I would have to conclude that Billy White didn't want me that badly.

Either that, or stuff went down at Moon Co, and he's been drowning in work because I haven't seen or heard from him since he bailed two days ago after Brick called.

Which is why I'm back to getting a rise out of him by tromping all over his boundaries.

Grayson, the beefy door guy, let me into Billy's apartment yesterday, and today with no explanation other than that Billy had told him to give me access. There was no note or text message from Billy. We are on radio silence.

Well, whatever.

Fine by me. I got a lot of work done on the first mural.

I also enjoy having Billy's place to myself.

Figuring he probably has nanny cams all over the place, I made myself at home today to annoy him, helping myself to his coffee in the kitchen and the food in his refrigerator, which is almost all meat, for the record. I guess he's one of those paleo diet guys.

Now I'm in his bedroom en suite's giant, two-person shower, washing off the paint before my date with Madi tonight. Yes, I did think it was appropriate to get naked in the same place he gets naked.

I pop the lid off Billy's shower gel. It's in a glass bottle–who brings glass bottles into a shower?

I truly hope he arrives home while I'm in the shower and finds me here, making myself at home like a bad hook-up who won't leave the morning after.

I haven't decided whether I'd let him have his way with me or leave him hungry as I flounce out in the sexy go-go boots Caroline gave me.

But I've been in his shower for a full thirty minutes, and he hasn't shown up. I guess I need to get a move on, so I can meet Madi. I was hoping we could go over together from here, but she texted to say she has to work late, and she'll meet me over there.

I still haven't worked out a plan for Pepper, who is sitting on the fluffy gray bath mat, waiting for me with his big brown eyes glued to the glass shower door.

I haven't found a home for him, which is a problem, since my apartment doesn't allow pets. So far, I've smuggled him in each night then brought him with me to Billy's. I didn't even have to use Billy's credit card to buy food and toys because all that stuff arrived at my door as if delivered by magical fairies.

I suspect the magical fairy was Billy's assistant. Am I surprised Billy went out of his way to help take care of a little puppy? Maybe a little, but less than I thought I'd be. Billy acts grouchy, but he seems to care more than he lets on. He pretends to be annoyed by Pepper, but when he washed the little dog, he was gentle. I think deep down I knew Billy would have hidden depths of kindness; otherwise, I wouldn't have brought a poor, defenseless puppy to his door.

But I still need to find a puppy-sitter for tonight. Pepper is doing well–he's already learned to only pee on the puppy pads or go outside. I was hoping if Madi and I left here together, I could leave Pepper with either Billy or Brick, but that plan didn't come together.

Which means...I could really annoy the hell out of Billy and just leave him a puppy surprise when he comes home tonight. While I sort of love the idea of being that obnoxious, I don't want Pepper to have a terrible time.

Hmm...decisions, decisions.

I help myself to Billy's razor–committing the cardinal sin of dulling a man's face razor by shaving my legs and bikini area then get out of the shower and help myself to a fluffy towel. I take my time getting dressed, rocking the skin-tight light gray t-shirt dress with the white go-go boots.

I rummage through Billy's refrigerator for dinner. He still hasn't shown up by 6:30, and it's time to go, so I put Pepper in the little carrier that I bought for him to sneak him in and out of the building–it could pass for a duffel bag if you don't look too closely–and I leave it by the door.

"I'm sorry, baby. I'm leaving you with the monster tonight. Hopefully he'll be nice and feed you something in the morning, but I'll come early to make sure you get taken out, okay?"

Pepper gives a little chirp of a bark.

"I know. I love you, too. Be good." I make kissing noises and swallow the pound of guilt coming up my gullet as I shut the door.

It will be fine. Pepper will be okay, and annoying Billy is worth it.

Especially after the disappearing act he played this week.

I step into the elevator, trying to ignore my misgivings. Everything about tonight feels wrong. Billy disappeared. Madi couldn't meet me here to go together. I hate leaving Pepper without being sure someone can watch him.

I feel off track.

I don't even know what I'm doing screwing around in Billy's building when I should be focusing on the Sentience case.

Saturday is their gala, and they will be unveiling my mural. That will be my chance to get the evidence we need for the case.

It will be my biggest risk yet, but there's no one else who can do it. As the artist, I have an invite. I also have a security pass.

It's the best chance we have at bringing them down.

* * *

Billy

I walk into my apartment at seven, knowing from the tracker on her phone that Aubrey just left.

It was purposeful timing on my part. I require a full reset where it comes to that female, and that means avoiding the temptation of her nutmeg scent and delectable body.

I lift my nose to drink in her scent. It's mingled with the flavor of drying paint, the damp of a fresh shower, and dog.

A small duffel bag is by the door, positioned over a puppy pad. Right. It's a dog carrier.

Pepper gives a sharp yip of joy at my entrance.

"Hey." I make my voice sharp, and Pepper whines.

I tug off my tie. Aubrey showered here and left the damn dog. Why in the hell would she do that? Does she not care about the well-being of this rug rat? Or does she harbor a higher opinion of my compassion for small animals than is justified?

Or...is she hoping to tempt me into punishing her? That thought gets my dick hard.

I unzip the carrier and lift the tiny fuzz ball out. "You don't bark at me."

He wags his body violently as he tries desperately to lick my face, my hands, any part of me that he can reach.

"I'm your alpha. Don't forget it."

More wagging.

He may be young and a mutt, but he's smart. I can see in his big brown eyes that he understands me perfectly. I give him a scratch behind the ears.

"Do you need to go outside?" I send the mental image of peeing on the grass in Central Park. That's how shifters communicate when we're in wolf form. We're not psychic by any means, but you can get a simple idea across well enough. Usually it's which direction to run or which animal to hunt.

Pepper's head whips around to look out the windows that overlook the park.

Yep. Smart pup.

Aubrey left a leash beside the carrier, but I'll be damned if I'm going to walk a small dog on a leash in public. Walking a small dog in Manhattan is beneath me, regardless. But signaling I can't control said tiny dog is absurd.

I set Pepper down on his feet. "Come." I open the door,

and he trots out with me and into the elevator, sniffing every corner of it. He picks up one leg to pee, and I growl. He freezes, drops on his back, and rolls to show me his belly in surrender.

I give him an alpha stare. "Outside only."

When we get to the atrium, I want to ask Grayson if Aubrey left a message for me—like why the fuck she left Pepper here—but I can't show weakness. I'm our alpha's right hand man. I look ridiculous enough walking out of the elevator with a tiny dog trotting behind me when I'm the kind of guy who should have an attack Doberman at his heels.

I nod at Grayson and stride out onto the sidewalk. Usually when I walk down the street, people avert their eyes, but Pepper makes them glance at my face with a smile. Of course, it quickly fades when they see my icy *don't fuck with me* return glare.

Pepper trots along as fast as his little legs will carry him to keep up with me. We make it around the corner to the grass of the park, and I point and tell him to do his business. He complies. I don't have a thing for babies, puppies, or kittens, but it's hard to deny how fucking cute he is. I may be a monster who's mostly dead inside, but there's something about the young—shifter, or animal—that brings out the protective alpha in me.

Especially when I see someone approaching with a bigger mutt that looks like it wants to eat Pepper. I make a low growl in my throat, too low for the human walking the dog to hear, but enough that the dog stops in her tracks, and hugs her owner's leg as she walks by.

My phone rings while Pepper is running from bush to bush marking his territory, and I pull it out to check the screen.

Madi.

She never calls me. While I have tried to prove my loyalty to her as my luna, we're still not on friendly terms.

I swipe my thumb across the screen. "Yes, Luna?" I don't need her to like me, but her trust matters. She needs to know I'm her loyal soldier, prepared to take orders. Prepared to lay down his life for hers.

"Billy. Hi. By any chance is Aubrey still at your place?"

I frown. "No. She left a half an hour ago. Why?"

"I was supposed to meet her tonight, but I can't get away from the office, and she's not answering her phone."

Something twists in my gut. It's not fear for Aubrey's safety although that is present too. It's something different. Something less clean than a protective instinct. Muddier. Tainted with jealousy and hurt.

Fuck. It's *empathy*.

I somehow know how Aubrey will feel about Madi standing her up.

I know, and I want to draw a sword and slay the dragon that made her feel this way.

"Where were you meeting her?" I try to keep the sharpness out of my voice. She's still my luna, and my loyalty should be with her over Aubrey.

For some reason, it's not, but I can't evaluate that right now.

"All Night. It's next to La Résistance in Brooklyn."

"I know the place. I'll go and give her the message."

There's a pause as Madi takes that in. "You will?"

"Of course, Luna," I say smoothly, like I'm doing it for her, not for Aubrey.

"Good. Make sure she's having a good time. Give her a ride home or something if she needs it." Madi uses a bit of alpha command in her voice, which isn't warranted in this situation. But she's a smart woman—sharper than most of us, and we're all Ivy League. I suspect she's onto me. I've shown too much interest in her best friend than is warranted. Now she's making this an order to give me the pretense of having Aubrey all to myself tonight.

I don't hate it.

"I'm leaving now," I clip and end the call before Madi can glean any more information.

I give a short whistle, and Pepper's little head whips around to look at me, ears pricked, eyes alert for my command. When I snap my fingers and point to my heel, he bounds over, tumbling a little when his body gets ahead of his legs.

"Let's go, Pepper. Your mom needs us."

* * *

Aubrey

She's not coming. And no, I didn't take her call when she tried the last ten times. Because if the call was just to say she's running a few minutes late, she would've texted. The fact that she's calling me means she wants to apologize, and honestly, I don't want to hear it. I will either say something I regret and permanently damage our friendship or burst into tears, and neither of those are appropriate when I'm at a live music event at my favorite venue. In a fantastic turquoise leather jacket that looks amazing on me.

I squeeze a lime into my drink and stir it with the mini straw. I haven't eaten anything, and the vodka tonic is going straight to my head. Of course, it's my second one, so that probably explains it.

A group of rowdy white and Asian college guys next to me at the bar keep looking over, giving me smiles. They're looking for encouragement to strike up a conversation, but I steadily ignore them and watch the band.

They're playing my favorite Pat Benatar song, "Invincible," and I would love to grab the mic and take over the vocals because their vocalist doesn't have the range for it. Not that I'm judging. I don't think you have to have a great voice to make music. Any voice will do. It's the desire to sing, to express yourself, that matters.

The door swings open, and there's a Wild West saloon moment when someone so very out of place walks in.

Billy Billions.

Still in his Wall Street suit. What is he doing here? And how did he find me?

He looks pissed as hell, like he's here to make heads roll. Heh. It's probably because I left Pepper there. I check his arm to see if he's carrying my dog, but he's empty-handed.

His gaze flicks to the guys standing near me then locks onto me.

For some reason, flutters start in my belly as he strides over. I'm not afraid of his anger. Hell, I want it. The flutters aren't fear–they're pure excitement. My pussy clenches at the thought of him trying to punish me again.

Will I let him?

That is the $10,000 question.

Billy doesn't confront me when he arrives, though. He pushes his way between me and the group of guys, angling his back to them and his front to my side.

I wait for him to say something, but he's signaling to the bartender for a drink. "Crown Royal. Neat." He drops a hundred on the counter.

He leans his hip against the bar in what for him is probably his most casual stance and looks at me. "Nice jacket."

"Thanks. It's vintage." I was hoping to show it off to Madi.

Now I doubt she'll ever see it.

Billy keeps studying me. I could make a comment on his stuck up suit, but I don't feel like it. I've really lost my mojo if I don't have the energy to make fun of Billions.

Then he says, "Madi stood you up."

Of all the things I expected him to say, that was not it.

Sympathy laces his words. Understanding.

I wouldn't have even thought him capable of such a thing.

My eyes widen, and my throat closes, nose suddenly hot and tight.

He touches my arm, his touch light at first then closing into a reassuring squeeze.

"It's like, the tenth time." My voice clogs. I sound like a teenager, but Billy's standing there, regarding me with something resembling warmth, and it all comes out. "I never see her anymore. I thought painting the mural in your building meant we'd at least get to hang out, but she's always either with Brick or at work. I've been trying to get together with her for weeks now." A tear escapes my eye, and I flick it away.

I feel like a fool.

"I know. Feels like you lost your best friend."

I blink rapidly at him. He must feel the same way with Brick. "Yeah. I mean, I think I did." That realization comes crashing over me.

It's time to face it. People change. Not all friendships last. Maybe I've been clinging to something that I need to let go of.

Billy shakes his head. "Madi needs and loves you. It's just an adjustment to a new situation."

I stare at him. I don't even want to talk about this anymore–it hurts too much. "Why are you here?"

"Madi called me when you wouldn't answer your phone. You want to get dinner? You haven't eaten, right?"

I narrow my eyes. Sparring with him is definitely better than talking about Madi. "Were you spying on me with a nanny cam or something?"

He scoffs. "Please. I don't need a nanny cam to know what you're up to, Silver."

I cock my head and adopt a teasing quality to my voice. "What was I up to?"

His lips curl slightly at the edges. I am coming to love that look on him. "I saw you made coffee and used my shower. And left me your dog." He raises his brows.

"Yeah, how'd you like that?"

"I'm going to punish you for it later."

A hot tingle washes over me. *Yum.*

He downs his whiskey and tilts his head toward the door. "Come on. Let's get dinner. You need a good meal."

"Okay, but how do you know I haven't eaten yet?" I press.

"I know you left not long before I got home, and I didn't smell any food."

"You have nanny cams set up to make sure I don't steal anything, and now that they're up, you no longer feel like you have to work from home while I'm there," I accuse. "Did you watch me shower?"

Billy's Porsche is parked a block away, and he stops in front of the passenger side without opening the door. "You think I'm afraid you'll *steal* something?" He sounds offended. Whether it's on my behalf or his, I can't be sure.

I raise my brows.

He catches one of my wrists in one hand, then the other,

and tugs them so my palms are facing out. His thumbs press into my palms, and he starts massaging. "I'm not afraid of anything, Silver. Least of all, you stealing from me. If you wanted to rob me, I suspect you'd do it while I watched to flaunt it in my face rather than sneak something out after I left."

That wrings a smile out of me. His smoldering gaze and rumbling tone make it sound like he admires that trait in me. He enjoys our sparring as much as I do.

"And if anyone ever nanny cams you showering, I will rip his fucking eyeballs out and stuff them down his throat."

A wash of heat rolls over my body. "That's...hot," I manage to croak in surprise. I didn't take him for a man of passionate crimes. I look up at his face. What seemed haughty before now appears achingly handsome–the firm line of his stubbled jaw, the smoky blue gaze framed by impossibly thick dark lashes. Yes, he's cocky, but when all that self-confidence is aimed in my direction, I can see the appeal. This new perspective makes it harder to maintain the barrier of resistance I've been holding up against him.

I reach up and pull his head down to mine for a kiss. His hand curls around the back of my head, and his tongue lunges into my mouth. He tastes of whiskey. His lips are soft except where the stubble on his upper lip scrapes my skin.

My ass bumps against the door of his car, and he presses me there, one hand sliding down my hip to grip my thigh and pull it up and open.

I hear a short yip from inside the car, and we pull apart. "You brought Pepper?"

"Of course I did." He glares through the window, and I twist to see my little dog outside his carrier in the front passenger seat. Pepper's little paws scratch the inside of the door as he stands on hind legs to look through the window at me.

Billy pulls back, releasing me from where he pinned me against the door, and opens it for me.

I pick up Pepper, but Billy takes him from my hands and sets his little paws on the asphalt.

"Don't put him down! What if he runs?" I exclaim. He's not on a leash or anything. I can't believe Billy drove with him out of the carrier. It's so dangerous.

Billy ignores me. "Pee there and get back inside," he commands, as if the little dog understands him. As if Pepper won't run off and make us chase him or get lost or run over or any of the things that could happen to a little dog in the city.

Strangely, Pepper does exactly as he's told, lifting one leg to pee, and then bounding back in the car.

"In the backseat," Billy growls. "Your mom sits there."

Once more, Pepper obeys. It's downright weird.

I climb in the car. "I guess you speak dog. He doesn't listen to me like that."

"I do." Billy shuts the door and walks around to his side. He pulls his phone out and opens up a restaurant delivery app then hands it to me and starts the car. "Order us some food to be delivered to your place."

A half dozen retorts flit through my head about how he's being presumptuous in inviting himself over to my place, but I realize I love it. I love his take-chargeness, and I love that he would even want to come into my place.

I wouldn't have imagined him ever setting foot through my door. But then I wouldn't have imagined him entering the door of All Night either.

Most of all, I don't say anything because I want this. I've

had a taste of Billy White in bed, and it definitely wasn't enough.

I scroll through the restaurant options. "What do you want to eat?" I ask.

He glances at me as he pulls into the street, and his eyes seem to glow under the street lights. "You."

I smirk. No objections here. He eats pussy like a champ.

"Get what you want because I'll be feasting on you tonight, Aubrey."

Chapter Nineteen

B*illy*
The moment she brings me upstairs—with the dog smuggled under her shirt because, apparently, she's not allowed to have pets—I start ripping her clothes off.

I've waited long enough for this. My self control is waning, and I am a man who normally controls every urge. I don't let anything or anyone master me.

I toss her shirt on the floor as I back her in the direction of the bedrooms.

She toes off her boots.

I unbutton her skirt and yank it down her hips.

When Pepper gives a little bark of excitement, I silence him with a growl.

One good fuck. One good fuck, and I'll get her out of my system.

The problem is just that I haven't come inside her yet. Once I get that relief, I'll have scratched my itch for a human, and I can move on.

That's what I tell myself as her scent invades my

nostrils in delectable nutmeg and honey notes. I'm on edge, a twisted coil of unmet desire and celebration at having her nearly naked.

I pick her up by the waist and walk her the rest of the way to the bedroom. When her eyes widen, I realize I forgot to make her look heavy.

Her room is like her–a jumbled mess of chaos and color. Her furniture looks like thrift market finds, mismatched wooden pieces painted in bright, cheery colors to pull it all together.

"This time I'm in charge," I assert, tossing her into the center of the bed. I let her have her fun last time, but tonight the leash on my control is frayed.

"You think so?" she challenges, but her pupils dilate so wide her cinnamon eyes look onyx. Her pillowy lips part. When I yank the straps of her bra down, I discover the points of her nipples hardened into stiff peaks.

"Don't pretend you don't want it this way." I slip my fingers between her legs, ghosting them over the gusset of her pale pink panties. "Lie to me, but don't lie to yourself."

Her panties instantly grow damp. The scent of her arousal makes my dick harder than steel. Aubrey's body is ripe for me. Ready for my plunder.

And tonight, I do intend to plunder.

I slide one hand over her ass cheek and squeeze.

"I think tonight we'll go for a good old-fashioned over the knee spanking."

Continuing to knead her ass with one hand, I slide the fingers of my other hand inside her panties. "Mmm. Nice and wet." I tease her sopping entrance, "You're excited for your punishment."

I make a show of unbuckling my belt. Aubrey's gaze tracks the movement, and I detect a ripple of uncertainty. I should keep up the pretense, make her believe I'm going to use it to whip her, but my wolf doesn't like the tinge of nervousness in her scent.

"It's for your wrists, Silver."

I sit on the edge of her bed and loop the belt over her torso, letting it catch her waist to drag her over to me. Her legs skid over the side of the bed next to mine, and she sits up, pushing her wild mane of hair out of her face.

"Unless you want me to use it on your ass."

"Pass."

"Come here, beautiful." I open my legs and manipulate her body, so she's lying over one thigh with her torso on the bed and her feet on the floor.

I take my time pulling the pink panties down below the curves of her ass. Her long black curls sprawl across her back and shoulders. She looks gorgeous as hell, and my wolf loves having her at my mercy like this.

Wait, no. Maybe that's my human side. It's hard to tell. We both want her under us tonight, screaming her pleasure when I finally get mine.

My hand claps down on her ass, a little harder than I meant to slap.

She gasps and looks over her shoulder at me, eyes wide.

Pepper barks. Good dog. He's protecting his mom.

I rub away the sting. "Sorry. That was too hard, wasn't it?"

Her shoulders relax.

I spare a look at Pepper. "Go lay down in the living room." I send a mental picture of him lying down in front of the couch, and the little pup whirls and trots obediently off.

That mutt is growing on me.

I deliver another spank to Aubrey, lighter this time, and she moans.

189

"Here's what's going to happen," I tell her, spanking her again. "I'm going to make you sore and sorry for leaving Pepper without asking, and then I'm going to reward you for offering this sexy body up for my punishment." I pick up the pace of the spanking, keeping them light but fast. She rolls her hips over my lap in pleasure.

Fate, this is good. The sound of my hand smacking her flesh, the dizzying sight of her upturned ass, the scent of her arousal growing stronger with each slap. I'm struck by a sense of disequilibrium. Nothing in my rational mind would have ever chosen this moment. To think that I would not just enjoy but relish being in Brooklyn with a human female who hates everything I stand for is illogical.

Yet I've never felt so satisfied in my life. The sense of rightness is hard to deny. Does that mean...?

No. Definitely not.

She can't be my mate. Fate would not put me with a human. I am the son of an alpha, born to rule a pack. I chose to leave my home pack and serve as the right hand of a worthy alpha, but that doesn't mean I'm any less of an alpha. I require an alpha wolf worthy of my bloodline. Someone to continue the purebred lines that can be traced back before America was a nation.

Fate would not put me with a human.

I spank Aubrey harder. She writhes and wriggles over my lap, making my dick throb.

No, this is lust. That is all. It's pent up frustration from earlier in the week when I pleasured her but didn't take my own release.

It's the rush of chemicals at knowing that tonight I will finally be inside her.

I stop spanking and circle my palm over her heated flesh. She has a perfect ass, full and round and heart-shaped. I love the heat emanating off her glowing brown skin.

She's magnificent for a human.

I slide my fingers between her legs, stroking her nectar up to her clit, circling it.

She comes, a shudder rippling through her body as her inner thighs clamp together around my fingers, and her core tightens in spasmodic pulsing.

That easily. A climax just from a short spanking and one rub of her clit. I can't deny how attuned this female's body is to mine. She may deny all affection for me, she may hate her attraction to me, but it's clear I am the master of her body.

"On your knees now." I put alpha command into my voice to make it sexier for her, and so she doesn't have to fight her pride when it comes to obeying.

She drops to her knees at my feet and looks up.

Fucking gorgeous. Her eyes are glassy with the orgasm, cheeks flushed. Her curls sprawl wild over her shoulders and back. I'm dying to fuck her.

She waits for instruction, like a good submissive, even though there's not a submissive bone in her body. Something in the back of my brain tells me that means something, too. That her body responds to my command because it already belongs to me.

But that's not right. It's just because I used alpha command and some part of her biology understands it.

"Take out my dick."

She licks her lips as she reaches for the button on my slacks and frees my erection. She strokes her fingertips slightly up the underside, teasing me.

It feels like heaven.

"Suck my balls." The last time she sucked my balls, the

silver of her nose ring blistered them, so I must be nuts—no pun intended—to ask her to do it again. But pain is irrelevant, and the burning only heightened the delicious sensation of her warm mouth around my most sensitive parts.

She takes her time, sucking my balls into her mouth, searing the inside of my leg with her nose ring. I'm in ecstasy.

"Now let me see those lips around my cock."

Again, she obeys. She opens those full gorgeous lips and slides them around and down my cock, sucking hard as she pulls away.

Fire ignites at the base of my spine as her head bobs over my cock.

Fuck, I need to be inside her. My control slips, an unfamiliar feeling for me. This female is my weakness. I shouldn't be here indulging because she feels like an addiction.

"Enough," I bark, sounding more harsh than I mean to. I grasp her waist and lift her. In my head, I only lift her to stand, but my body has a will of its own, and I find her pussy directly in front of my mouth. I settle her thighs over my shoulders and feast.

"Holy...oh my *gawd*." Aubrey grasps the back of my head. "You're so...strong." The breathy quality of her voice drives me to a frenzy. I can't wait any longer.

This need has ratcheted beyond my control.

I stand and turn, supporting her upper back as I lower her to the bed. I shove her knees up to her shoulders, so I can really get at her core, but there's no nuance. I'm sucking and licking like a starved man. Like a drunk man. Her juices coat my tongue. My teeth graze her soft flesh.

Wait...my teeth?

What the fuck?

No. No, that can't be. She's not my fated mate. I don't want to mark her. That's insane.

A growl rises in my throat. I pull back and blink. My vision has domed, like I'm seeing through my wolf's eyes.

I quickly turn away, so Aubrey won't see.

Condom. I need a condom. I just need to release inside her, and this lust will subside.

I keep my back to her while I shuck my clothes, then grab a condom from the nightstand. I rip it open and sheath my cock.

When I turn back, I have my breath under control. My vision still seems sharper than it should, but it's dark in here, so she probably can't even see my eyes.

"Spread those legs for me, Silver," I command when I crawl back on the bed.

She bends her knees and opens them for me, holding my gaze as she reaches one hand between them to play with herself.

"Fuck, that's sexy."

She knows it. The taunt in her smile tells me. This woman loves to torture me with erotic power.

I should hate being on the receiving end of that torture, but there's no part of me that's dissatisfied. I like her attention focused on me. I like her wielding her body's potency against me. She's enchanting.

"Are you going to take my cock like a good girl?"

Her lids droop to half-mast as she strokes herself. "What happens if I say no?"

I flip her to her belly and smack her ass. "More punishment. Or should I fuck this ass?"

"No, but I like it from behind." She hollows her lower back to lift her ass in my direction, legs spread wide.

I nearly come from the sight. My control disintegrates.

193

Renee Rose & Lee Savino

A growl fills the room, and I'm balls deep in Aubrey before I realize the sound is from me. Being inside her is like coming home.

The mythical home. The religious home. Not the shitty one I grew up in.

I grip her hips and pull her onto her knees to plow into her. Her back makes an elegant slope to where she braces on her forearms.

I know I need to hold back. There's no trace of gentleness in the way I'm handling her, but I can't slow down. Can't rein my lust in.

She's mine now. She's under me. I'm inside her. I fucking *need* this. I need her.

I slap her ass with my loins harder. Deeper. Faster. I'm feverish. The chaos of her small bedroom closes in on me, then recedes. I'm riding a wave, chasing ecstasy, and its name is Aubrey Cook.

Through the roaring in my ears, I realize she's crying out. I try to focus through the frenzy of my thrusts. Does she sound pained?

There's a plaintiveness to the mewls.

I'm hurting her.

Fuck.

"Too rough?" I grit out. I try to slow down but my body won't obey.

"No," she wails. Her fingers fist the sheets, the muscles in her long, slender back tense as she takes me. "Fuck me, Billy."

Fate. The last threads of my sanity snap as her words shoot me into overdrive. I roar, bucking so hard her knees lift from the bed with the force of my thrusts. I hold her nape to keep her from slamming forward into the wall.

She screams.

194

I dimly register someone banging on the wall from the other side. Right. A neighbor. She lives in close quarters here.

I roar again and shove in deep to empty hot ribbons of cum into the condom. It doesn't stop–I keep coming and coming. The fingers of my free hand find her clit and rub.

Aubrey comes, too, shrieking her pleasure. Her hips jerk against mine, her ass pressing back to take me deeper as her internal walls pulse and milk my cock for more.

I'm still coming.

She's still coming.

It seems to go on forever.

And then I find myself on my side, my body curled around Aubrey's, holding her like we just birthed a new universe.

And that's when I realize how truly fucked I am.

Coming inside Aubrey didn't free me.

It transformed me. I'm not the same man who walked in here tonight.

In fact, I don't know if I'll ever be the same.

Chapter Twenty

ubrey

Tonight's the night of the Sentience Gala.
They're going to reveal my mural to the world.

And I'm going to steal what I need to take them down.

They're throwing a fancy party and bankrolling it with
the money they stole from artists. I feel no moral qualms
about drinking their champagne and then setting a match to
their whole company.

Burn, motherfuckers. Burn.

I'm deliberating what to wear when there's a knock on
my door. It's a delivery person with a large black box.

"Delivery for Aubrey Cook. Sign here." I do, even
though I'm not expecting anything. Curiosity gets the better
of me.

I set the box down on the kitchen table and open it. A
dry sandalwood scent wafts into my face as I part the tissue
paper and uncover a gorgeous silvery gown. It's the most
glamorous thing I've ever seen. It even smells expensive.

Did Madi send me the dress as an apology? After she
missed our girl's night out, she kept calling all night. I finally

answered after Billy left, and she apologized in tears. She's been stressed with the wedding and running her family's company, and Thursday night they had some crisis at work that she couldn't get away from.

I forgave her, of course. It sucks, but I'm accepting that Madi's life is changing. She's got new obligations and a relationship that eclipses ours. I want her to be happy, but I'm also grieving the loss of our closeness. She'll never be my roommate again. We won't have endless late nights eating cookie dough ice cream and singing "Push It" in pajamas.

But we can still be friends. We caught up a little on the phone. She asked about the Sentience job, so I filled her in, including the law-breaking parts. I also told her about screwing Billy. We ended the call agreeing that we'll have plenty of time to connect on the trip to Monaco.

She didn't mention that she was going to send me a gift. She didn't need to, but it does make me feel good that she was thinking of me.

Feeling warm all through, I rush to strip off my paint-splattered clothes and pull the sheath on. It fits like it was made for me. The gown is cut in a mermaid style, and without high heels the fabric pools at my feet like liquid mercury.

I have just the heels for the dress too—from Madi's engagement party. I was going to wear that silver dress tonight, instead, but this one is far more expensive.

I look beautiful and formidable. Like a queen from a sci-fi fantasy show. The sort of character who can shoot lasers from her eyes.

I finish up my hair and makeup. I got my hair braided this morning, and I must have been on the same wavelength as whoever bought me this dress because instead of gold and red, I switched to box braids with a little silver tinsel. Just a little glam–that matches the dress perfectly.

Some silver jewelry, and my look is complete. I still have a metallic clutch that matches the heels. The only part of me that isn't red carpet ready are my nails. They're neat and polished but there's some white oil paint around the cuticles. I leave it. I am an artist, after all.

And if people don't like it, I'll incinerate them with my laser eyes.

There's another knock on the door. This time, the delivery is a big floral arrangement of sunflowers, my favorite flower. The note reads: "Congrats on your big night! You're going to kill it. Good luck and Love, Madi."

Huh. I thought the dress was from Madi, but now I'm having second thoughts. It's possible Madi sent both the flowers and the dress, but wouldn't they arrive at the same time?

Maybe Madi didn't. My parents called earlier congratulating me, and Jan and Caroline told me in person. They could've all pitched in to buy the dress, but it's not really their style.

If my closest friends and family didn't send the dress, who did?

I exit my apartment to wait for my ride and notice the limo idling in front. It's blocking one side of the street. There are no other cars waiting, but I'm about to shout and tell it to move when the back of the limo opens. A man steps out, and I lose my train of thought. He's in a classic black tux and radiates enough confidence and aplomb to make James Bond jealous.

Then I zero in on his face.

"Oh my God, Billy?" I hitch up my dress and glide down the stairs to go to him. "I didn't recognize you at first."

I was too busy admiring him in the tux, not that I'm going to tell him that. "Quick, say something insulting."

His gaze roams over me, as if checking for flaws. I wait for him to make fun of me, but instead he seems to zone out, mesmerized by the glittery silver dress.

"Well?" I wave a hand, calling his attention back. "I'm waiting."

His mouth quirks even as the heat in his eyes sears me. "No overalls tonight?"

"There he is. And there's my rideshare." I wave to the poor driver of the blue sedan, who can't get any closer because Billy's limo is blocking the road.

"Not tonight. I'm your ride."

"What?"

But Billy's already moving, and in my heels I can't move fast enough to intercept him. He pulls out his wallet and peels off some bills, making sure the rideshare driver leaves happy.

When he returns, I notice the light grey vest he's wearing with his tux.

"Ready, Silver?" He offers me his hand.

I hesitate. "How did you know there was a gala tonight?"

He gives me that signature Billy smirk. "I saw the invite on your dresser. Figured you're the guest of honor tonight. You should ride in style. Unless you want to take the subway."

"There's nothing wrong with the subway." I take his hand, feeling a zing as his large palm engulfs mine. His warmth steals through me, and my cheeks heat. It feels like we've crossed a line. We've had epic sex, but this is a step beyond fuck-buddy territory. This is a date.

He helps me into the limo. My body responds to his

easy, assured touch. And my arousal is still on overdrive, distracting me.

Once we're in the limo, I place a hand on his shoulder, making him go still.

"Silver," I murmur, stroking the silk vest. The color subtly compliments my dress. "It was you, wasn't it? You sent the dress." He noticed the invitation and decided to play the part of fairy godmother by sending me the dress and coming in a limo to pick me up. Except he's both the fairy godmother and prince rolled into one.

It's arrogant as all hell but also so thoughtful.

With the lights down low as we share a seat, it's almost painfully intimate. Emotions clog my throat. Happiness, confusion, a little regret. He showed up the night Madi stood me up, and now this? It's too much.

Am I having a moment with William White the Third? A man who recently bragged about how he's going to claim my artist fee as a business deduction, which is basically borderline tax fraud?

Impossible.

"I don't know what you're talking about." He sniffs. "I'm just glad you're not in overalls."

I burst out laughing. That's the suit I know and love to hate.

"Only you can give me a gift and turn it into an insult." Satisfied we're back in safe territory–sniping at each other–I sink back in the limo seat. "I'm guessing you want to be my date. You could've just asked."

"I don't ask, I command."

I roll my eyes. When he says douchey things like that, it's almost like he's daring me to call him on his BS. "Or you assume because you know nine times out of ten, you can get away with it." Perks of being a rich white guy.

"Sometimes it's easier to beg for forgiveness."

"So you're going to beg?" I cross my legs, showing off the wicked slit in the dress. I don't get dressed up often, but when circumstances call for it, I love to shine.

"Begging is always on the table. But it might not be me doing the begging."

My breath catches as hot liquid pours through me. The thought of Billy kneeling between my legs, kissing my inner thighs, has me ready to combust. And he's right–after a few minutes of torment by his talented tongue, I will be begging for more.

I squeeze my thighs together. Billy's gaze flickers down. His eyes grow heavy, and he blinks, inhaling deeply. I search for a way to change the subject and distract us both before we're tempted to have limo sex.

"Thanks for coming tonight. My parents wanted to come, but I asked them not to."

"You don't want them to see how you've become a corporate shill?"

I roll my eyes at him. "You're the one who's a poster child for capitalism."

"You've done a good job diverting your money into art. Once you graduate, are you going to paint full time?"

I catch my breath. I wasn't ready for a compliment and a serious question. I ponder it. "I do want to create art full time..."

"But?"

"I'd planned to become a lawyer. Like Jan, my mentor. I want to make a difference."

"And art doesn't make a difference?" His blue eyes are open and honest. He's not baiting me, he's genuinely curious.

"You know it does. I just..." I pause, trying to articulate

why I never wanted to make art my career. When I think about it, I don't really want to go to law school. I want to focus on art. I subconsciously decided that wasn't possible.

Leave it to Billy to be the only one to question why.

"Until Sentience and now you, there was no money in it. I don't need a lot of money, but this city is expensive. A lot of artists struggle. I'm lucky I even have a place in my apartment to paint. I guess I never thought about actually making it work."

I gnaw my lip. I should hate sharing all this with Billy, but he's a good listener. Better than I thought he'd be.

"If you keep finding shameless capitalists who will pay through the nose for your work, you would be golden."

"I want more. I'd like to really help the community. Make sure everyone has an opportunity and space to make their art. I don't know..." This is frustrating. These are big problems requiring big solutions. "I guess I thought becoming a public defender would be the best way to contribute to society."

"Now who's the capitalist? You don't have to contribute to society. Your mere existence is a gift." He blinks, as if he didn't expect to say something so kind.

I want to joke that I am a gift, and he should be grateful for being in my presence, but instead, I say, "Thank you."

"You're welcome. And if you want a business plan on how to become a full time artist, my rate is a mere $100,000 an hour."

"Oh fuck you."

I'm smiling when we pull up to the Sentience building. They've hired a valet and rolled out a red carpet for their execs and the Who's Who of New York they want to impress. My stomach drops to my feet as I remember why I'm here. It's not to trade insults with Billy Billions. At some point in the party, I'm going to need to slip away and break into the subfloor server room.

How am I going to do that?

Billy helps me out of the limo and offers me his arm. We move up the red carpet and into the party. After a short meet and greet with the COO of Sentience and a few other execs, I'm no longer smiling. These people exploited artists to create a tech machine that will lead to more exploitation, but tonight they're celebrating their "commitment to art." Spending all this money on a mural and a party to show it off. "Look at us, we love artists. We're not stealing from them at all."

I can't wait to take them down. I just have to figure out how to do it.

Billy gets me a glass of white wine and a G&T for himself. We sip our drinks and watch people ooh and ahh over my mural. I know I only took the gig to get access to Sentience, but knowing my art is being used as a form of color washing only makes my mood more sour.

Noticing my sober silence, Billy turns on the charm and makes excuses for us to leave and head to the open bar.

"Nervous?" He nudges me.

I'm busy thinking of how I'm going to sneak off unseen with all these people milling around. My throat is full of acid, but I swallow and sniff dismissively. "No."

"Good. Because you have nothing to be nervous about. You're the realest person here."

I blink and turn to him. "That sounded like a compliment."

He smiles. "Because it was. These people," he gestures with his glass at the crowd. "Aren't adding anything to society. They're just cogs in a corporate machine. Whereas you are creating something from nothing. And living true to your values."

My throat clogs again. I never expected Billy would say anything like this. "I try."

"You succeed. And that's why your art is so powerful. Because you put all of yourself into it. Everything you believe, everything you are." When he turns to me, I see every striation in his blue eyes.

My heartbeat's picked up, and my hand holding my wine glass shakes a little. I'm overcome with emotion, and it's not just because Billy is paying me a genuine compliment. It's because it sounds like he sees me, fully. It's caught me off guard and makes me want to run. Or fight.

I pick a fight because with Billy, that's what I always do. "And what about you? What are you creating and putting out into the world?"

He puffs out his cheeks, accepting my censure. "That's a good question," he admits. "I know you think Moon Co is just another cutthroat corporation out for profits."

"Isn't it?" I set down my wine glass and face him. "You talk about everyone here being cogs in a machine. But aren't you just like them?" My cheeks are hot. I'm being harsh, driving him to admit my accusations are valid. But I don't want him to give in, I want him to defend himself, and I'm not sure why.

"I am focused on profits. But there's a lot of good my company can do."

"Please," I scoff. "You got your start in crypto. You're just like these AI guys, getting rich off of speculative tech, all the while destroying the environment."

"Except that Moon Co is a leader in green investment," Billy says mildly. "Solar power, lithium batteries–tech that has the capability to provide reliable green energy all while reversing climate change."

"I didn't know that." I thought Billy was just another business bro out for profits.

"We're very interested in saving the planet. And we have the vision, and we have the funds to invest in R&D. Think of it–" he holds up his phone and shakes it, his eyes lit with excitement, "One day, a battery the size of this cell phone will power this whole building for a year. We'll be able to capture solar energy in long term storage, and when that happens, electricity will be practically free."

"Really?"

"Really." He tucks his phone away, grinning boyishly. A bit of hair falls in his face, and he brushes it back, as if self conscious that he shared so much. "You sound surprised."

"I am." I feel like I just met a whole new Billy, one who I have a lot more in common with than I thought. "I didn't think you cared about anything other than making money."

"Ouch. I guess I deserve that. There are plenty of examples of corporate greed and capitalism destroying the earth and society. But we create the world we want–and I choose to create one where I can create solutions to humanity's biggest problems."

"While still making billions." I narrow my eyes.

"Money is power. Power to create. To protect the things we hold dear. Why do you think the Blackthroat Foundation is focused on land preservation?"

"For tax write-offs?"

"I know you think billionaires should be taxed out of existence, but remember, businesses make money by providing value. And if we provide trillions in value, why shouldn't we earn billions?"

I roll my eyes. One day I'll sit Billy down with Jan and

let her give him her argument about billionaires and taxes. "Agree to disagree."

"I'll take it." He raises his glass in a toast to me and drains it. "Another drink?"

I open my mouth and remember I'm supposed to be breaking into the subfloor server room. "Uh, yes. Will you get it for me? I need to use the ladies." The hall leading to the bathrooms will allow me to use the key card I stole to get up to the offices.

He pauses before answering, which makes me think he notices my distraction. "All right," he murmurs eventually. He raises my hand to his lips and presses a kiss to my skin. My insides flutter. "Don't keep me waiting."

"I won't." My voice is breathy in a way I hope is sexy, not nervous. I wait until he's at the bar to glide to the hall. There's an exec on the phone there, and I smile and nod to him before placing my hand on the bathroom door. He wanders off, and I change direction, moving to the stairs at the end of the hall. I slip inside and start the long descent to sub floor three.

The stairwell is empty, but my heartbeat booms in my ears as I descend. Jamie told me the company doesn't have many layers of security. And tonight, the team will have their hands full managing the party. Still, I walk on tiptoes, so my heels don't make a sound on the concrete floor. At the bottom of the stairwell, there's a locked door barring my way, but no sign of a security guard.

I have the keycard in my purse, and I hold my breath while I swipe it to gain entry. It feels like eons before there's a beep, and the light flashes green.

One hurdle down, several more to go.

My heartbeat pounds in my ears as I take careful steps towards the room Jamie told me about. I have to use the keycard again, but it works. The door opens, and the chilly air hits my face.

The room is quiet except for the hum of air conditioning and machines. I hustle down the rows of equipment and insert the special flash drive Jamie gave me into a server at the end of the rack, where it shouldn't be noticed. If this works, she'll be able to see all of the company's backed up files.

I let out a long breath. They keep the temperature low in this room to protect the machines. Goosebumps pebbling my skin and my nipples are showing through my silvery sheath.

"Are you finished with whatever you're doing?"

I nearly leap out of my skin.

There in the shadowy doorway, is Billy. And he doesn't look happy.

"Aubrey?" He frowns, coming closer. "What *are* you doing in here?" His gaze flicks behind me then back to my face. "Taking down their servers?"

"I can explain–" I say, but then stop. Billy caught me red-handed, and even if I do tell him the truth, he's more likely to side with Sentience than me. Right?

"We need to get out of here." He beckons to me. "A security guard will be walking by any minute."

"How'd you get in?" I whisper, hustling toward him.

He arches a brow. "I could ask you the same question." He takes my arm and propels me out of the room. "You missed the cameras." He nods to the ceiling.

"Shit," I breathe. I didn't even think of it. Neither did Jamie. But of course, Sentience has cameras. Maybe Jamie will be able to do something to alter the footage when she breaks into their servers.

"I'll take care of it," he mutters.

"What?" I jerk back, but he puts an arm around my waist and hustles me along.

"Shhh, someone's coming."

I don't hear anyone, but I don't argue. We hit the stairwell and hustle up the stairs. We're almost back to the main floor, when he tugs me back.

"What are you doing?" I hiss. I'm breathing hard, but Billy barely looks winded.

He pulls me close, so I'm practically leaning against his body. "Follow my lead." He tucks his head into the crook of my neck and shoulder and inhales. Goosebumps prick my skin again, and this time, it's not from the cold.

No, I refuse to be aroused right now. We're in the middle of our escape, for fuck's sake. But Billy is acting like we're teenagers in the back of a car.

I'm about to push him away when I hear voices approaching.

I gasp, and Billy cups the side of my face. "Just breathe. I got this."

For some reason, I trust him. I give him a tiny nod, and he leans back in to claim my lips.

It's surreal, being kissed right now, while waiting for a security guard to find us. Exciting but scary. I'm hot and cold, trying to get my breathing under control. Adrenaline roars through me, and my pussy tingles.

Then Billy's scent washes over me, and I lose myself in his soft lips. It's just an act, but it doesn't feel like it. His mouth is making filthy promises, and I can't help relaxing into him.

I close my eyes, letting Billy kiss me while the footsteps get closer. The door beside us opens and a harsh voice snaps, "What are you doing in here?"

It's a pair of execs, one looking confused, one glaring at us with suspicion.

Billy angles his body, so he's in front of me, giving me shelter. "Is there a problem?" His voice drips with condescension.

"You're not supposed to be back here," the angrier one says. "I'll ask you again, what are you doing here?"

"Isn't it obvious?" Billy drawls. His body is relaxed, while I'm vibrating with nerves. "I finally got this perfect woman to give me the time of day. I wanted to get her alone for some private conversation. But since we're no longer alone, we'll go." He sounds bored and annoyed, as if the execs are trespassing on his turf, instead of the other way around.

"How did you even get in here?"

Billy shrugs with every ounce of his arrogance. "The door was unlocked. If you don't want people in here, you should make sure it's secure." While the exec is sputtering, he puts a hand at my back and guides me away. They call after us, and I flinch, but we're back in the mix of guests, and they don't seem to want to follow and make a scene.

We keep a sedate pace, wandering almost aimlessly towards the door.

"Thank you," I breathe once we step outside.

"Don't thank me. We're not out of the woods yet. But once we are," he fixes me with a narrow-eyed look that makes my stomach swoop again. "You owe me an explanation."

* * *

Billy

I don't know what's going on. I just caught Aubrey attempting some sort of corporate espionage.

And I helped her. I don't know how I got involved in this mess, other than I saw the gala invite on Aubrey's dresser and couldn't bear the thought of her going with anyone else but me.

Now I'm on the phone with Sully, getting him to wipe all evidence from the security cameras to make sure neither of us are caught. I can hear his curiosity in his voice, but I don't bother to explain. I'm not sure I can, even if I made a habit of explaining myself to my packmates.

I hang up with Sully. "It's done," I tell her.

She sighs and nods, sinking back in the limo seat. She's a vision in the silver dress I chose for her. The thought of laying her down and feasting on her pussy right here in the back seat makes my mouth water. But I'm not ready for that distraction yet.

"You're not off the hook yet. Talk."

"It's a long story–"

"I just helped you avoid a few felony charges. I think I've earned the right to hear why you were doing something so reckless."

She blows out a breath, but she must realize I put my neck out for her. I'm not too worried about the consequences, but my wolf is geared up, wanting to protect the little human from any threats. "Sentience is stealing from artists," she blurts. "A whistleblower has proof that they uploaded artists' work illegally."

"It's an LLM. It was trained on tons of data."

"It's still wrong." She blinks her big brown eyes at me. "This hurts people, Billy. Artists like me."

"That's for the law to decide."

"The law is about a century behind the times. When laws are unjust, it's our duty to resist."

"It still was reckless. We could've been caught." I'll never forget the way my heart lurched at the sight of her in the server room. She's lucky I scented the security guard and got us out of the server room in time.

"But we weren't." Aubrey smirks. "And now Jamie–the whistleblower–will be able to get the incriminating evidence we need."

I run a hand down my face. While I admire Aubrey's loyalty and commitment to justice, I wish she had a little more self preservation. This little human will be the death of me.

"Relax, Suit, it worked. And you were brilliant. The way you told off those Sentience guys. How did you know they were coming?"

"Heard them," I lie. I caught their scents.

"I wouldn't have thought to cover our tracks with a make out session."

"Maybe I just wanted to kiss you."

Light glints off her silver nose ring with the movement of her smile. "How did you follow me?"

I followed her scent trail, but I can't tell her that. "Saw you sneak into the stairwell. So I stole a keycard and followed." The last part is true.

"Huh, I thought I was stealthy enough."

"You were good, Silver. But I'm better."

She snorts at my bravado, as I knew she would. "So suave. You know, I thought you looked like James Bond when I first saw you tonight."

I curl my lip. "Ugh."

"What? I thought you'd take that as a compliment."

"I don't drink weak-ass martinis. *Shaken, not stirred,*" I mock. "Please."

"Whatever. We make a good team."

"Yeah, Silver, we do." We share a grin, and it does something peculiar to my chest. "But now you owe me."

"Excuse me? You're the one who decided you were going to tag along as my date."

"You're lucky I did. You couldn't have pulled this off without me. What were you going to do if you were caught?" I put some force in my voice, trying to get her to see the seriousness of the situation.

She lifts one shoulder in a lazy shrug. "Play dumb."

"Yeah," I snort. The image of Aubrey trying to act clueless makes me want to laugh despite myself. "That never would have worked."

"Excuse me?" She sits up, looking outraged. "I can pretend to be ditzy."

"No one would ever believe it. You needed me, admit it."

She shakes her head, muttering to herself.

I put my hand on her calf and slide it up to her knee. "You owe me."

"Oh really?" She raises a brow, but I catch the quiver in her voice.

"Nothing comes free." I slide my hand up further. Her skin is silky and warm, and when she parts her legs a little, her heady scent hits me and sends me reeling.

"Wrong, Billy Billions. The best things in life are free." And with a foxy smile, she puts her hand on the front of my tuxedo pants. My cock throbs under her touch.

"Careful..." My breath hisses between my teeth as she rubs her palm along the ridge of my erection. She's in dangerous territory. My wolf is on edge. He wants me to pin

213

her down and ravage her. Wear her out and keep her in my bed, so she'll never do anything so dangerous again.

She leans in, letting her braids trail over my upper torso while she bears down, rubbing me harder. It's perfect until she says, "Maybe this is how I would've gotten out of a tight situation. Did you ever think of that?"

Instantly, my brain goes there, giving me an image of Aubrey playing seductress with a security guard. I bite back a snarl. "Anyone who touches you, loses that hand."

Her eyes widen a moment. Her gaze searches mine, as if she's wondering where that intensity came from. I don't care how possessive that sounded. I mean every word.

After a moment of hesitation, she smirks. "Jealous?"

Before I think, I've moved, pulling her across my lap. She gasps, and I smack her perfect ass. "No one touches you. I mean it."

Her dark chuckle tells me she's into it. "And if I touch them?"

"I punish you." But she's punishing me, torturing me with thoughts of her with other men.

I rub her bottom over the dress, getting lost in the sensation of the firm muscle under my palm, her weight pressing on my dick. I slide my hand under her dress, seeking her softness, her heat. We both sigh when I find it, pulling the slender gusset of her G-string aside. She's dripping wet.

"No one else. This" –I stroke her lightly– "belongs to me."

She's limp over my lap, too focused on the movement of my fingers to argue. And I'm suddenly desperate. I need her to be safe. I need her to be mine.

What the hell am I doing?

"Promise me, Aubrey. No more breaking into server rooms. Or anything reckless like that."

"I make no promises."

"Then you won't come until you do." I give her clit a tap and smile at the conundrum. Her own ideals against her desire to come.

Another tap.

She wiggles her hips over my lap, making my cock thrust out in my tuxedo pants.

"How about this? If I want to do any B&E, I'll call you first."

"Deal." I penetrate her with my finger.

She gasps, looking over her shoulder at me with her berry-painted lips parted. She's so gorgeous. I want to satisfy her. Make her scream my name. Make her mine.

Wait, no.

Not that part. I just don't want her to ever be with anyone else.

Fate. I'm getting muddled.

I finger-fuck her slowly, and she bites her lower lip, holding my gaze. "I want to suck your cock." Her voice sounds husky, like honey and gold dust.

My upper lip lifts in a snarl of approval. I remove my finger, and she slides down to kneel at my feet. I help her by freeing my erection.

She grips the base of my cock and slides her tongue around the head.

I draw harsh breaths in through my nostrils. She's making me lose control, and I hate to lose control.

She drags her tongue up the underside of my cock, then engulfs it with her mouth.

She's trouble, this human. I give her full points for courage back there, but fuck, she's reckless! Careless with her safety and her future.

I live a controlled, curated existence. That's how I

ensure superiority over every other male in the pack but my alpha. That's how I manage pack and business politics.

Aubrey is clearly disrupting the order in my life. The fact that I came tonight when there's no possible financial or strategic gain for me or my pack proves it. What could I possibly hope to gain by mixing with this human? She is trouble for me and my kind.

But then she cups my balls and picks up the pace, bobbing her head over my cock.

Pleasure rolls over me in a tidal wave.

It shouldn't feel this good. Being with her shouldn't feel like this.

Fuck. I'm losing control again. Anger at that fact mingles with pleasure.

Her eyes are on me. Her lips stretch around my cock. I just spanked her luscious ass, and I plan to fuck her senseless when I get her home tonight.

It's too much.

I put my hand around her throat. It's a threat to her very existence. Proof to myself that I still have the upper hand. I'm still in charge, no matter how out of control I feel.

Her eyes widen, but she keeps sucking me off like a good fucking girl.

And that's what does me in. The fact that she's kneeling at my feet, working to please me—it is too much.

I let out a snarl as my climax rockets down my shaft. "Coming," I manage to grunt, tightening my grip on her throat. "Show me how you swallow."

Because she's Aubrey and disobedient as fuck, she pulls off and takes my cum between her tits.

My laugh is sudden and harsh.

This female is ruining my life.

Chapter Twenty-One

Aubrey

I am sore when I sink into the gorgeous white leather seat of Brick's private jet for our trip to Monaco. I spent the past two weeks exploring the darker side of sex with Billy.

Spanking. Bondage. Rough handling.

I love the way his cool control slips when he gets passionate. The way he tries to keep it all together then combusts. I suspect he hates it, which makes it even better. Like I've gotten under his skin. Like I've won.

We're not in a relationship—that is plain. He tells me nothing personal. He never talks about business or pleasure. It's just verbal sparring and searing interludes.

Which is fine by me—he's not the kind of guy I'd ever date.

Still, he's growing on me.

On the night of the Sentience gala, my landlord was waiting outside my apartment when I got home. I guess Pepper was crying for me, so the jig was up over having a pet in the building. I was afraid I was going to lose the apartment, but Billy smoothly handled it, claiming the dog was his, and apologizing with a fat wad of cash that made the whole problem go away.

The same way he made the videotape of me in the server room go away. Jamie says she has everything she needs now. She's busy compiling documents that can be used for a full class-action lawsuit.

After that night, Pepper slept at Billy's house.

So yeah. We may not be in a relationship, but apparently, we're sharing a dog. And fucking like rabbits.

An attendant walks through the jet handing out champagne glasses filled with prosecco.

"Let's get this party started!" I turn on the portable Bose speaker I brought and play Billy Idol's "White Wedding" to get us in the mood.

Billy gives me a long-suffering look, and I smirk.

I lift my upper lip in my best Billy Idol snarl and sing along. For a moment, I think Madi's going to let me make a fool of myself alone, but then she joins in, lifting her fist in the air with her own version of the song.

I've never been on a private jet. Or hung out with Brick and his buddies, other than at the engagement party. This is really not my kind of scene. They're all billionaires, and apparently Nickel is some sort of duke. Or about to become one via an arranged marriage. It's wild.

I down my glass of prosecco, trying to relax and enjoy the experience, and stop wondering how much this trip is adding to my carbon footprint.

As if he reads my mind, Billy leans in. "This jet is electric. No emissions."

I gasp. "Really?" I peek out the window at the wing as if I'll be able to tell the difference between a gas and electric engine.

"Yep, prototype," Brick says. He and Madi sit across from me. Billy somehow ended up beside me. We look like we're on a double date, again.

"That's awesome," I say. "Billy was telling me about battery technology the other day."

"Was this at All Night?" Madi asks. She knows Billy met me at the club the night she stood me up. But I haven't gotten the chance to tell her about how we've been hooking up since then. We're overdue for a girl chat. "Actually, it was at the gala. Billy was my ride." My date, really, although I don't know if we want to label it like that.

Madi blinks. "I didn't know you went to that, Billy. How was it?"

Billy and I share a look, silently agreeing that we're not going to share how we broke into a server room and almost got caught.

"Good," we say in unison.

Madi stares at us, taking in our newfound camaraderie. Brick looks amused.

"How is the team at Sentience?" Brick asks.

"Bunch of blowhards," Billy answers. "Their tech isn't as impressive as they think it is, but these days, angel investors throw money at any mention of AI. Also, their security is shit."

Brick nods. He's got Madi's hand cradled between both of his. Every so often, he raises it and kisses it as if he can't stand to be physically separated from her.

It's a lot of PDA, but it's kind of sweet. I'm glad my friend has found a man who worships her like she deserves.

I'm also glad that Billy isn't hanging on me like that although he does seem to be sticking close to my side. We're not in a relationship, but we are hooking up, and he's made it clear that he doesn't want anyone else touching me. I thought it was just in the heat of the moment, but I've caught him glaring at the other business bros on the plane as if warning them off. His possessiveness should be off-putting, but I kinda like it. I have no interest in fucking any of his friends.

Madi's younger brother Brayden couldn't get away to join us because he was in finals at NYU. It's my last semester at City College, and I only have two classes this term, so taking a few days off won't kill me. Brick's buddies are all here, minus Eagle, Ruby's husband. He and Ruby are meeting us over there with Scarlett, Brick's youngest sister who goes to college somewhere in Europe. Other than the pilot, Madi and I are the only women on this plane. But the other Moon Co guys have been carefully polite to both Madi and me. I'm not sure if they'll relax enough to let their hair down in front of me, but it'll be fun to find out.

"I'm glad you guys had fun." Madi tilts her head at me, obviously wanting more of the story about the gala, knowing that I won't spill the beans until it's just the two of us in private. "And I'm grateful for the work you both put in planning this whole trip. We need to catch up."

"We do," I say. "I need to tell you all about how Billy and I are co-parenting a puppy."

Madi's mouth drops open. "You...and Billy? Co-parenting a puppy?"

Brick frowns like he can't believe it.

"Yup." I pop the "p." I can feel Billy grumbling next to me.

"I knew you were harboring a dog," Jake accuses him.

"It's not mine," Billy protests. It's too easy to rib him. "We're not co-parenting. Aubrey just brings the dog over when she paints."

"You're the one buying all the stuff for Pepper."

"You charged it to my credit card!"

"That was just food and a bed and puppy pads. You're the one buying the toys." I'm aware that we're bickering like an old married couple in front of everyone, and I'm enjoying every second. "Every time I come over, there's another ten toys for him. Soon you won't be able to see your floor."

Billy denies this.

"I have proof." I hold up my phone. My screen saver is Billy cuddling Pepper close. I snapped the picture when he wasn't paying attention. The affection on his face as he looks at the little dog is apparent.

"Who has the puppy while we're gone?" Madi asks.

"Billy's assistant took him." I met Annabeth—a gorgeous redhead who stopped by the penthouse to pick up Pepper—and I developed an instant irrational jealousy of her. But Pepper took to her instantly, so at least I know he's in good hands.

"Awww, look at that little guy," says Jake. He and the white guy sitting next to him—his name is Vance, I think—explode in laughter, jeering at Billy. I feel a little bit of regret that I showed them such a tender moment. I like seeing Billy with his guard down. It's so rare.

But he can hold his own. "Pepper is smart. I've already got him trained. If you're not careful, I'll train him to do your job." He wads up his napkin and throws it at Vance's head. Vance catches it and lobs it to the back of the plane, where Sully is sitting. He catches it without even looking up from his phone.

"Okay, Doggie Daddy, we got it," Jake says.

Billy raises his hands and makes several emphatic gestures. I've seen Madi signing enough to know he's speaking ASL.

I didn't know Billy knew sign language. Even more

surprising, is that Jake and Nickel seem to know it too. They both start signing back.

Madi laughs.

"Wait, what is he saying?"

"He's insulting their parentage." Madi grins. "And everything about them, really."

Now Vance is trying to get in on the signing, but he doesn't seem to know much of the language. Instead, he uses both hands to give everyone the middle finger. Madi and I both crack up.

"When did you all learn to sign?" Madi asks, delighted.

"We've been taking lessons ever since Noah moved to the executive floor," Billy tells her. "Couldn't have you outshine us all with your skills."

"Noah's an executive? That's awesome," Madi says. "He was always my favorite co-worker at Moon Co."

Brick clears his throat, and she gives him a small smile. "Except for you," she clarifies.

"In training," Billy says. "He's got a ways to go. But I think we should get him into our club. He's paid his dues, he deserves membership."

What club? Athletic club? Social club? What, are they all Masons? I feel like they're speaking about more than just a membership.

"We'll talk about that later. This weekend is for relaxing and fun," Brick says, and everyone settles into their seats as if his word is law.

"And practicing for our big Queen number," I say. "Brick, Madi volunteered you as Freddy Mercury."

He glances at her for confirmation, and she nods, her eyes twinkling. "Oh yes. I got an all white outfit like the one he wore at Live Aid. You're going to look amazing."

Brick's brows draw together in alarm, and Madi and I crack up all over again.

He relaxes. "That was a joke, wasn't it?"

"Yep."

"You should've seen your face," Madi crows. He shakes his head and lifts her hand to his lips and kisses it.

Billy and I make eye contact. I roll my eyes, and he smirks.

Chapter Twenty-Two

Aubrey

"So what's the scoop with you and Billy?" Madi asks, not missing the fact that he escorted me to my private cabana last night.

And, yes, he did come in and wear me out, so I could get to sleep in a new time zone.

Yes, it was incredible, as always. The man can make me orgasm over and over again until I'm wrung out.

Madi's stretched out on a comfy blue chaise lounge beside me. We're both in fluffy bathrobes provided by the amazing spa, lounging by a salt pool. We've just gotten massaged and manicured and pampered, and now we're snacking on hummus and crudites in between sessions in the sauna and dips in the hot tub.

Madi's two soon-to-be sisters-in-law are still getting their massages, so this is our chance for girl talk.

"I have so much to tell you." I start with the Sentience gala and give her the details of my shared days and nights with Billy. She's a good audience, gasping and laughing at appropriate times.

"He what?" Her jaw drops when I tell her about him giving me the credit card. I describe all the ways I charged it up, and she snickers. "Get it, girl. Torture him."

"At first, I was doing it because of how he treated you. But then it was just fun."

A spa attendant comes by with tiny white cups of lemon sorbet, and Madi and I take two each. The lemon flavor is both cool and sharp on my tongue, refreshing.

"He's so good with Pepper, though. I never would have guessed there was a softer side to him."

Not for humans, apparently, but for puppies. That must mean something.

"Let me see that picture again." Madi holds out her hand, and I give her my phone. She studies the photo, frowning.

"I wouldn't have guessed he had it in him, either." She shakes her head and hands me my phone back. "He hates weakness, in anyone. I guess puppies are exempt from his disdain, though."

"I think it's just an act."

"No, I had to prove myself to win his loyalty. And even then it was because Brick basically ordered him to."

"Yeah, about that. It's weird how they take orders from Brick. I mean, aren't they basically college friends. I guess it's because he's the CEO?" But that wouldn't affect their personal lives, would it?

"These guys, they do better with a leader," Madi says. "They were raised by hard asses. They trauma-bonded in college and started Moon Co to prove themselves. Brick led the way."

"So they take orders from him all the time? Like they're a military unit?"

"Something like that." I get the sense that Madi wants

to wave this away. She's not telling me the whole story, and I don't like it.

I get that some of this might be proprietary information, but I'm used to Madi spilling all her secrets to me. I fight disappointment that she isn't going to open up to me like she did before. I guess some secrets are meant to be kept.

"You know, Billy is a lot like you."

She wrinkles her nose, not liking that comparison.

"Loyal," I explain. "Committed to his friends. You say he hates weakness, but I think he just expects the best of himself and requires that of the people around him. If you're in his circle, he'll fight for you to the end." I think of him in the stairwell of Sentience, kissing me like his soul required it. Playing the part, but now that I remember the moment, his muscles were tense. He was intent on me, but if those guys had tried anything, I have no doubt in my mind that Billy would've done what was required to get me out. Even punching one of them.

He didn't need to resort to violence. He just acts like he has the biggest dick in the room and dominates everyone in it.

It helps that he *does* have the biggest dick in the room, I grin to myself.

I realize I've been reminiscing while Madi is frowning at me.

"Aubrey..."

"What?"

She looks away as if figuring out how to phrase what she wants to say. "Billy is committed. To Moon Co. To Brick and the rest." She's trying to tell me something, but she's dancing around it.

"I know that," I say.

"He's not the type to settle down."

Ugh, is this what she's trying to tell me? Billy's not looking for a relationship? I know that. I'm not looking for one either.

"Billy is the last guy I'd want as a boyfriend. We're just hooking up," I say. "Having some fun."

"Okay." She forces a grin. "Good."

A flash of irritation ripples through me. "But *why* is that good?"

"I just don't think he's capable of a relationship. Brick said he came from an abusive home with an uber-exacting father."

That news hits me square in the chest.

Well, no wonder he's so contained. So cold and controlled.

"It seems to me he's been hard-wired for ruthless success at any cost and not much else," she says.

That fits. Sorrow for the pain he's endured drowns me.

Dammit, I don't want to start seeing him as a three-dimensional human. Meaningless sex is working right now. I don't want anything else.

I rise and undo my robe, dropping it on the chaise lounge. I have a scrunchie on my wrist, and I whip it off to gather up my braids into a loose bun. "I'm going for a dip."

Without waiting for Madi's response, I turn and walk down the steps into the long infinity pool. It's heated to the perfect temperature, and the sensation of pristine water lapping against my bare skin relaxes me. I swim to the edge and lean against it, letting water slosh over the infinity edge. This side of the spa overlooks a gorgeous stretch of the beach. There are a group of guys down there, running back and forth over the sand, shouting to each other and tossing around a ball shaped like a rounded lemon.

I realize it's Billy. And Brick, Jake, Nickel, and the rest.

They're playing some sort of sports ball. Maybe rugby? All but Nickel have stripped off their shirts, and I'd be lying to myself if I didn't admit that they're all premium grade, A grade beefsteak. I didn't know guys really had abs like that. Tight and chiseled with enough contour to keep Michelangelo busy sculpting for a lifetime.

When do they even have the time to work out so much?

* * *

Billy

What started as a relaxing morning on the beach has turned into an intense game of shifter rugby.

Shifter rugby and human rugby are pretty similar. At least, when we're in public. In private, there are a lot less rules–and wolf forms are allowed. We have to play with a special ball because our wolf teeth puncture the traditional rugby ball and deflate it. I've played games where the ball was the jawbone of a deer or a piece of antler.

Now that I think of it, shifter rugby and human rugby have nothing in common. There are a lot more fights, a lot more biting. And howling.

Our game on the beach is pretty tame. Until my skin prickles, and I realize that someone is watching us. I turn and spot the culprit. The fancy spa Madi took her bridesmaids to overlooks this stretch of the beach. Aubrey's there, watching me from the pool. With her braids piled on her head, she looks like a queen.

My chest swells. Time to put on a show. I huddle up with Vance and Sully, facing Brick and the others. We sign our plans to each other and then break apart.

I do the kickoff, and immediately start running. Sully races to catch the ball, narrowly missing Nickel and Jake, who dive to stop him. Vance hollers and Sully passes the ball back to him. It's tricky because Brick is barreling down on them both.

But then I tackle Brick. I aim for center mass and slam into him, driving us both into the surf. We fall into the water.

The next thing I know, he's trying to drown me. He's got some new moves—he slipped my hold using a technique his werebear sparring buddy must have taught him. "Submit," he growls.

Normally I'd give in, but Aubrey's watching. "Never," I shout, and dive at his legs. I get a kick in the head and a mouthful of seawater, but Brick goes crashing into the water again.

"Are you kidding me?" Brick roars. It comes out garbled because I splash him when his mouth is open, and he swallows seawater.

"Smile." I splash him again. "We're on candid camera." I turn and wave to Aubrey. Madi has joined her on the edge of the pool, and they're both waving and laughing.

Brick grumbles but waves, and his face brightens when Madi blows him a kiss.

"Did we win?" I ask Vance, who's watching us from the beach, covered in sand.

"Yeah. Nickel and Jake tackled me, but Sully got the ball to their goal when we all stopped to watch you guys wrestle."

I pump my fist into the air. Our distraction tactic worked this time. It won't work again, but winning once feels nice.

"Dumbass," Jake signs at me, and we start insulting each other again in ASL.

A scent on the breeze alerts us that we have company.

We turn as one to face the group of shifters walking up the beach towards us.

Jake signs in ASL, "Who are they?"

Shifters have a heightened sense of hearing. Knowing sign language gives our pack an edge when we don't want to be overheard.

"King of Monaco and the top wolves in his pack," Sully answers. "We sent word that we'd be here. As a courtesy."

"Let's say hello," Brick says out loud in English, and we follow him up the beach, arranging ourselves in a loose formation with Brick at the head and me by his right hand.

The wolves facing us are big and burly. In the human world, they'd be clocked as body builders. The leader has a dark beard and a wild tangle of hair down his back. With his deeply tanned skin, he looks like a pirate. Sully gave Brick and I a dossier on him and his pack, so I know his family were shipping tycoons.

"Luka Atlantea," Brick greets him. "Wolf King of Monaco."

"Blackthroat." Luka's voice is deep and resonant. "The Wall Street Wonder. Welcome to my kingdom. We're honored by your visit."

"We're the ones who are honored," Brick must have dug deep to find some respect for King Luka because his words ring true.

"You are here to celebrate your upcoming nuptials, no?" Luka looks around as if searching for Brick's mate.

"Yes. My bride is here with her friends." Brick sweeps a hand out, indicating Madi and Aubrey at the spa. I tense slightly. My wolf doesn't like calling attention to Aubrey. We don't know these wolves.

Out of the corner of my eye, I see Sully shifting on

either foot. He's our security. He probably has wolves stationed all around the spa.

The thought makes me relax.

"We're celebrating with a bachelor and bachelorette party," Brick says. "It's a human tradition."

"Ah," King Luka says. I don't know what he's thinking. His scent is overpowered by a thick cologne. His face is shadowed as he looks up at the human women.

I'm on edge. Brick being mated to a human is still a shock to other wolves. Human shifter pairings aren't unheard of, but an alpha of a pack as large as ours would normally stick to tradition and find a strong shifter mate to keep the pack strong. At least, that's the older way of thinking.

It's my father's way of thinking.

It used to be my way of thinking. But Madi proved her strength and proved me wrong.

Still, other packs might see Brick's pairing as a weakness and decide to challenge him.

Is the King of Monaco one of them?

The guarded look disappears from Luka's face like it never existed. His mouth stretches into a wide smile and opens his arms like an exuberant host. "Well, you cannot go to the casinos. They are owned by the vampires. Come aboard my yacht, and I'll show you what Monaco is all about. Let us celebrate your mating, Atlantean style."

"Thank you, we would love that," Brick says.

I catch Sully's eye. Looks like we're going to party on a yacht with a bunch of strangers. Alcohol, a huge group of shifters, and two human females–including one who doesn't know our kind exist.

Fuck.

What could possibly go wrong?

* * *

The *Sea Maid* is a two hundred million dollar superyacht owned by Atlantean Enterprises. At 75 meters, it's the largest yacht in the dock. I heard the docking fees are over six figures a month.

At dusk, it glows like a jewel. It's so huge, it might as well be a bright white city floating on the water.

I watch over Aubrey as we board the boat. For some reason, she and Madi were singing "You're So Vain" by Carly Simon on the ride over. Now she, Madi, and Brick's sisters Ruby and Scarlett ooh and ahh over the luxurious wood floors and white leather lounge area. Staff members in white and navy uniforms offer us glasses of prosecco. I wave mine away, and Aubrey grabs it and drinks it for me, her eyes sparkling. I'm glad she's having a good time.

I notice our males are a lot less relaxed. I keep myself between the ladies and the Monaco pack wolves at all times. Luka allowed Sully's team aboard the ship to do a security sweep. Sully himself okayed the trip, so I shouldn't be on high alert.

The biggest danger is the King himself. And he's drinking. It takes a lot of alcohol for a shifter to maintain a buzz, but he seems determined to accomplish it. He also insists on giving us the full tour, including the cinema, gym, spa, and ice room. The ladies love it.

"Instead of the spa, we could've come here," Scarlett giggles.

"You are welcome anytime, my lady," Luka captures her hand and bows over it.

I don't like watching him flirt with Scarlett, who I think of as a little sister, but she's a she-wolf who can handle her own. Brick makes her train daily in self defense.

We're mingling on the party deck, next to the glass bottomed pool.

The other wolves stand back, murmuring politely. Everyone's behaving themselves.

I don't know how I ended up next to Luka, but he's talking to me, and it'd be rude to rebuff him.

I'd rather be with Aubrey. After a day at the spa, she is glowing. Right now, she and Madi are on the top deck, taking in the view.

"Your luna is lovely, for a human," Luka murmurs.

I give him a nod although I want to grill him on what he meant by 'for a human.' Is he a shifter supremacist like my father? Like I was raised to be?

"You're also here with a human," Luka says. He raises his head and sniffs the air. "The one with the delectable scent. Spiced oranges?"

Talking about scents is super personal. I tense, my wolf hating that he's speaking of Aubrey so intimately and so casually. But maybe it's an American thing.

Luka swirls his drink. He's drinking ouzo, and the strong anise smell hides his own scent.

"I, too, enjoy a human now and then. They are so weak. Dominate them a little, and they become eager to please. Easily kept as pets."

I have a gift for staying unemotional. Controlling my reactions, so I can manipulate situations with the correct angle, but anger explodes in my brain. Did this dickhead really compare Aubrey to a pet? Like she's a dog like Pepper?

I want to kill him. Right here, right now. It'd be so easy. He'd never see it coming, I could just jump on him, tear out his eyes, and strangle him before he knew what was happening.

My wolf is howling, all for it. No one talks about Aubrey like that and lives.

Except...I can't. This is the Alpha King of Monaco. We're in his territory.

This is another example of how much Aubrey disturbs my ability to function. Fuck.

Nickel notices my tension and signs the equivalent of "Easy, tiger." I signal back, "Fuck off." I'm not going to lose control of my wolf in the middle of a foreign country.

I smile at the king, showing my canines. "Our pack treats humans like equals. We share their world, after all. And I don't know about other packs' practices, but we don't fuck our pets." I hide my sneer, but I don't need to. My derision comes through.

The king hears it loud and clear. His eyes flare amber–the same color as Brick's–and then he gets his wolf under control. "You misunderstand me. I was merely curious why the alpha of such a strong pack would stoop to mating a weak human. He will dilute his bloodline. His pups will be duds."

That's it.

I know he's just saying out loud what many older wolves in our own pack think. But this insult cannot stand.

"Our luna is not weak," I say loud enough that everyone on the deck can hear me. "She provides strength to our pack."

Luka's lip curls, but he seems to realize he's crossed a line. "I mean nothing by this, of course. I am just curious."

"See that your curiosity doesn't make you less courteous," I say. His eyes flash–I've just given the king of this territory an order. On his own yacht, no less.

Nickel must sense danger because he heads our way to intercede. "Luka, I'm glad to meet you, at last. I believe our families are connected by marriage. Our cousins in Gibraltar?"

Luka ignores Nickel. His gaze locks on mine. I tense, expecting a challenge.

Instead, he laughs and downs his drink. "Indulge me one more curiosity. Your human?" He gestures towards Aubrey, who's laughing and leaning into the wind on the upper deck. She lifts her braids away from her neck, and a fresh bloom of scent hits the breeze. "What does she provide? Other than a few holes to please you–"

I don't think, I just act. The king usually stands with both feet planted, like a ship captain used to stormy seas. But he's made the mistake of leaning back on the railing to point Aubrey out.

I drop and grab his leg then heave. He isn't expecting an attack, certainly not one that involves me dropping to my knees in front of him. In a split second, I get him off balance, and gravity does the rest.

The king's mouth opens wide, and then he falls backwards. Not to the lower deck–we're on the lowest part of the ship.

No, he spills right over the edge. I watch in slow motion as he roars–the sound splits the night–and falls into the dark water with a splash.

What have I done?

I just threw the king of the Monaco pack over the side of his own boat.

His two bodyguards are already moving towards me, shouting. They're going to grab me, lock me down.

I don't let them. I feint and dodge and weave, getting behind them, and then use their own momentum against them. One of them trips, and I make myself the fulcrum to send him flying. The other slams into me. I twist, deflect, and kick him over the side, too.

Now there are three wolves in the water far below. Which is fine–I'm sure they all can swim. The king's body-guards can protect him from sharks.

I have bigger problems. There's more bellowing above me, as the king's pack rushes to get to this deck to take me out.

Someone sidles up beside me, and I almost drop kick him, when I realize it's Nickel. He smells like gin, and his perfect polo shirt is soaked with the juniper-scented liquid. He's breathing hard, and I realize he moved to trip one of my attackers. He's taking his place to fight beside me.

A howl, and Jake lands on the deck beside me. He's shirtless, his abs gleaming wet from the pool. His eyes are bright, his wolf's come out to play. He skids to my side, opposite Nickel. I signal for them to fall into a rugby forma-tion, facing the King's enraged wolves.

"The humans," I mutter. I glance up, but I can't see Aubrey or Madi anymore.

"Brick's on it. He, Sully, and Vance will get them to safety, if they have to commandeer a boat to do it."

That makes me feel better. I've already fucked up, starting a fight with our hosts. I'll have to explain to everyone later. "We better give them a distraction then."

Jake whoops. His fangs flash with his grin. "Let's kick some shifter ass."

* * *

"So what really happened?" Brick demands. We're in his penthouse suite, debriefing just the two of us. On the boat back from the super yacht, I explained to the group that

Luka got drunk and rude, and things escalated to a brawl. Fortunately, everyone was flush with adrenaline and still in a party mood. Aubrey and Madi started singing, "You're so vain" again, and Jake and Vance even joined in. Our escape from the super yacht was just another bit of fun.

Now Nickel and Sully are holed up in a comms room. Nickel is on the phone with his family, using his personal connections to smooth things over with the pack here. Sully is adding layers of security to make sure our pack is safe. Everyone else is getting some sleep, worn out from all the excitement.

Except me and Brick. He wants answers.

"They insulted Madi," I tell him, and his eyes go flinty. He's not happy about the way things turned out, mostly because the humans could've been hurt. But he understands the need to defend our luna. He would do the same. "And humans in general. Are we getting kicked out of Monaco?"

"It's up in the air, but I think we can smooth things over long enough to finish out our trip. Nickel's connections will help us appeal to reason. Luka is a known hot head, and even though he's the king, he's still guided by the wiser members of his family. We'll want to avoid this country in the near future, but I doubt Luka wants it getting around that we beat him on his own boat."

I snort, remembering his outrage as he fell into the water.

"You're usually more controlled than this," Brick observes. I've been waiting for him to read me the riot act for starting something, but he looks less angry than thoughtful.

"He got to me. He was spouting the same stuff my

father says." Brick is one of the few people who knows how bad my father was. "And...he mentioned Aubrey."

"Ah." There's a lot of weight in the syllable. I wonder how much I've revealed–or if my guardedness is announcing my deeper feelings for the chaos human. "A year ago, you wouldn't have lifted a finger to defend a human."

I inhale, my cheeks burning with shame. I treated Madi like shit because I thought she was going to tear our pack apart. I didn't trust her, and I thought she'd end up being a weakness we couldn't afford. And, yeah, my dad's fierce anti-human prejudice played a part in this. "I've changed."

"Yes, you have."

Brick leans back in his chair and crosses his arms over his chest. "Aubrey is Madi's best friend. Like a sister. I need to know what this human means to you."

I feel like a kid getting grilled by the father of my prom date. *I promise to get her home before ten pm.*

"I've treated her well," I say defensively.

"That's not what I'm asking. I know that, when it counted, you treated her with respect. If you hadn't, she would've chopped your balls off. And Madi would've helped."

This is accurate, but I wince.

"And then I would kill you," he continues in that even tone. "I wouldn't want to, you're pack second, and my closest friend, but–"

"I understand. If I hurt her, I wouldn't be able to forgive myself."

"Hmm," Brick murmurs again. He narrows his eyes, studying my face. I've given myself away.

What does Aubrey mean to me? I can't answer because I don't even know. She's chaos to my control. Bright splashes of paint on a monotone palette. The scent of orange, cinnamon, and nutmeg filling the back of my limo.

What can I say? She has a silver nose ring that burns my skin. Kissing her is better because it hurts a little.

I can't tell Brick any of this.

"She's special," I say.

"What does your wolf think?"

"He wants to protect her." He wants me to do more than that.

Brick tilts his head as if waiting for me to confess the rest. How my fangs have sharpened when she's in my bed. How feral I get near the full moon. How I imagine claiming her and keeping her in my life...forever.

I'm not ready to admit what she could be to me. *Mate*.

Brick seems to understand this. He nearly went moon mad trying to avoid claiming Madi. Of all the wolves, he knows what I'm going through.

After a long pause, he nods. "Your punishment is patrol duty for the rest of the trip." Not much of a punishment; we're all taking security posts to make sure Luka doesn't have an opening to retaliate. "Let's get some sleep. We'll take the dawn shift."

"Are you punishing yourself, too?" I follow his lead and rise from my seat.

"It's my fault we were on that boat in the first place. I should've made sure I knew his stance on humans before allowing him so close to ours." He claps my shoulder. "I'm grateful you stood up for Madi and Aubrey."

"Even if it cost us?"

"Even then. That's the lesson fate taught me when I met Madi. No matter what, your mate always comes first."

Chapter Twenty-Three

B*illy*

The next morning, Sully gives us the all-clear, security wise. The bridal party heads into the city center because the females–mostly Brick's sisters, Ruby and Scarlett–want to do some luxury shopping. I would opt out to preserve my manhood, but my wolf doesn't want Aubrey to go unescorted.

My assistant, Annabeth, did a great job with the logistics, and she somehow arranged a bullet-proof limo driven by one of Sully's top security wolves, and we pile in. Scarlett pours champagne for everyone.

On the way, Aubrey's phone rings. She glances at the screen and frowns. "I'm sorry, I have to take this."

Through the phone, I hear the tinny voice of a panicked female. "Aubrey! Yesterday I got home, and my computer was gone. My apartment had been broken into, and they ransacked the place."

I frown as Aubrey goes rigid.

"Did you call the cops?" she asks.

"No! Are you kidding? This isn't a normal break-in. It's

241

Sentience! I told you someone was watching me! I'm in hiding. I don't know if you're in danger, but I wanted to give you a heads-up. Tell Jan, too."

The scent of fear that comes from Aubrey turns my wolf ferocious. Everyone in the limo notes the change and focuses on Aubrey.

"I'm so sorry I got you involved in this—" the person on the other line is babbling.

"Hey, it's okay," Aubrey soothes. "I'll be careful and will make sure Jan is too. We'll be okay. Let me know when you're somewhere safe."

"What is it?" Madi asks.

Aubrey hesitates then shakes her head and forces a smile, clearly not wanting to ruin the festive atmosphere. "It's nothing—just, um, someone I know had their house broken into."

It's clearly not nothing, but I let it go until I help her out of the limo, and we can talk in private. She doesn't want to disturb Madi's weekend, and I respect that. We're at a group of luxury shops located in an outdoor courtyard with fountains and gardens.

The group scatters, agreeing to meet back up in a couple of hours.

"What happened?" I escort Aubrey away from the others. "That had to do with the Sentience espionage, right?"

She swallows. I hate the edge of fear I see behind her normally confident expression. "The Sentience whistle-blower had her place tossed. She told me before she thought someone was following her. That's why I freaked out that night you were trailing me in your car."

"Fuck. I'm sorry I scared you."

She gives her head a quick shake. "No, don't be. I just..."

"I'll have someone check on your place and keep an eye on it while we're gone. Who's Jan?"

She gives me a surprised look, and I realize I revealed too much. I shouldn't have heard her conversation over the music playing in the limo.

I play it off with a shrug. "I overheard. You were right next to me."

"Jan is my lawyer friend. She and her partner own La Résistance, where I work. She might take the case if we get enough evidence."

"Do you want me to put security on her as well?"

Aubrey's eyes go round, but her body relaxes. I've given her relief. "You would do that?"

"Absolutely." I dial Grayson, our front door guy. He's one of Sully's security team members, but he'll answer to me as pack beta. "Call Jan and let her know," I say to Aubrey.

We both have brief conversations, and I text Aubrey and Jan's addresses to Grayson.

"Thank you." She looks up at me with her warm brown eyes. "You really are a fixer, aren't you?"

Something shifts in my chest. I refuse to work to earn anyone but my alpha's approval. But hearing the admiration and appreciation in Aubrey's voice affects me. I want to earn her gratitude again. Want her to look up at me this way, like I'm strong and powerful. Like I'm the male who will hold her steady when things get rough.

"Who said that, Madi?"

She nods.

I lean over and kiss her forehead. It's a decidedly affectionate gesture–completely unlike me–but I like the way it makes me feel.

Like for a moment, I'm not an island in the middle of the fucking ocean. It's not me against the world.

I could choose between keeping the world under meticulous control to ensure survival, or I could become this guy. Someone who has a lovely female to care for and protect.

It's a role I never thought I wanted. It involves vulnerability. Not just between me and the female but because there's a female in my life. She becomes a vulnerability. A liability. Another place danger could strike.

Brick chose this life. Allowing someone in to weaken everything he built. He's not the razor-sharp shark I met in college. The one looking to take back everything the Adalwulfs took from him anymore.

But Madi has strengthened him, too. As a couple—as alpha and luna—they are more than the sum of two parts. Their strength is exponential. And he smiles now. He's found a satisfaction that seemed out of reach to me.

But maybe it's not.

"Feel better?" I ask.

"Yes."

"Good. Come on, let's shop." I take her elbow and steer her toward a jewelry store.

"Really?" She peers up at me through thick lashes, a sensual curve to her lips. "You don't strike me as the shopping type."

"I'm not."

"I'm more of a thrifter. I love to haunt the sales racks or flea markets. I can't afford anything here."

"You have the hundred grand you charged me."

She throws me an impish smile. "True. But that money doesn't even feel real. I was just pushing you to see where you'd push back. I never expected you to actually pay me that much."

"You negotiated what it was worth to you. I paid what it was worth to me. Come here, let's check this place out." I lead her into a jewelry shop that I noted when I researched where we were going on the way over. "This place has lab-grown diamonds. No children dying in mines for their jewelry."

Aubrey peers at me. "I can't decide if you're making fun of me."

"Not at all. I know what's important to you." I look at the woman behind the desk, who greets us in French.

"Good afternoon. I would like to buy my girlfriend a diamond nose and navel ring. Do you have any?" I ask in French.

She beams at me. "We do. I have a wide selection. Look at these." She pulls a tray of diamond studs out from a locked cabinet behind her.

Aubrey flicks a glance around with disinterest. I get it. She's not impressed by money or expensive gifts.

"This is a pink diamond. It would look stunning on her." The saleswoman still speaks in French. "And there is a matching set with two diamonds for her belly. I will get them now." She bends down to open another cabinet and produces another tray, this time with pairs of diamonds–one large, one small–set on curved studs.

I pick up the pink diamond nose stud and hand it to Aubrey.

She peers at it. "Oh!" She lifts her gaze to my face in surprise. "It's a nose ring."

"What, did you think I'd buy you a cheesy pendant or something, Silver? I pay attention. I know what you like." I slide a mirror over to her. "Is this the one?"

"You're buying me a gift." She sounds stunned. "Wow." She holds the pink diamond up to her nostril. "You do pay

245

attention. It's lovely. I...I love it." I can almost see the inner wrestling, and I celebrate the small victory of picking the right gift. One she won't reject out of her disdain for money. One that reflects my respect for who she is, as she is.

"There's a matching one for your navel."

"Really? Thank you." Her lips turn up at the corners as she gazes at me in surprise. "This is...unexpected. Very sweet–and generous." She lifts her lips to kiss mine.

It takes all my control not to grab her and tongue-fuck that sassy mouth until she's breathless. But I don't do PDA.

"I didn't think you were capable of sweet."

"I'm not." I make my voice extra dry. "But I'm allergic to silver."

Understanding dawns on Aubrey's face. "That's why you always get red after we kiss!" She claps a hand over her mouth. "Oh my God, why didn't you tell me?"

"I didn't want you to stop. I've accepted that you, Aubrey Cook, are my own personal kryptonite."

Aubrey's expression is warm as her lips turn up into a smug smile. "Love that."

"Of course you do."

"We'll take these," I tell the saleswoman, indicating the pink diamond nose ring and matching belly button ring. The larger stud on the navel ring is at least two carats, and it's surrounded by a ring of tiny white diamonds.

"Excellent choice." The saleswoman seamlessly changes to English. "Would you like to wear this out?"

Aubrey nods and slides her silver nose and belly button rings out as I pay the five thousand dollar bill as Aubrey puts the new jewelry on. "I love them, thank you." She reaches for my face and pulls me down for a kiss.

I experience a moment of alarm. What am I doing? I'm acting like a boyfriend to Aubrey, which I'm not.

I can't be. Things are spiraling out of my control. A sense of danger crawls up my spine. Life or death danger, but that doesn't make sense.

My phone rings, and I whip it out.

"Billy, it's Grayson. I stopped by Ms. Cook's apartment, and it's been trashed. The lock was busted. Her neighbor says it must have happened yesterday. She saw a guy coming out of her apartment, and she asked him if he was watching her place while she was in Monaco. So he's got a heads' up on her location now."

Fuck.

That was the warning I had from my wolf. It wasn't that giving Aubrey gifts was unsafe. It was about *her* safety.

Which I suddenly realize means everything to me.

I step outside, and she follows. "Okay, file a police report. See if you can catch a–" I stop myself before I say *scent.* "Any trace of who was there. And check the surrounding area. The place may be watched. If so, take them down and bring them in for me to deal with when I get back."

"On it, boss."

The warning prickle at the back of my neck doesn't ease. I scan our surroundings, even though we're 4000 miles away from Manhattan. My body's in motion before I even register what I've seen.

A sniper, 200 feet away.

I tackle Aubrey to the ground as a bullet pierces my skin and embeds in my back.

* * *

Aubrey

I scream.

I'm not sure what's happening. Why Billy threw me onto the ground. The pavement scrapes and bruises my knees. His body blankets mine, heavy as a rhino.

The way he covers my head with his arms makes it clear what's happening even before he rasps, "Stay down. There's a shooter."

A shooter. What the fuck?

Is this random gun violence or related to Sentience?

Billy has his phone out, and he barks. "I need back up *now*" before he pulls me to my feet. His hand stays on my head, pushing me, so I'm folded in half at the waist like him ducking from whatever or whoever is after us.

That's when I see the blood soaking his clothes.

"You're hit!"

Oh no. No no no no. Oh my God.

"Billy!"

This is unreal. Catastrophic. I gulp breaths to try to think.

He pulls me in a ducked run behind a low garden wall, keeping his gaze on a point in the distance.

I don't hear the sound of shots, but glass explodes behind us.

Screams sound from every direction. They must be using a silencer. No one heard the first shot, but now everyone in the outdoor mall knows there's a shooter.

My heart beats so hard I swear it will come out of my chest.

"You're hit. Oh my God." The amount of blood that soaking Billy's clothes scares the shit out of me. We need to get him to an ER. "Help!" I scream, looking around. "Someone call an ambulance!"

He's going to die, and it was because he was saving me.

He can't die.

A bullet hits the brick wall to my right. I bark a sharp shriek of surprise.

"We're okay," Billy says calmly although he has to be seconds from collapsing from the amount of blood he lost. "Just keep your head down, and he can't sight us."

"Are they here for me?"

He scans the environment again then pulls me at a crouched run behind the next wall. "I won't let them get you, Silver."

Sully, Vance, Nickel, and Jake race around the corner.

"Shooter, two o'clock. Aubrey's the target. Get transport," Billy barks information with military precision although his movements are slowing, like the blood loss finally caught up.

He wasn't in the military, was he?

Even more baffling, the guys react as if they are part of an elite navy SEAL team.

"Already on it. Jake, Vance, find the shooter. We'll cover Aubrey," Sully replies. Sully and Nickel flank us, providing me with even more body coverage as we run, en masse, toward the street.

Billy collapses, dropping to one knee.

"He's hurt!" I cry, stating the obvious.

Nickel hauls him up, putting his shoulder under Billy's arm.

"Cover Aubrey." Billy's voice sounds thin.

Oh my God. He's going to die. I can't let him die.

This can't be happening.

"We need to get him to a hospital," I cry.

Brick, Madi, Scarlett and Ruby, and Eagle run around, and one of the guys barks, "protect the Luna."

Brick and Scarlett sandwich Madi.

Sirens sound in the distance.

The limo stands out front, doors open. The guys hustle us toward it. Billy's still hanging onto me like I need protection when he's the one about to bleed out.

"Wait!" I call, pointing in the direction of the sirens. "That might be the ambulance. Billy should go in an ambulance."

They ignore me.

"Put Aubrey in the front," Brick snaps from behind us. He takes my arm to try to separate me from Billy.

"Right," Madi agrees.

In the front? With the chauffeur's glass separating us?

Hell, no.

"Why?" I screech.

"Aubrey–" Madi's also now trying to tug me away.

Billy collapses at the door of the limo, and Nickel and Sully have to pick him up to toss him like a hay bale onto one of the seats.

The reality that Billy may die turns me icy cold.

"No!" I wrench away from Brick and Madi and throw myself in behind him. "I'm riding with him."

"Fuck," Brick mutters, but everyone tumbles in, and the limo takes off with tires squealing before the door even closes.

"Billy." I drop to my knees in front of the seat where he's curled on his side. His face is colorless, teeth chattering.

Nickel sits toward his feet, and he rolls Billy forward to examine the wound.

I frantically skim his body with my palms as if I can heal him through touch alone.

"What in the fuck just happened?" Brick roars.

Billy's lips move, but no sound comes out. He starts shaking like he's having a seizure. His eyes seem to turn an icy silver.

"The bullet didn't go through," Nickel reports. "Lucky for Aubrey."

For me? What in the fuck does he mean? Oh–because it would've hit me too? But everyone who watches mafia thrillers knows bullet wounds that go straight through are better. If he has a bullet lodged in an organ somewhere, he'll need massive surgery.

"It's my fault," I choke. "They came for me."

A strange cracking sound comes from Billy's back, like it's breaking apart. God, did the bullet hit his spine?

"Fuck," Brick mutters again.

"He took a bullet for me." Tears streak my face. "Now he's going to die."

"He won't die." Nickel sounds calm. It's weird how people handle emergencies differently. Billy was calm, too.

And now he's going to die.

Billy's face contorts. The snapping bone sound gets louder. There's a tearing of fabric, and then suddenly, Billy's gone.

My breath stops.

In his place lies an *enormous white and gray wolf.* Billy's clothes lie in shredded tatters around him.

A strange whimpering sound escapes my throat. What...just–

The wolf's white fur turns red from blood.

"That's it, Billy." Nickel's hand is on the wolf's flank. "Let your wolf heal you."

"The...the wolf is Billy." My voice sounds far away to my ears.

Billy is a wolf.

I twist to look over my shoulder to gaze at the rest of the group. Every face I scan looks unsurprised. Pale and sober but unsurprised. Even Madi's.

"Billy is a werewolf?" It's like one part of my brain–the one indoctrinated with fairytales and fantasy–understands perfectly, but the other says this is impossible.

"A wolf shifter," Madi says.

That's when it hits me. "You're all wolves."

All except for Madi? Or has she been turned?

"He's going to be okay," Madi says, and this time I believe her. Because if men can turn into wolves, I certainly can believe other magic and miracles are possible.

I bob my head, tears still streaming down my face. "Okay," I sniff. "That's good." I realize the other people in the limo are looking at each other.

I'm in on their secret.

I lean my face close to the wolf's. He's ginormous–way bigger than a normal wolf. My body has a biological fear response to the huge head and giant teeth, but this is Billy. The guy who just took a bullet for me. "Please be okay," I murmur.

He licks the tears from my cheek.

"Please."

"The bleeding already stopped," Nickel says quietly. "His body will expel the bullet in a day or two. He'll need to rest up to recover, that's all."

Relief pours through me, and I cry harder. "Oh. That's good." I stroke his silky ears. "That's really good."

"What happened, Aubrey?" Brick asks, without the bark this time.

I wipe the tears with my wrist and turn to look at him, keeping one hand on Billy's head. "I'm involved in some corporate espionage. To take down Sentience, the A.I. company that stole everyone's work."

Brick's eyebrows pop.

"Did you know this?" he asks Madi, who winces.

"Yes."

"I didn't know it would come to this," I say.

"There was a whistleblower of an AI company who ended up dead in a hotel room," Brick says. "His death was deemed suicide...but his parents protest that claim. These guys don't mess around."

I shiver. Jamie was right to be paranoid. "Then I guess they're trying to get rid of me. Billy's guy said they ransacked my apartment yesterday and must've found me here. It's just... crazy." I shake my head, unable to believe things have come to this.

"A heads-up would've been nice," Brick mutters. "From either one of you." He splits a look between Madi and Billy.

It's weird to see someone talk to an animal like they understand.

Suddenly, his relationship with his friends makes more sense. They're wolves. They follow an alpha.

And no wonder Madi pulled away from me after she got serious with him.

I think back to how she felt marginalized by him at first–sequestered in a separate wing of the house when she got snowed in with him in the Adirondacks. That must've been before–

"Madi...are you a wolf, too?" I croak. I have to know. Are they going to bite me and turn me into one of them now? How does this work?

She lets out a chuff of laughter, but her eyes are sorrowful, like she regrets that she couldn't tell me. "No. Still me. They're a different species. It's not a contagion like movies would have us believe."

"Okay." I turn back to Billy. That's all I can handle right now. I keep stroking his head and ears.

I don't care if they're a pack of donkeys. What matters is

that Billy is so much more than I believed. I'd pigeon-holed him into the role of asshole billionaire. A big, bad bully. I thought he only cared about money and business when he actually had a depth and history I never saw.

Now I want to know the real Billy. The one who is fiercely loyal to his alpha. The one who protected me with his life. There's so much more to him than I realized, and I want to see it all.

Chapter Twenty-Four

B *illy*

I wake with Aubrey's nutmeg and honey scent curling into my nostrils. I draw it in, finding it deeply soothing, like I'm in the right place.

Wait—where am I? Aubrey and I don't sleep together. We have sex, and I leave.

I force my eyelids—heavy with grit—open and look around. I'm in Aubrey's cabana. She's curled beside me, her myriad of braids sprawled across the pillow. The pink diamond nose ring looks delicate and beautiful in her nostril.

That, along with the sharp pain between my shoulderblades, brings it all back. Someone shooting at her. Getting her to the limo. Then it gets fuzzy. I vaguely remember Aubrey weeping. I licked her face.

Fuck.

I shifted. Of course I did—I was shot. My body repairs much faster in wolf form.

I remember Aubrey insisting on caring for me, so Nickel carried me here to her cabana.

I reach for Aubrey and tug her body up against mine. Her eyes fly open, startled.

"I didn't mean to wake you," I murmur.

"You're awake!" She pushes up to sit, but I pull her back down. "How do you feel?" She twists and reaches for a bottle of water by the nightstand. "Here, drink some water. You lost a lot of blood."

I find a smile tugging at the corners of my lips. I normally hate feeling out of control. I want to be the guy orchestrating everyone and everything around me. Definitely not someone who wasn't even aware of where he was sleeping. But waking up next to Aubrey doesn't disturb my inner control freak. And Aubrey taking care of me feels... sweet. Tender.

Which is strange because tenderness isn't an emotion I normally allow. Not even for my mother or sister. I accept the water bottle from her and drink it down. She was right–I'm thirsty.

"Are you hungry?"

My hand slides to grip her ass. "Ravenous."

Some of the worry in her expression melts away. "You're really okay, aren't you?"

I glance at the clock. "How long was I out?"

"Sixteen hours." She blinks at me. Gold starbursts decorate her brown irises. "You saved my life."

Remembering that there's still someone after her makes me draw a sharp breath. I sit up, wincing a bit at the pain between my shoulder blades. "Did they find the shooter? What's going on?"

This time it's Aubrey pulling me back down to the bed. "I don't know. Jake and Vance went after him, but I haven't heard if they found him or not."

I study her, bringing my hand to cradle her cheek. "So

now you know our secret."

She nods. "Wow."

"You seem pretty unfazed by it."

"It was sort of eclipsed by the fact that you were dying." There's a tremble in her voice that makes my heart squeeze.

The image of her tear-stained face next to mine after I shifted rises in my mind. She was worried about me. This girl who once hated me was devastated when I was hurt.

"I would never let them hurt you, Silver," I tell her. "I will find who shot at you and rip his spine from his pelvis."

Her eyes fly open wide. "That's, um, scary but hot." I scent the honey of her arousal.

Her body needs me. Just like mine needs her.

My lips twitch again. My dick lengthens for her. I push her onto her back, climbing on top of her. I'm still naked from the shift. "I'm going to fuck you now."

She rolls her pelvis to meet mine but says, "Are you sure? I mean, are you up for it?"

"I need your pussy, Aubrey. It will help me heal."

She lets out a breathy laugh. "I'm not sure that's true, but okay." She reaches for a box of condoms I left beside the bed when I escorted her here when we arrived. It feels like so long ago.

She wears a matching lavender lace cami and panty set. Now that she knows what I am, I don't have to hold back. I grasp the hem of her panties with both hands at the top of her thigh and rent the fabric in two.

She gasps then giggles. "Oh my God! You're super strong. It all makes sense now."

I rip her cami straight down the front.

"I missed so many clues."

"Like what?" I ask because I need to know where I was

careless. The control freak in me has to log all potential weaknesses.

"Your strength. How you potty trained Pepper with one look. Why Madi never included me anymore."

I roll a condom over my erection.

"I thought you were a dick, but you're just protective of your secret."

"No. I'm a dick," I assure her. "Nobody would argue with you there."

She shakes her head. "You're not."

I rub the head of my cock between her legs. She's slick and ready for me. I ease in. My body's still weak, so I don't have that urgent drive I've had every other time I was with her.

I want to take my time. To just experience the incredible sensation of being inside her without the need to turn myself inside out to pleasure her and get my release.

She's still synthesizing it all. "Madi said you're classist. I thought it might be code for racist. But now I understand. You don't relate to outsiders. Or what do you call people like me?"

Something akin to pain stabs at my chest. I don't want to be the person she's describing. I don't like the way it feels. I usually operate without compassion for others because compassion makes it impossible to make clear decisions.

But Aubrey doesn't sound hurt or judgmental. It's more like she sees me–really sees me–and doesn't flinch.

"Humans." My voice sounds rusty. I arc in and out of her slowly, relishing the tight squeeze of her channel and the way she arches her full breasts and rocks her pelvis to take me deeper. "I was raised in a small town made up entirely of shifters. My dad was a shifter supremacist."

Fate, am I telling this story? I never tell this story. I haven't since I told it to Brick Freshman year at Yale.

I find her hands and pin them beside her head, interlacing my fingers with hers.

"Am I your first?" she asks.

"First what?"

"First human?"

I wince. "Yes," I admit.

She doesn't seem offended. "You're my first, too." She smiles.

"First wolf?"

"Billionaire. And wolf. I've had a white guy before, though."

I can't help it. I laugh. Things feel so different with Aubrey right now. Like all our barriers are down. All that sniping at each other, all the power plays are absent. We're suddenly on the same team.

I lean over and nibble at her neck while I continue to glide in and out of her. "I wanted you the moment I first caught your nutmeg and honey scent at the cafe. You were so fucking sassy. I wanted to bend you over that counter and smack your sweet ass."

Aubrey gushes fluids, turned on, as always, by any suggestion of dominance. I go with it, caging her throat with my fingers.

"Did I make you break your rule?" Aubrey's lids droop.

Warning bells go off. I shouldn't share this with her–shouldn't give her a reason to hate me, but she doesn't seem offended.

"Yes," I admit.

She gives me a satisfied smile. "You made me break mine, too."

Fate, she's gorgeous. I like her like this–soft and open to

me. I like her feisty, too, but this is something special. She's letting me in.

"Your no billionaires rule?"

"Yep. I wanted to keep on hating you, but you were too damn sexy. And then you started with the capability porn."

"The what?"

"Capability porn. The way you solve problems so easily. Like training a puppy and getting security footage erased. Protecting me from snipers. You're pretty swoon-worthy, Billy." A vulnerable look creeps over her face. "I consider myself a strong, independent woman, but I like how you make me feel taken care of. You see me for who I really am, despite all the fronting I do."

My wolf revels in hearing that she feels protected with me, as she should. It occurs to me that I am attracted to Aubrey's strength, even though my bias said she must be weak because she's human. I was wrong—just like I was wrong about Madi. Aubrey is strong in ways I can't comprehend. She's brave and loyal and has a sense of justice that doesn't flinch or wither beside self-preservation.

She's one in a million. I thought she was an itch to scratch, but she's so much more.

She's everything.

"Silver, I'm about to make *this* into capability porn. Me capable of making you come with my fingers around your throat."

She smiles.

I tighten my fingers—not enough to block any airflow, just enough to make it exciting. I ride her harder, plowing deeper with each thrust. Making it mean something.

She starts moaning, and the sound brings out my feral side. I pick up speed, slamming into her harder now. Her eyes roll back in her head. Her mewls make me harder than stone.

My body finds a new reserve of energy–probably drawn straight from Aubrey–and tension builds. My balls draw up.

"Come, Aubrey," I command.

"Yes! Yes!" she cries. "I'm right..." Her muscles squeeze around my dick.

I come at almost the same time, thrusting deep and filling the condom. When we finish, I drop to my side and wrap my arms around Aubrey, inhaling her scent into my being.

It wasn't supposed to happen this way. This wasn't part of my master plan. Aubrey shouldn't know what I am. I shouldn't be lying here with my arms around a human, forgetting to care about anything but her and her safety.

But no part of me regrets this.

Aubrey is mine. I'm going to hunt down her enemies and end them, one by one.

I will put myself between her and danger every time.

Even if it costs me everything.

Chapter Twenty-Five

ubrey

After sex, Billy falls back to sleep with me in his arms, so I quietly slip out of bed and go out to the balcony to call Madi. I called Jamie last night to tell her that someone shot at me, and I fear it could be related to Sentience. She's in hiding still, so hopefully, she will be safe.

We were supposed to fly back this morning to get ready for the wedding, but they decided to delay the flight for Billy to recover a little more. The plan was to leave this afternoon whether he was conscious or not–which terrified me.

But I guess after that spectacular display of virility, I don't have to worry. They were right–he's going to be just fine.

Which is just crazy. All the pieces are still clicking together in my head. All the hints I had but didn't recognize. The allergy to silver–OMG!

Werewolves are supposedly allergic to silver, at least

according to the lore. But they aren't werewolves, they're wolf shifters.

I have so many questions.

Madi answers after a couple of rings. "Hey, how's he doing?"

"He woke up. We had sex, and he fell back to sleep."

Madi laughs. "Well. I guess that means he's good to fly back."

"Yep. Thank God."

"Jake and Vance couldn't find the shooter."

I suck in a sharp breath. "They didn't?"

"But Nickel determined through his family that it wasn't Luka or his pack. So you're probably right—the shooter was sent from Sentience."

"So...you're marrying a wolf, huh?"

"Yeah. I'm sorry I couldn't tell you. It killed me. I know we were drifting apart because of this secret, and I just didn't know how to fix it."

Tears spear my eyes. Suddenly, I'm crying. "Yeah, I've missed you so much."

"Me too! I'm sorry, Aubrey."

"Well, now I know. It makes sense why you were warning me off Billy."

"No, I think I was wrong about that. He used to have a bias against humans. He initially didn't think I was the right mate for Brick because I'm not a wolf, and alphas have to protect their blood lines or their kids won't shift. But I think you may have changed things for him. I think you might be his mate."

There's a reverence to the way she says *his mate* that clues me in to a deeper meaning. "What does that mean?"

"Well, wolves can have ordinary relationships, like humans. But supposedly every wolf has one true mate. A fated match. Someone they instinctively know–primarily by scent–is The One. But it's not that common to find your true mate. You'd have to search the whole world over. So it's pretty special when it happens."

I remember what Billy said to me when we were making love. *I wanted you the moment I first caught your nutmeg and honey scent at the cafe.*

Am I his fated mate? It would explain why he pursued me even when I was so prickly. Perhaps he was pursuing me against his own best judgment.

"Are you Brick's mate?"

"Yes. I guess it's unusual for an alpha wolf to have a human as a fated mate, so his pack had a hard time accepting it."

"Oh my God. That must've been so hard. I wish you had come to me." It breaks my heart that she couldn't talk to me about it.

"I wanted to. So badly. I felt so alone. But part of being in the pack is following the strict secrecy rules."

I think about it. "That makes sense." If word got out there were men who could change into wolves, they'd be hunted or experimented on. They'd lose their freedom forever.

"Anyway, they finally came around after I proved myself."

"And you think I might be Billy's fated mate?"

"He's been fascinated with you from the start. I should've seen it earlier, but I just didn't trust him. Now it seems obvious. He got into a brawl with the local Monaco pack when their alpha said something derogatory about you on the yacht. And protecting you was all he cared about yesterday. He would've died for you. Considering the fact that Billy is pretty self-serving, I would say you mean far more to him than a duty to please his alpha."

I chew on that.

"But more importantly, how do you feel about him?"

How do I feel? I told myself this was just a fling. Billy wasn't relationship material for me. We're just too different. I have a set of ideals and a self-image that don't include flying on jets across the ocean for parties or living in a penthouse on Billionaire Row.

But Billy's shown me there's a depth beneath the dollars. He does care about climate change and protecting the environment. I thought he was selfish and standoffish, but I learned he'd do anything for the people he cares about, and the hard protective outer shell stems from deep wounds.

I take a deep breath. "Honestly? I'm falling for him, Madi. Hard. I tried not to. I told myself it was just about the sex because he's everything I normally despise in a man, but I can't help how I feel with him."

"Safe?" Madi asks.

"Yes! Is that how you feel with Brick?"

"Yes."

"I feel seen by him. Protected. He takes care of me like my dad takes care of my mom. Yesterday he bought me jewelry—and not some dumb tennis bracelet. He somehow found a lab-grown pink diamond nose ring and matching navel ring."

"He really thought about what you would like."

"Exactly!"

"Yeah, he pays close attention to people even though he pretends to not give a crap. Probably a result of his childhood abuse."

My chest squeezes. I've judged him way too harshly.

Now, after all my delight in tormenting him, I just want to make his life easier. I want to be there for him the way he was there for me yesterday. To get him to open up and share himself with me.

I want to be his mate.

"Yeah, I'm falling hard, Mads. I hope he is, too."

* * *

I step out of the shower. Billy was still asleep after my convo with Madi, so I decided to get cleaned up and start packing.

As I towel dry, I hear the deep baritone of Brick's voice in my suite.

Oh! Billy must have woken and let him in.

Awkward. I don't want to walk out there in just a towel. I put on my moisturizer.

Their voices are low, and I can't make out what they're saying until the A/C stops blowing, and it suddenly gets clear. "I need to know your intentions. Today. The more memories she accumulates, the harder it is to wipe them."

I freeze. *Wipe. Memories?* Excuse me?

My heart starts pounding hard.

Is he talking about *my* memories out there?

Madi didn't say anything about wiping my memories. But then again, why would she if she knew it was going to happen? Telling me would just produce more memories to wipe.

My stomach turns over, suddenly queasy.

"I'll take care of it."

"Take care of it, how? You'll take her to the vampire king to get her mind wiped? Or is she your mate?" Brick asks, still keeping his voice low. "Do you plan to mark her?"

"Fuck." I hear the sound of Billy's heavy footsteps, like he just got out of bed.

Was the *fuck* because it pained him to get up? Or because he doesn't know if I'm his mate?

I suddenly feel like I'm untethered on a space walk. A few weeks ago, I wouldn't have cared about his answer. A few weeks ago, I didn't want any kind of relationship beyond sex with Billy.

Now, I just decided I want him forever.

But Billy had a rough childhood that involved heavy abuse from a shifter supremacist. That would make it hard to accept a fated match with a human. *If*, in fact, I am his mate.

God, this is complicated. I press my hip against the sink counter for support, my knees suddenly weak. I'm trembling although I couldn't describe the emotion associated with it. Not fear. Not pain. Just...vulnerability. My whole world feels like it's teetering on end.

Someone tried to kill me yesterday.

I found out wolf shifters exist, and the guy I've been screwing is a huge white beta.

Turns out my best friend didn't abandon me for her fiance, she joined a wolf pack.

They know how to wipe memories for people who find out.

I may or may not be Billy White's fated mate.

That's the piece that makes me feel most unmoored. I want Billy to pick me. Not because I smell good to him but because he loves me.

"I don't know," Billy says finally.

My lips tremble, and I draw in a deep breath.

"But either way, I'll handle it, Alpha."

Chapter Twenty-Six

B *illy*

The night before Brick's wedding, I return to Sentience.

I left Aubrey sleeping in my bed. She'll be safe in our pack building. I hate to leave her after the rehearsal dinner, but I can't sleep until I've made this right.

I need to find out if Sentience is behind the hit. It was easy to reach out to the founder and CEO team and get an invite for a private meeting.

I invited a co-conspirator along to make things go smoothly.

The security guard greets me and lets us both into the Sentience building. It's after hours. I timed it so that no one would be here but the leadership team and their security.

I pause in front of Aubrey's mural. I'd destroy this building with my bare hands if it weren't for that beautiful piece of art. Instead, I have better plans for it. I just need to evict the current hosts, permanently.

I'm not perfect, but Aubrey's rubbed off on me. I do want to leave the world a better place.

"This way," the guard says and leads us to the elevators.

Thaddeus, Vampire King of Manhattan, strolls beside me. He's my co-conspirator. He decided to help out, just for shits and giggles–and a ten million dollar fee.

Once the guard swipes his card to allow us to go upstairs, Thaddeus faces the man and stares deep into his eyes. The human goes still, a deer frozen in headlights.

"Hand me the keycard," Thaddeus orders. The man does so.

"Good boy," Thaddeus purrs. "Now listen, you've decided this job isn't for you. You're going to quit and follow your dreams. What is something you've always loved to do?"

"Surf," the human answers.

"Excellent." Thaddeus instructs the human to pack up his life and head to San Clemente, California. "Go." The human turns like a robot and heads out of the building.

I've never watched a vampire glamour a human, but it turns my stomach to watch.

It's necessary, though.

"He'll be happier," Thaddeus says, as if he can sense my discomfort. He shakes the keycard, a knowing smile on his face, and saunters off. He'll take care of the rest of the security team. There will be no one left in the building but the people who called for the hit on Aubrey.

No one to hear them scream.

The elevator drops me off at the C-suite. I exit, noting every detail about the room. We're in a large open space that showcases the amazing view of the city. There are six guys here milling around–the founders and CEO team. Two of them are at a foosball table, playing while their friends watch. Three of them are drinking beer, and one is eating barbecue potato chips–I can smell it. There are a few more scents layered in. Someone is smoking weed, and one of the guys has sweated through his deodorant. There's also a bitter tang that tells me they're sampling harder drugs like cocaine.

Finally, one of them notices me and strolls over. He's an Asian guy, almost as tall as me, and his eyes are a bit glassy.

He spreads his arms in welcome. "William White, right?"

I raise my chin, but don't bother greeting him. My wolf and I are both ready for violence.

If this guy tries for a handshake, I'll end up breaking his hand.

"Man, it's so great to meet you. We've all been looking forward to it, right, guys?"

The other guys cheer.

These are the men who tried to take Aubrey from me. If I hadn't been a wolf with razor sharp senses and heightened speed, the bullet would've found its mark, and she would've died in my arms.

It's unthinkable.

They will pay.

I just have to keep control a few minutes longer, long enough for Thaddeus to clear out the security team.

"So great to meet you, man. So great," the guy in front of me keeps saying. He's definitely on something. We actually met briefly at the gala when Aubrey's mural was unveiled, but I'm not going to remind him.

Behind us, the elevator dings, and I tense because I don't know who might be coming up behind me. Did Thaddeus take care of the rest of the security?

The doors open, and Brick walks out, followed by Nickel, Jake, and Vance.

Brick smiles at me. His eyes glow, and his fangs are

longer—his wolf is out. "You didn't think you'd be doing this alone?"

Relief rushes through me, followed by gratitude. My pack brothers always have my back. Even my alpha is here on the night before his wedding. I hold out my hand, and he clasps it. I use our connection to pull him closer and speak, so only a shifter can hear, "They went after Aubrey. I want them to suffer."

"Agreed."

"Uh, guys? What's going on?"

I paste a bland smile on my face. "I was so looking forward to meeting with you, I brought my whole team."

"Wow, that's great. So great." He waves a hand, inviting us over by the foosball table. "You want to talk business or IPOs or something?"

"Or something." I give the CEO a real smile, one that shows my fangs, and he takes a step back. And then I pull off my shirt.

The gasps from the humans tell me they weren't expecting this.

The one closest to me swallows, his pupils growing wider. "Whoa. You're super ripped."

The foosball players have stopped their game. One of them frowns. "Hey man, what's this all about?" They probably think I'm about to propose an orgy.

"After tonight, your company will cease to exist." The guys blink, surprised, but I don't let them speak. "You're going to have a change of heart. You'll be shutting down your company and offering compensation to all the artists you stole from."

The guys look at each other, their heads jerking in an automatic rejection to what I'm saying. A few of them are growing angry. "What the fuck—"

"Stop talking," I say. I use a mild tone, but it's an order. I don't bother to use alpha command on these guys. They recognize our dominance. "You're going to do what I say and release a public apology. Your board will be surprised, but they'll come around." If not, we'll have the vampire king glamour them.

While I'm talking, Jake and Nickel take a little stroll on opposite sides of the room. They head to the back half of the C-suite, to make sure there aren't any witnesses lurking in an office. The humans unconsciously huddle together for safety when they pass.

I kick off my shoes. Beside me, Brick does the same. We're both undressing, so we can let out our wolves. By the time we're chasing these idiots around their C-suite, they won't be fit to leave their house, much less run a company. Then, to be sure of their cooperation, Thaddeus will compel them all to do our bidding.

By morning, Sentience will be no more.

But first, I want answers.

Jake and Nickel return from checking the offices and use sign language to tell us the coast is clear. I signal back to wait a moment.

"You tried to take the life of someone very precious to me. And now you're going to answer to me." I let my wolf out, and the humans recoil at the bright glow that lights my eyes. "Tell me why you hired the hitman to kill Aubrey Cook."

"What?" the CEO gasps. He's gone pale and looks a little green around the edges.

One of the foosball players steps forward, his fists clenched. "Dude, we didn't hire anyone to kill anyone. We don't even know who the fuck–"

The guy next to him elbows him. "Aubrey Cook. Wasn't she the one who did our mural?"

"Oh yeah, she was sneaking around at the gala," another guy says.

"You tried to have her killed," I snarl. They all recoil, holding up their hands like they're fending off an attack.

"No, no," they shout.

"We just sent someone to scare her. No one should've been killed," one says.

"She was trying to steal secrets from us," another guy adds. "Along with a disgruntled employee. We sent someone to toss her and Jamie's apartments and find our stolen files. That's all."

I don't smell a lie.

I glance at Brick. He's frowning. "So no hitman?" he asks.

"What? No!" They all protest. "Why would you think that?"

"A hitman came after her. In Monaco," I say. "She almost was shot. The bullet came inches away." My own vertebrae stopped it from exiting my body and killing her. She's lucky she had a shifter shield.

The CEO's eyes roll back in his head. He keels over, slumping to the floor.

"Somebody help him," Brick orders, and two guys rush to obey. They prop him up and give him water when he rouses.

We shifters go into a huddle. "They're telling the truth," Jake says. We can smell when someone is lying.

"Could someone else in the company have hired the hitman?" Nickel asks. "Someone from the board?"

"They probably wouldn't want the board getting wind of intellectual theft. They said it themselves, they hired people to toss the apartments. I don't think they hired the hitman at all." Brick turns to me and asks the question that's going to keep me up at night. "If Sentience didn't try to kill Aubrey, who did?"

My stomach roils. I don't know, and I need to. It's the only way to ensure that Aubrey will be safe. "We're sure it wasn't Luka's pack?"

Nickel nods. "I can bark up that tree again, but my family connections didn't think he had anything to do with it. Not his style."

The elevator dings. It's Thaddeus. He must be done taking care of the security team.

"How's it going?" he asks.

"Not great," Brick glances down at the CEO.

"Is it my turn?"

Everyone looks at me. I was looking forward to roughing up these guys and putting the fear of wolves into them. Now, I just want to get back to Aubrey and make sure she's safe.

"Go ahead," I say.

"Gentlemen, look this way," Thaddeus says in smooth tones. The humans all focus on him.

We back away, letting the vampire do his work. He'll convince them to shut down their operation and issue payments to the artists they stole from and sell the building to me.

By morning, Sentience will cease to exist. I didn't get the hitman, but I can do this much.

Chapter Twenty-Seven

Billy

B Weddings are worse than galas. I'm playing usher in my tux because for some reason, that's the tradition for groomsmen.

The street in front of the Plaza Hotel has been flooded with limos dropping off well-heeled society members. The doormen hold the doors, but our job is to check invites and escort guests to the banquet hall.

Everyone's pitching in on usher duty–even Noah, who isn't part of the wedding party or the pack but was invited at Madi's request.

It's been two days since we returned. I slept most of the flight back to the States while my body was still regenerating. I insisted Aubrey stay with me, citing the threats on her life from Sentience. We now know the hit didn't come from Sentience.

Eventually the news of their demise will come out, but Brick and I decided to keep all this under wraps until after the wedding.

I'm hoping the target of the sniper was me–someone

sent by Luka to ruin our vacation after I embarrassed him on his yacht. If that's the case, Aubrey is safe, but I won't sleep easy until I know for sure.

Aubrey's been subdued since we returned–quieter than usual. I can't tell if she's freaked out about discovering I'm a wolf or still shaken up by the shooting. She's definitely processing it all. I'm just grateful she hasn't completely closed herself off from me.

I made love to her an hour ago–after she showered for the wedding–because my wolf needed my scent all over her for tonight's event.

In a few moments, I'll be escorting her down the aisle, Best Man to her Maid of Honor. As much as I scorn these human traditions, I'm looking forward to having the most beautiful female in New York on my arm. Most of the guests have arrived by now, but Noah and I stand outside in case there are any stragglers.

"What's going over there?" Noah signs, pointing to the socialites heading in the hotel next door. It looks like there's some other kind of gala or formal affair there.

"I don't know," I sign back. "It seems strange they would book two major events here the same night."

A white limo pulls up. When a pale blond man gets out, I growl.

Noah must sense the vibration of it because he shoots me a look, then looks back.

My lips curl back from my teeth, and I spit out, "Aiden Adalwulf." I start to finger spell *Aiden,* and Noah nods before I'm halfway through, understanding. His gaze jerks back across the street.

"He has to upstage Blackthroat's wedding," Noah observes, "by throwing his own event right next door."

"Yes." I make the sign at the same time I speak the word, my fist nodding with my head.

A slender, waifish female with the same moon-pale hair as Aiden climbs from the limo behind Aiden.

Noah's body lurches forward, like he's suddenly alert.

Aiden doesn't wait for her or help her out of the limo. He walks in alone. The young she-wolf walks behind him demurely, head bowed like a servant.

"Who is that?" Noah signs.

I shake my head and sign back, "I've never seen her before, but I think that's Aster. She's a distant cousin to Aiden. I hear she's the new pack seeress." I have to finger spell *seeress* because it's not an ASL word I've learned.

Noah stares until she disappears inside, as if mesmerized. His throat bobs on a swallow.

"Do you know her?" I ask.

He hesitates, then signs, "no," but his brows are down like what he saw disturbed him.

I don't believe him, but I let it go for now. The most paranoid part of me originally thought he could be an Adalwulf spy when he arrived at Moon Co, but Sully's background checks showed no contact with our rival pack, and he's proven himself loyal. I have no reason to distrust him.

An older couple exits the nearest limo, and the female holds up her invite. They're pack members, so I don't need to check the list. "Good evening. Welcome. Right this way, please."

When I drop them off, the wedding planner beckons me over to where the rest of the groomsmen and ushers stand. There's a complicated order and timing for who walks down the aisle. We went over it last night at the rehearsal, but I only paid attention to my job—escorting Aubrey.

I catch my breath when she rounds the bend with Ruby and Scarlett. All three are in strapless brick red gowns, tight around the torso and flared at mid-calf, like mermaids. Aubrey is stunning. Her hair is piled high on her head and tied with a red scarf. Her breasts swell at the bodice of the dress, looking ripe and eager for my handling. Like Brick's sisters, she's wearing pearl-drop earrings and a three-strand pearl choker–probably gifts from the bride.

I like seeing her in finery.

I like her in paint-splattered overalls, too, but right now she looks more royal than any of Manhattan's elite. My hands are on her waist, my lips tasting her neck before I even realize I moved.

"You look incredible."

"You look like a billion bucks. Oh yeah, you are a billion bucks." She flashes me a smile.

I keep my hands on her waist. It occurs to me that I don't want this moment to end. Initially, this thing with Aubrey had a limited timeline. We'd work together, perform our joint duties for the wedding, and after that, we'd go our separate ways.

But I don't want to give her up. My wolf seems to think she belongs to me.

She's busy doing her Maid of Honor duties, though–squeezing Madi's mother's hand and glaring in solidarity when Madi's paternal grandmother walks down the aisle. I think I heard something about her father not being invited since he's never taken an interest, and it would be uncomfortable for her mom.

Aubrey fist bumps Ruby's pups, April and August, before they trot down the aisle as flower girl and ring bearer. Vance, Jake, and Sully walk down the aisle by themselves. Nickel escorts Scarlett. Eagle escorts Ruby. And then it's our turn. I wrap Aubrey's hand around my elbow and walk down the aisle with her.

Halfway down the aisle, I catch a scent that sends my wolf roaring to the surface with life-threatening danger. One second. Two. I have the adrenaline rush back under control, just as I taught myself years ago. I grind my teeth and take a quick sweep of the guests.

There. I see the back of his balding head.

Mother. *Fucker.*

My asshole dad somehow wormed his way into the event. If he does anything to ruin this wedding for Brick and Madi, I will serve him his own liver on a platter.

* * *

Aubrey

I straighten Madi's gown as she and Brick walk down the aisle together to the applause of their guests after the ceremony.

It was perfect. Madi looked incredible in her custom Dior gown. Seeing her mom and brother walk her down the aisle together was poignant and sweet and a good reminder to her wicked grandmother, Eleanor, who ensured that those two–and me–were the only family Madi had growing up.

Madi's bouquet of dark red roses matches the brick red–for obvious reasons–of our bridesmaid dresses, and we hold white bouquets to contrast. Catherine, Madi's mother-in-law has on a beautiful red dress, which makes sense, since it's her favorite color. She did name all three of her children with shades of red.

Good thing I wore waterproof mascara because I cried through the whole wedding. It wasn't over losing my best friend–I am so genuinely happy for her. Especially now that I understand Brick is a wolf, and Madi literally took on a new pack. There was so much she couldn't share with me before that she can now.

Billy offers his arm to me, but his face is wooden. His eyes flashed silver when he saw me in my gown–a sign I now realize means his wolf is showing because he's turned on. But now he looks distant. Something happened when we were walking down the aisle.

I want to ask him about it, but ever since the conversation I overheard between him and Brick, I've been giving him space. He's trying to figure out if I'm his fated mate, and I'm sure that's complicated by his long history of bias against humans. It hurts a little, but I'm trying to be understanding. If he chooses me, I want to know it is out of love, not scent. Not some animal instinct that he's trying to resist. I don't want to be the mate he wished he wasn't attracted to. I deserve a man who truly desires me.

He escorts me out to stand beside Brick and Madi in the receiving line, the way we rehearsed last night. I steal a glance at his face again, but it's a cold mask.

"Are you okay?" I ask.

He doesn't answer me. He doesn't even look at me.

Ouch.

But then he says in a rusty voice, "My father is here."

Oh. Oh shit. His abusive, *shifter-supremacist* father. No wonder he went wooden in there.

Brick overhears and shoots him an inquiring look.

"I have no idea how he got in," Billy says, "but I'm about to handle it."

"Let him stay unless he tries something. I have nothing to hide."

A muscle jumps in Billy's jaw. He doesn't answer,

but his eyes flash with the silver hues of his wolf. We stand and greet the guests. I only know Madi's family, so my job is to stand and look pretty. Most everyone in attendance is here for the Blackthroats. Ruby is a natural hostess, but Madi exudes a certain power and leadership I haven't seen in her before. She's no longer the nerdy Princeton grad who can out think anyone. Now, she has CEO energy. Boss Bitch energy. Alpha of the pack vibes.

I love seeing her like this. No wonder I felt left behind. She's evolved with quantum leaps.

The last of the guests exit.

Billy scans the place.

"Did he not come out?"

Billy shakes his head. "No."

"Maybe he left."

Billy nods, but he still looks grim.

"I have to pee," Madi murmurs to me, grabbing my hand. She can't do it by herself with the long train of the dress. Besides, it's time to take the train off, so she can mingle and dance at the reception.

"On it." We go into the bridal dressing room where the women got ready for the ceremony. I carefully unhook the six hooks that attach the train. "Okay, you're free. I'm going to go back out and make sure Billy's okay."

Madi blinks at me. "You two are really a thing, aren't you? It's so crazy. You're as different as they come, and I never would've seen it coming."

I hesitate. "Honestly? I don't know if we're a thing or not." The dull ache that's been there ever since overhearing his indecision gnaws at me.

I find Billy waiting for me just outside the dressing room holding two glasses of champagne, and I want to hug him. Even when he's torn up inside, he's always a gentleman.

I accept a glass. "Any sign of your dad?"

"No." Billy suddenly stiffens and swivels to the right like he smelled him first. "Yes."

A tall man with the same grey-blue eyes as Billy's, salt and pepper hair, and an expression that looks like he sucked a lemon advances toward us.

"Who's this?" the man demands, giving me a disdainful up and down. He lifts his nose in a decidedly canine gesture, then wrinkles his nose. "You've been slumming, son."

My natural instinct is to throw all my sass at this guy, but I don't want to make things worse for Billy, so I remain quiet, my chin lifted, a matched look of disdain on my face.

"You weren't invited, old man." Billy's voice is flat. Lifeless.

"I was next door at the Adalwulf party, and I just thought I'd pop over to say hello," Billy's dad says. "I have powerful friends too, son. You forget how far my reach goes." He sends another narrow-eyed glance my way.

What a pompous asshole. I don't care what he thinks about me, but I want to kick him in the balls for being a horrible father. But maybe I'm the one making this worse for Billy. Should I walk away, so he doesn't have to try to shield me from his dad's derision?

"You're not welcome here. Leave before I throw you out." Billy still sounds deadened. Like all animation leaves his persona when he's near his father.

I'm sure a child who was in physical danger all the time would learn to mute his very being. Adult Billy's nervous system still reacts in the presence of his tormentor. He remains perfectly still, but I hear the air ripping in and out of his lungs like he's running a marathon.

His dad's gaze rests on me as he speaks to Billy. "You'd better not be following the path of your weakling alpha." He shakes his head slowly. The way he looks at me makes my skin crawl. I see evil behind those eyes, and it's directed right at me.

Billy stops breathing altogether.

"You should know that I wouldn't allow my son to make that mistake."

It's a threat, and I register it. Ice sluices through my veins.

"Fate makes no mistakes." Billy's tone could freeze lava.

Rage ripples over William White the Second. His eyes flash silver. "Are you trying to tell me *fate* chose this trash for *my* son?" he roars. "She's a pet, no more."

Before I even see him move, his hand snaps out, grasps the pearl choker Madi gave me as a bridesmaid gift, and yanks. The pearls explode from their strings, rolling onto the floor.

Billy delivers a powerful kick to the older man's gut, driving him back with so much force he flies eight feet through the air and crashes against a wall. Good thing we're out in a hallway where the guests can't see us.

He thrusts his champagne glass into my hand and stalks after his father, who seems to be struggling to breathe. Billy must've kicked his diaphragm.

Madi comes out of the dressing room. "Oh shit," she mutters. "I'll get Brick or one of the guys."

I just stand in place, frozen. I live in Brooklyn, but I haven't seen violence like that. Never like that.

Billy's father struggles to his feet but not before Billy grasps him by the throat and picks him up with superhuman strength. The older man is tall, but Billy lifts him above the ground and bashes his head against the wall. "You don't touch her. You don't look at her. If you speak of her again, I will fucking end you."

* * *

Billy

Rage pours from me in waves. He reached for Aubrey's throat.

He wants her dead.

The cold steel of a blade seems to rip across my chest. I never should have let on what she means to me.

Flashes of my father murdering the human hunter years ago throw me off balance. Bring back the stench of blood to my nostrils. Screams in my ears.

I'm that five-year-old in the woods–horrified and afraid. Forced to watch him torture a man for wandering across the line onto pack land.

Fear grips me. I can't let him torture *her*.

But I'm not small anymore. I can fight back.

I punch my dad in the gut, even though he hasn't recovered from having his head smashed yet. I should kill him right now. My wolf wants to. He attacked our mate.

I'm sure now–Aubrey is my mate. I knew it all along, but I was in denial.

I think this is why.

I'd locked up the memory of that hunter's murder until now–but the five-year-old in me still fears for Aubrey's life if I claim her.

In my mind, the hunter is replaced by Aubrey. I see my father circling her with a knife. Her legs broken. Flesh torn from her by wolf jaws. Her screams cutting through the forest.

Look how weak she is. Don't look away while I end her, Billy.

No! I almost shift to wolf form to save her.

"Not here." I hear Sully's calm, efficient voice through the screaming in my head.

I blink. I'm not in the woods.

Not five years old watching Aubrey die.

"You're scaring Aubrey."

I suck in a sharp breath and look over my shoulder. She's frozen where I left her, in a blood red dress, holding our two glasses of champagne. Her eyes are wide with horror.

He's going to kill her.

I deliver four more punches in rapid succession, reveling in the sound of his ribs cracking.

"*Not. Here.*" Sully growls between clenched teeth.

Right.

Not here.

He, Vance, and Jake stand behind me. They have my back—not that I need it. I'm bigger now. The days of my father's torment are over. I could snap his neck right here.

But Aubrey's watching. I didn't want my father anywhere near her. I definitely didn't want her to see this.

And Sully's right. It's my alpha's wedding. Our luna would be horrified.

Vance and Sully each grasp one of my dad's arms.

Jake tilts his head toward another hallway. "Back door."

"You can deal with him later. Go to your mate—she's scared," Sully says.

Your mate.

They know already.

I haven't marked her, but everyone knows. I'm the only fool still denying it.

I turn slowly to face my beautiful female. Pearls are scattered across the floor. I can't quite remember how they got there.

Aubrey swallows. "Billy?" She sounds unsure. Like she's scared of me.

Like my mom was when my father raged.

Fuck. Shame floods me. I'm just like him.

It's my deepest fear. Far worse than the instinctual terror he'll kill Aubrey because my logical brain knows I won't let that happen.

But I just reenacted the violence I saw as a pup on the man who delivered it in front of the female I love. The female who I've been denying was mine.

Somehow I make my feet move. I make them arrive in front of her. My lips move, and a rusty sound comes out. "Fuck, Aubrey. I'm sorry."

Her chest heaves, full breasts spilling from the strapless bodice.

"Are you okay?"

Very lightly, I brush my thumb across her neck. There's a scrape there. What happened? I'd thought he was going to choke her, but he'd had restraint. He'd yanked off her necklace.

She nods. "Are you?" she whispers. Her hands find my face.

One part of me wants to pull away. It's not safe to be touched. But I catch her scent, and it soothes my wolf. I lean my cheek into her hand.

"Billy...am I your mate?"

My body goes rigid, ice stiffening my spine. I glance at the direction they took my father.

288

Did he hear? If he knows she's my mate, he'll try to kill her.

Once more, I'm in the woods. The hunter's on his knees. My father presses a knife into my hand. I'm supposed to stab Aubrey.

No, not Aubrey.

It's a wedding. She's safe. She's not in the woods on her knees.

"I think...I think things are really complicated." I see a depth of sorrow in Aubrey's eyes, but I don't understand it.

I barely know where I am.

"Billy, I don't even know if we're in a relationship. I don't think we are because if we were, we could work through this stuff together."

Wait. What is she saying? I catch sadness in her scent, and it makes me want to fall to my knees.

I made her sad. I lost control.

I'm a violent, dangerous wolf. I'm not safe to be with a human. I'm not fit to mate.

Her hand still cradles my cheek. I catch it and hold it there. I don't want her to ever let go of me.

"You need to figure out what you want. So do I. Let's take some space and do that."

Take...some space?

Fuck.

She's breaking up with me.

I can't make my lips move. Can't figure out any words to say. I'm the fixer for the pack and the company, but I'm at a complete loss for how to fix this.

"Aubrey." There. I said something. Except I don't know what to say next. I don't know what the right words are. Where to take the conversation.

My brain is unwired. Powered down. I don't know what Aubrey wants or how to make her stay.

I don't know how to be anything but the man I hate.

William White's scrappy runt of a son. The one who learned to be violent, ruthless, and cunning to survive.

I don't know how to be the kind of mate Aubrey deserves.

Her face comes closer to mine. I blink as she stands on her tiptoes and presses a kiss against my lips.

"Don't," I murmur.

She lets out a little whimper as she pulls away.

"Wait." I catch her elbow.

She looks into my eyes. "I love you."

My heart detonates. My head explodes. I want to say it back. I want to drop to my knees and beg for forgiveness except I'm not sure what part upset her. I'm confused because she doesn't seem upset. Just sad.

I love you.

I want you.

You're my mate.

The words ring out in my head, but no sound comes from my lips, and she's already walking away.

Already leaving me behind.

I stand perfectly still and watch the best thing that ever happened to me walk out of my life.

Chapter Twenty-Eight

ubrey
The next day, a knock sounds on my door.

I'm still in my pajamas even though it's two in the afternoon. I have no intention of getting out of bed today, much less getting dressed.

Tomorrow I will drag myself back to school, get through finals, and graduate. I have the money from painting Billy's mural to live on while I figure out next steps.

I still owe him the second one, but I can't be in his penthouse right now. Not even with him at work.

The tears I've been holding at bay would overwhelm me.

Getting through the wedding last night was painful, but I couldn't run away and cry my eyes out. It was my best friend's big night. I had to put on my game face, smile, dance and cheer her on until she and Brick drove away in the limo we decorated with shaving cream and tin cans. I had to hide the fact that I was dying inside.

Billy haunted me like a ghost last night. He remained in robot mode—withdrawn and silent—but every time I turned around, he'd positioned himself on the sidelines where he could watch me like a bodyguard. Available to jump in and help when I needed it. Hanging back when I didn't.

He's still worried about my safety, but I refused to stay at his place, so he had two burly guys drive me home. They're still parked outside on the street.

Sensing that he was hurting, too, made my heart break even more.

I kept questioning myself. I know he was in a trauma response from seeing his father. It's not that I don't cut him all the slack.

But twice he's been directly asked whether I'm his mate—once by Brick and once by me—and he couldn't answer.

I have too much pride to let myself get dragged around in his mess without even knowing if he wants me to stick around.

I figure I'm doing him a favor. Either he'll decide he wants me, and he'll show up for this relationship, and we'll get it all out on the table, or I let him out of a complicated situation, and he'll feel relieved that he didn't have to slum with a human anymore.

The knock sounds again. "Ms. Cook?" Even if I didn't recognize that formal baritone, the accompanying yip of my dog forces me to sit up.

How did Grayson even get into the building? I didn't buzz him in.

I groan and roll out of bed. I wrap a purple robe around my shoulders, so I don't reveal too much in my braless state, and I stumble to the door.

The idea that Billy sent Pepper to me via Grayson stings. It more than stings—it's like being flayed and having salt poured over the wounds. I guess he made up his mind.

292

We're done. Have your dog back even though you're not allowed to have pets in your apartment.

I pull the chain back, unlock the door, and open it. "Hey."

Pepper is on a leash rather than in his travel bag, and he goes crazy for me, making joyful whimpers like a squealing pig and wagging his butt so hard it turns him in circles.

Tears spear my eyes. "Hi, buddy. I missed you, too." I pick him up, and he licks my face frantically.

I blink hard, trying to keep from crying in front of Grayson.

"Mr. White thought you might want the company of your dog today. He worked things out with your landlady. He paid a generous pet deposit, so she's willing to bend the rules for Pepper." He unhooks the leash and folds it up.

Oh. I guess he does care. That makes my nose burn even hotter. My throat clogs with emotion. This might be easier if he was a big jerk. Then I could hate him and move on.

Right now, I just miss everything about him. I mourn not just what we did have–because that wasn't much more than mad, hot sex–but I'm mourning the glimpse I had of more. Of getting Billy to open up and be vulnerable. Of me showing more of myself to him, even though he seemed to see more than I thought I was sharing. Of me being a part of his world–not the billionaire world because I'm still uncomfortable with that but the wolf world.

But maybe I'm not supposed to know about that anymore.

With a sharp spike of fear, I remember Billy and Brick discussing wiping my memories. How did that work? Was that why Grayson was here? What if I never remembered any of this?

At least my heart wouldn't be breaking.

But no. I wouldn't give up these memories of Billy for anything.

I draw a breath and lift my chin. "Anything else?"

Grayson shifts on his feet, looking uncomfortable. "Mr. White ordered 24/7 bodyguards on you until we've found whoever shot at you. He didn't want you to be scared if you saw them."

Oh. He definitely cares.

God, I really need to cry. Why didn't I let myself last night when I got home? Holding it in now chokes me.

I manage to bob my head, holding my breath. "Okay." My vision swims.

Grayson looks alarmed at the tears. He clears his throat. "I would like to offer you a hug, but I'm not sure if Mr. White would cut off my balls for touching you."

A watery laugh tumbles out of my lips. "I would like to accept, but I'm about to fall apart."

Pepper tries to lick me some more.

"Tell Billy thank you."

Grayson nods and thrusts the leash in my direction and steps back after I take it. "Our guys are outside in a black Range Rover. If you need anything, let them know." He bows his head.

"'Kay. I will," I choke. "Thanks." I shut the door and lean my forehead against it as the first sob rockets from my throat.

God, this hurts.

I let the emotion spill in tears and sobs. I stumble to the sofa and throw myself on it.

Fuck.

I wish I could call Madi to talk this through with me,

but there's no way I'm going to bother her on her honeymoon.

I can't control the outcome of this situation. Either Billy will show up or he won't.

Or he'll try to wipe my memories, in which case I will throw down to keep them.

I'll get through it. I've had breakups before.

None of them felt like my heart had been ripped out of my chest still beating, though.

I roll to face the back of the couch and close my eyes, letting another wave of sobs roll through me.

For all my efforts to stay in fling territory, Billy White wormed his way firmly into my heart. Now it's flayed open, bleeding, and still beating for him. And there's nothing I can do but grieve the loss and hope he figures his shit out.

* * *

Billy

Aubrey is gone.

I'm alone.

I know she's safe—I've done what I can to ensure that—but there's a sense of loss that's unfathomable. Like I'm missing a part of me I never knew I had. And never will have.

My wolf whines, wondering why we're not with her.

"She doesn't want to see us," I tell him. He doesn't understand. To him, things are simple. A mate is the one person in the world you want to be with. So you be with them. You protect them. You hunt for them. You help lick

Renee Rose & Lee Savino

their wounds. And when it's night and you're together, you howl at the moon.

It's taking everything in me not to go to her. But ...she asked for space, and I respect that.

I also have some things to deal with on my own.

That's why I'm in Maine, back on the lands where I grew up. I've always loved the woods here. The vibrant green moss and ferns, the lichen-covered rocks. The cold, spring fed lakes and deep quiet.

But the beauty is tainted because when I'm here, I hear my father's voice from the past. Right now it's morphed into an angry mocking. "Are you sad? What, are you going to cry? Stop moping, boy," followed by a punch to the head.

And if he knew I was broken-hearted over a human? I can't imagine what he'd do to me. If I was small and weak again.

I pace through the woods, heading toward the pack houses. I pause when I come to the clearing where my father made me watch a human die.

A twig cracks.

"I know it's you," I call. "And I know you stepped on a stick on purpose. You're usually quieter than that." I look back, and there's a giant wolf. A white and gray wolf, like mine, except she has a splash of black on one ear.

"Hey, Boo."

My sister shifts to human form and stands.

"You're nuts," she informs me.

"This is going to end today." I told her everything on a phone call on the way up.

"Mm hmm." She walks past me to a tree with a big hollow about head height. She rises to tiptoe and pulls out a black waterproof bag, the sort that campers use. It seems she has a stash of clothes at the ready.

Once she's dressed, I study her. She's in jeans and a faded "Dark Side of the Moon" t-shirt. Even dressed, she looks a little wild. Her bare feet are tanned, and her long hair hangs snarled down her back.

I remember how, when she was first exiled, she showed up on pack land in an old pickup truck, desperate to see me. I was so scared my father would order his enforcers to kill her. She was strong enough to fight him, but if he sent enough wolves, they would all be able to overpower her.

Back then, I wrote a note to her and had a trusted pack member smuggle it to her. In it, I told her to stay away and not worry about me. I wanted her to be happy and free. I planned to escape as soon as I could. I just had to survive my teenage years under the tyranny of my father.

And now I have, and I'm back for closure.

"Are we doing this?" she asks.

"Might as well. I came all this way." We grin at each other.

We review our plan. I ask her how she's going to hide her scent until the right moment, and she just gives me a smile. "I have my ways."

"You've come here before," I point to the tree where she stashed her clothes. "Visiting friends?"

"Someone has to watch over this pack."

"And that someone is you?"

She nods, and I accept it. "Let's do this then."

She disappears, and I walk deeper into the woods to find my father.

After a few minutes, the wind shifts. It was blowing past me towards the pack. This would carry my scent straight to my father's door. Now it carries his scent back to me.

He's coming. He has a few enforcers with him. Of course he does.

Not Chip and Dale but some other thugs. My father is a bully, but he's also a coward, and he's incapable of fighting his battles alone.

When he appears, he keeps his enforcers close. There are six of them I can see and more in the woods out of sight.

"Son?" he asks warily. "What are you doing here?" He sniffs the air, and his eyes light a little, probably because he can't scent Aubrey on me. "Are you here to atone?"

"For what?" I scoff.

"For defending a human."

I suppress a growl. I can't lose control now, it'll ruin my and my sister's plan. But I want to hurt him for spitting the word human like a curse. *Soon.* "Why would I need to atone for that?" I bait him.

My father's lip curls. "Look at him," he says to his enforcers. "My son, the human lover. You know, I raised you right. A real son of mine would never consort with a weaker species–"

"Enough."

He bares his teeth at me, realizing I just gave him an order. As an alpha, he should be able to resist me. But he can't.

Because I'm stronger.

It's time I prove to him that I'm not his son any more. I reject him and his toxic worldview, once and for all.

A cold wind blows through me, bringing me to that empty place where I feel nothing. I know what needs to be done, and I'm ready. "Call the pack. All of them. There's something they need to see."

His face grows red as he tries to resist the alpha command in my voice. Then he barks the orders to his enforcers. "Call everyone." He stomps his feet, wanting to make the decision seem like his idea. But we both know what happened: I gave him an order, and he had to obey.

The pack gathers quickly. They're used to being called to this spot to hear my father's rants.

"I'm here to pass judgement on William White the Second. My father. You are no longer fit to be alpha."

My father rocks back on his heels. "What?"

"You heard me. You need to answer for your crimes."

"My crimes?" My father's teeth are sharpening and growing too large for his face. His wolf is taking over in his rage. "What about yours? Consorting with a human. I saw you." He points at me and turns to the pack to accuse me of my so-called crimes. "He picked her up in a limo. She was in a dress, and he was in a tux. He was courting her." My father spits this like it's the worst crime imaginable.

My wolf is on high alert. *He saw me with Aubrey.* The night of the gala, he must have been following me. He's known I was with Aubrey for longer than I thought. If I missed that, what else did I miss? Something niggles in the back of my mind, a premonition of what's to come.

"My own flesh and blood," he rants. "And now he thinks he'll challenge me? Take over my pack?"

"No," I interrupt his raving. I need to get us back on track. "This isn't about me. I have no intention of leading this pack. I'm just here to stop you, once and for all."

"You want to fight? Prove that you're stronger? That human has made you weak."

I almost laugh in his face. Aubrey makes me stronger. I need to be the best version of myself just to deserve to breathe her air. "We'll see just how weak I am." I shrug off my jacket and toss it to the ground. We'll fight as wolves.

My father won't win.

And he knows it. So does the pack. Everyone's watching closely, the mated pairs, the greybacks, the enforcers. Mothers hold their pups close, shushing them when they'd make a fuss. There's an energy in the air. Change is coming.

My father stops ranting and turns to me. His voice turns whiny. He's trying a different tack. "I tried, you know, son," he says. "I tried to take care of the problem for you. I thought if the human was gone, you would see reason, but–"

"What are you talking about?" Goosebumps break out on my arms. "What did you do?"

"I did what needed to be done! I did what you'd do if vermin overran your home. I hired an exterminator to take her out!"

The world goes black for a moment. When I come to, I've crossed the clearing and am holding my father by the throat. Everyone's shouting, but all I can see are the whites of my father's eyes. If I just squeeze a little harder–

"Billy," my sister's voice is calling. "Billy! Stop," her voice takes on a tinge of alpha power. The command rolls down my arms, making them weaker.

"Not like this," she says. "I know you want to kill him, but there's a right way to do this."

I drop him and step back, and my sister orders everyone to step back. They all do although the enforcers don't look happy about it.

My gut feels hollow, like I'm going to be sick. My father was a bigger threat than I thought. I missed it and almost lost my mate.

"Is this true?" my sister asks my father. "Did you try to harm Billy's human friend?"

"Mate," I say, needing to publicly claim Aubrey. "The human is my mate."

A murmur ripples through the watching wolves. Half

the pack looks stunned, but some look curious. This seems to incense my father.

"Harm her? I tried to take her out! She poisoned his mind."

The hitman in Monaco. Sentience wasn't behind it. Luka's pack wasn't, either. My father was.

My own father tried to take my mate from me forever.

"How?" I ask. "Where did you get the money?" He'd need a hefty amount to hire a hitman.

"He bankrupted us," one of the elders speaks up. She's a stooped, grey-haired woman with gnarled hands resting on a carved wooden cane. "He's been draining the pack funds for his own personal gain for years, but it's been getting worse. And a few days ago, I discovered he's cleaned our savings out."

"Is this true?" Boudicca asks gently. The elder nods, and a few others murmur agreement. The pack seems to drift closer to my sister, looking to her for guidance. She confirms a few details and then looks back at me, "I knew it was bad, but I didn't realize it was this bad."

"You shouldn't even be here," my father snarls at her. I can't even look at him right now. If I do, I'll tear off his head. "You're exiled, you traitor–"

"Be silent," Boudicca says. She gives the order without even raising her voice.

My father's mouth snaps shut. He looks surprised that she can command him, but much of the pack doesn't.

A few of the enforcers start to move towards her, and she says, "No," the power rolls out of her, stopping the enforcers in their tracks.

"Alpha," the elder murmurs. Everyone stares at Boudicca. My sister sighs.

If it were any other moment, I'd say "I told you so," to

my sister. I knew she had the alpha ability. But I'm not in a joking mood. Not when I've just realized my father tried to murder Aubrey.

The wind shifts again. It's time.

"Today is a day of reckoning. It's been a long time coming." My sister faces our father. "William White the Second, I now declare that you are unfit to lead this pack as alpha."

"I second this," I say. I'm following protocol, so no one can dispute the way we removed our father from command. But I can't stop myself from adding, "You are cruel. You've tortured humans and your own children. You've exiled good wolves and brought out the worst in this pack." I see some heads nodding slightly. Many of the pack members don't think it's right that Boudicca was exiled. They still think of her as pack.

"You think that weakness should be punished, not protected," my sister says. "You've confused cruelty for strength."

"You're a bully," I add. "And it's time to show you how pathetic you are."

I kick off my shoes, continuing to disrobe.

"Billy," my sister says. "Let me—"

"No. He tried to kill my mate."

Her blue eyes hold mine. She wants to be sure I'm willing to take on the burden of fratricide. She's protecting me even now.

That's why she'll make a great alpha.

"You're the true alpha of this pack," I say. "Not me. I belong with the Blackthroats. But first...I want vengeance."

"All right." She steps back to give me space. At some point, a black wolf came to her side. I recognize the wolf as her mate, Kali. The black wolf presses against Boudicca's legs, and my sister rests a hand on her head.

I turn back to my father. "Face me like a wolf," I tell him. "It's time for you to die."

My father's face turns red. He wants to argue, but he can't. He fights the compulsion, but he's not strong enough to resist my softly spoken command. In the end, his eyes roll a little with fear.

It's a little sad.

I wait until he undresses, and then I call my wolf and surrender to the change.

The fight goes quickly. Two wolves sparring. But my father is old and grey, and I'm snow white and fast. I slam my shoulder into him, and he goes sprawling. I'm on him in a flash, and from there it's the work of a moment to sink my teeth into his soft belly and rip out his guts.

Then I shift back, and order him to shift, also. He morphs into human form. He's sprawled in the dirt on his back, wheezing, trying to hold his organs inside his body. Trying and failing.

I feel no pity. No sorrow. This is simply a job that needs to be done.

I take a knee and clamp a hand around his neck.

"There's something you should know," I say. I speak softly, but I know every shifter can hear me. "I love my human mate. I will fight every day to deserve her. She makes me a better wolf, and I will love her to the day I die, even if she never thinks about me again."

My father's eyes widen. He tries to speak, but can't do much more than gurgle on his own blood. I don't let him speak. I will not allow my mate's name to be soiled in his mouth. I choke him until his eyes grow glassy, and his body stills.

Power passes through me. I feel it. Everyone in the clearing does.

But it doesn't rest on me. It moves through all of us–the power of an alpha–and settles on my sister. Her eyes flare bright blue, and then it fades.

"Alpha," I greet her.

"Alpha," the rest of the pack murmurs. One by one they begin to kneel.

It's like I told her earlier. She always fought for this pack. Protected the weak. That's because she was meant to lead. She was always an alpha, and it's time for her to take her place. It won't be easy. Some of the enforcers will challenge her or leave. But she has more allies than she thinks. And she has her mate at her back. I'm learning that a wolf can do anything if they have a strong mate.

This execution should've been done a long time ago. But I didn't do it for me or my sister, or even the pack.

I did it for Aubrey. Now, she'll be safe.

And now I can go home.

Chapter Twenty-Nine

ubrey

A I sit alone at All Night. It's karaoke night and some drunk guys murder Queen's "We are the Champions" up on the stage, shouting lyrics with raised beer glasses. Very original, guys. That song never gets sung on karaoke night.

But whatever. No shade. Music heals. That's why I'm here. Drinking a gin and tonic because that's what Billy likes. It's been twelve days since the wedding, and it hasn't gotten much easier.

Classes are over. I officially graduate Saturday. I have no job lined up, other than my part time hours at La Résistance, which means I have nothing to do.

Nothing to take up the time and give me focus.

Way too many hours to ruminate on why Billy didn't decide we were worth it.

The first week after the wedding, I held a thread of hope, thinking Billy might show up or call. I wanted to work things out with him.

I feel pathetic to admit it, but I wanted him to choose me. I wanted him to say I'm his fated mate. I'm the one.

But he didn't.

I haven't heard a word from him.

I still have two guys tailing me at all times. They're even here tonight, sitting at a table by the door.

I order another drink and try not to check my phone. I still have Billy's picture as my lock screen's wallpaper. When I first snapped the picture, I saved it there to annoy him. *Look at us, co-parenting a puppy.* It's the sort of picture a girlfriend or partner would take and save. Now, there's no hope of us becoming a couple, but I can't bear to change it.

Madi got back from her honeymoon in Greece yesterday. I wanted to give her time to settle and get over the jetlag before I called her, but I ended up leaving a message an hour ago telling her I needed a shoulder to cry on.

I need someone else's perspective.

And music. Music helps.

"Aubrey Cook is up next," the emcee announces.

I'd signed up when I got here in case I felt like singing. I sigh. Do I?

Fuck it, why not? I stand, find my way up to the stage.

"Which eighties song tonight?" the emcee asks.

Yeah, they know me here.

"'Pictures of You,' by the Cure."

The emcee nods, and I take the mic and close my eyes, swaying to the melancholy intro. It's a seven minute ballad, and I intend to indulge in the entire thing. And yeah, I know I'm bringing the mood in the place down.

Too bad.

I let the music wrap around me. Swallow me up. I'm the kind of person who feels emotion as music—the two are inextricably intertwined for me.

I pace around the small stage with my eyes mostly closed singing–not for the audience, but to get this sense of gloom out of my chest. For catharsis.

They're patient with me for about half the song, and then the crowd gets annoyed.

"Too sad!" someone yells.

"Why you gotta bring us down?" someone else heckles.

"Shut up and let her sing."

My eyes fly open. I recognize that voice.

Madi's sitting at the table right in front of the stage. She must've come in while I was indulging. She's rocking with the sad music, showing her New Wave appreciation like a good emo girlie with melancholy glee.

I jump off the stage and lean into her, sharing the mic, so she can sing the last lines with me.

The crowd boos, and I laugh into the mic before handing it back to the emcee.

He puts on the original Eric Carmen version of the song "All by Myself" to mock me. "Come back up, Aubrey. We know you're sad. Get him out of your system."

I flip him off.

Madi chuckles and hugs me. "Ugh. I got your message. What happened? Is it Billy?"

I try to swallow the walnut-sized lump in my throat as I nod and sit down across from her. I spill the thing about overhearing Brick ask him his intentions and saying my memories might have to be wiped by a vampire.

Madi winces.

"Is that a real thing?"

She nods. "It's how they protect their secret."

"Nobody's touching my memories," I snarl.

She hesitates then nods, reaching across the table to squeeze my hand. "I won't let it happen. I let the wolf's secrecy pull us apart once. No matter what happens with Billy, you're my inner circle."

A huge pressure lifts off my chest. "Thank you." I draw a breath. "Anyway, when Brick asked, Billy said he didn't know if I was his mate. And then his dad came up to us at the wedding."

Madi nods. "Right. Tell me what happened."

I tell her about the altercation and me asking Billy again if I was his mate and him just standing there with a blank look on his face.

Madi stares at me. I can practically see the wheels in her head turning. I hope that brilliant mind of hers can save me from my messy, tangled thoughts. "Billy doesn't show emotion. I imagine he learned to disassociate around his dad. So instead of showing you how angry or upset he was, he might have just checked out."

My nose burns for Billy. Maybe I did the wrong thing, walking away. Maybe he needed me to pull him close in that moment. Bring him back to life.

"Also, he was probably ashamed. Both of his father's insults and maybe even of how he reacted. He doesn't like to lose his cool. He prefers to have thought three steps ahead and then coolly take his opponent down. Messy violence isn't his normal thing."

Sorrow sweeps over me.

If I had it to do over, I would try to draw Billy out more. Make him feel safe expressing his true self with me. I was too busy protecting my heart before, playing games sparring with him while telling myself it was just a fling.

I thought he needed some space to sort things out, but maybe he needed the opposite. Maybe he needed me to crawl in his bed and tell him I wasn't leaving. But I was too hurt over his indecision. I didn't like feeling like I was the lesser choice because I'm human. Like being with me would be some kind of sacrifice for him.

But it's probably no different than my bias against him for being a Wall Street billionaire. I wasn't sure my self-image included having a boyfriend who could end child hunger in New York with his annual salary. I thought I'd be selling out or giving up on my ideals to be with someone like him.

Until I walked away, I hadn't realized that he was worth it. That money doesn't make a man evil. I hadn't realized how far I had waded in with him while telling myself I was holding back.

I consider Madi's words about Billy not liking to show his hand. "When we were having sex, there would sometimes be a moment when passion took over, and he lost control. I could tell he hated it. Afterwards, he'd leave or withdraw, like he needed to put himself back together."

Madi raised her brows. "That could have been his wolf trying to mark you."

I frown. "What does that mean?"

"If a male wolf finds his fated mate, he knows it because she brings up the instinct to mark her." She pulls the neck of her shirt down to point at four pale scars at the place where neck meets shoulder.

"Brick *bit* you?"

"It's a mating bite. It leaves his scent embedded in my skin, so all other males know I've been claimed."

Um, wow.

"Did his eyes ever change when you were having sex?"

I suck in a breath. "Yes. To silver."

"Sounds like he was fighting his instinct to mark you. Brick nearly lost control of his animal side because we broke up, and his wolf wanted to mark me."

Renee Rose & Lee Savino

"Do you think...do you think I'm his mate, Madi?"

She stands. "Come here. I need to show you something."

* * *

Forty minutes later, we get out of the limo Madi took to Brooklyn–yes, I rolled my eyes about it–followed by the two guard dogs Billy put on me. Madi invited them to ride along in the limo because they'd had to tail me on the subway and had left their vehicle near my place.

"This would've been a lot easier if you'd just let us drive you in the first place," one of them mutters, but one quelling look from Madi, and he bows his head. I swear I can see the tucked tail in his posture.

We're in front of the Sentience building. Madi tugs me to the front door. My bodyguards hang back.

As we draw closer, I see the front wall of windows are covered with plywood from the inside. A vinyl banner stretches across the entrance reading SILVER ARTS GALLERY AND ARTIST SPACES COMING SOON.

"Oh my God." Shock pushes me off balance, and I drop to a squat and touch the ground to find my bearings. I stare up at the building. "What happened? Billy did this?"

Madi lets out a soft laugh. "I guess he's been busy dismantling Sentience since we got back from Monaco. He and Brick had a conversation with the owners. They had a change of heart and decided to use their funding to pay back the artists they stole from. Then Billy bought this building and turned it into this."

A tight band closes around my throat. Tears spill from my eyes. I cover my mouth.

Billy took down a billion dollar company. For me.

And then he turned it into a place to make and show-case art. He listened and parsed the deepest desire of my heart and made my dream come true.

The man I thought wasn't sure about me just made the grandest gesture possible while I was licking my wounds at home believing he'd decided I wasn't worth the trouble.

"So...I am his mate?" I don't know why, but I just need someone to say it out loud. Billy won't.

"He may not have marked you, but he's clearly yours. He's slaying your dragons, even when you're not together. He's trying to make your dreams come true."

God, I'm crying like a baby. I cover my mouth to hide the ugly sob.

Why did I doubt him?

Billy is broken, that's for sure. But it doesn't mean we can't work. He may not be willing to admit yet I'm his fated mate, but I can admit he's mine.

It's time for me to fix this.

If he's not willing to claim me, I'll go over there and claim him.

I swipe at the tears under my eyes and lift my chest. "Take me to your place."

Chapter Thirty

Billy

I sprawl on my couch and attempt to get drunk while I stare at the grey flower study spanning my wall. It's bold and brilliant and begging for color.

Aubrey did that on purpose.

She did that to me.

She walked into my life, showed me texture and beauty, and pointed out how colorless I am. How soulless. How empty and flat and grey.

Until I met Aubrey, I thought I was satisfied. I clawed my way out of my childhood, and fate delivered me to the side of the most powerful alpha in the country. I wasn't the biggest or strongest wolf in his pack, but I was the most vicious. The most paranoid, calculating, and conniving. I won every challenge for dominance and made myself indispensable to Brick when his life imploded. I helped him hold his pack together when the Adalwulfs nearly took them. Helped him more than replace the wealth that was ripped from his pack.

I had my life in complete control. I was wealthy,

successful, and stood at the side of the most powerful pack in New York.

Then she waltzed in and set everything on fire.

Fuck.

I chug from a bottle of gin. I've downed almost the entire container, but with my shifter metabolism, the buzz is hard to maintain.

Someone opens my door without knocking. My teeth bare in a snarl as I tear to my feet to eviscerate whoever it is.

"Honey, I'm home."

I go still.

She's here.

Mate, my wolf howls.

I know.

I froze when she asked me.

Froze when my alpha asked me.

But as soon as she ended things, it became crystal clear: I've known Aubrey was my mate since the first time we met at La Résistance. I resisted fate because on some level, my subconscious registered her as a threat.

Love isn't clean or simple. It isn't orderly. I can't control it.

The abused child in me feared for her life as well as my own because he was frozen in time, not knowing I'm all grown up now.

All grown up, and my tormenter's dead.

No one will ever threaten my mate again.

If I can make her my mate.

But I'm frozen again now. At a loss for the right words to say to the female who means everything to me.

Mate, my wolf snarls.

Yes, *I know.*

I need to move. Need to say something.

Aubrey's taking in the liquor bottle in my hand. The mess on the coffee table in my usually immaculate living room. I must look the way I feel–like I took a dive into Hell and stayed there. She struts over to me.

I have to speak. I am the man who brokers billion dollar deals. I can make my lips move.

"You're my mate." The words sound wooden and rusty.

Aubrey freezes her advance, staring at me.

I clear my throat. "I'm sorry I didn't answer you at the wedding, but yes, you're my mate. I would do anything for you, my Silver. My perfect poison. My Kryptonite. I...I need you in my life. I won't make it without you."

She runs to me, clomping over in her Doc Martens and taking a flying leap.

I catch her in the air, and she straddles my waist. "I love you, Billy White, the third."

"I love you, Aubrey Cook, the first."

"I'm here to claim you and mark you as mine, however the fuck I do that," Aubrey declares.

The smile that forms on my face nearly breaks my cheeks. A strange sound comes from my lips. I don't recognize it at first, then I realize it's a laugh. "I can't wait to see what you come up with."

She licks my ear, then bites it. I slowly rotate us, savoring the feel of her in my arms. The incredible lightness that suddenly takes over my being. This female broke my heart and then waltzed back into my life like nothing happened.

"I'll figure something out," she promises. "A tattoo on your ass, maybe?"

Another laugh spills from me. "You want to tattoo my ass?"

"Uh huh. With my name. Or maybe a picture of my face?"

I press my face between her breasts and inhale her scent. I kiss her breastbone. "You came back."

"For future reference, the next time I walk away, I want to be chased."

A third laugh comes out of my mouth. I'm so buoyant, it's a wonder I don't just float up to the ceiling.

"There won't be a next time," I growl and carry Aubrey to the couch. I sit with her straddling my waist. "I'm going to claim you, Silver. I'm going to mark you as my mate, so every wolf knows you belong to me. And if you leave me again, there will be consequences."

"What kind of consequences?" She waggles her brows, her full lips stretching into a megawatt smile.

"The kind that involve you naked over my lap for a good spanking."

Aubrey's eyes grow dark. The scent of her arousal reaches my nostrils. "Mmm." She squirms against my dick. "Maybe you should show me."

"I will. After you tell me why you left." Some of the heaviness descends again, like a cinder block on my chest. "Was it the violence?"

Aubrey holds my face and leans her forehead against mine. "No," she says softly. "I mean, it scared me, but I understood. Your dad sort of assaulted me. It triggered you."

I study her face. I don't want to say these words. They physically pain me to speak, but there's so much that's been unsaid between Aubrey and I. We need to get it all out on the table now. "I have a violent side. Shifters are more phys-ically violent in general, but I was forced to fight for my life throughout my childhood. I...didn't want you to see that side of me. I was ashamed. I am ashamed."

Aubrey pulls her forehead away from mine, and her eyes brim with tears. They alarm me. I tighten my grip on her hips as if afraid someone might try to yank her off. Take her away from me.

"I shouldn't have chosen that moment to ask you if I was your mate. It's just...I overheard you and Brick talking about it in Monaco. About wiping my memory." Her lips tremble.

"Fuck." Self-recrimination rips through me. "Fuck, I'm so sorry. I would never let a leech wipe your memories. I don't know why I couldn't bring myself to admit to Brick that you're my mate. I knew it. Every one of the guys knew it. My behavior was so erratic. I started an international pack incident when the Monaco king insulted you. I worked from home to be near you. I co-parented a puppy, for fuck's sake."

Aubrey gives me a reluctant smile.

"I guess I subconsciously knew marking you would force things to a head with my dad. Things I'd put off for far too long. So I stalled and pretended I didn't know for sure. But I did, baby." I stroke her cheek with my thumb. "And I'm so fucking sorry I hurt you and made you feel like you weren't good enough. That was never it. I was the one who wasn't good enough for you. Not yet. But I took care of it. My dad and those assholes from Sentience will never threaten you or your friends again."

She studies my face. "What did you do?" she whispers.

I hesitate. This is the violent side I don't want her to see. But if she's my mate, she needs to know who I am. What I'll do to keep her and our family safe. "I put my dad in the ground."

She sucks in a breath.

"As long as he was alive, you and our pups would be at risk, and I could not have that."

Aubrey's eyes mist again. "Our pups?" she chokes.

My throat closes, too, but the words are flowing now. I can't hold them back any more. "Please marry me. Let me protect you, provide for you, and be your family."

Aubrey breaks, clapping her hand over her mouth to stifle a sob.

I hold my breath, watching her. Bracing for her reaction.

"Yes." She nods. "Okay. I'm in, Billy White, the one and only. I'm all in."

I fall back on the couch, limp with relief. I've been a zombie for the last twelve days, barely living, barely breathing, barely keeping my shit together.

But it's over.

Aubrey's mine.

I know we still have work to do. I have to learn to make her happy. Keep her interested. Please her in ways beyond the bedroom. I have to learn to open up. It was my silence that made her walk away.

"When you didn't contact me, I thought you were relieved that I ended things," she tells me.

My heart squeezes painfully. "Fuck. I was just trying to honor your wishes."

"Yeah, don't do that again." She flashes a sad smile. "Tonight Madi took me over to Sentience and showed me what you did for me. I realized you must still care."

I sit up, pressing my chest against hers. I grip her nape. "I care. I care so fucking much, Silver. I'm sorry I don't know how to show it."

"No, you do. You show it perfectly. You're an 'acts of service' guy. I was looking for 'words of affirmation.' But now I know how you express love."

My brows dip in confusion.

"It's a love language thing. We have to learn to speak each other's love languages."

I hold her gaze. "I'll learn," I swear like I'm making an oath to my alpha. "I'm a quick study."

She gives me another one of those brilliant smiles. "I know. You're the guy who just mastered ASL in the last few months. Madi told me you can read a 50-page contract in five minutes and demand extensive, thoughtful changes. You're way smarter than I am."

"I'm an idiot compared to you."

She kisses me. "Not true. I let my pride *and* prejudice get in the way of us. But now we're a team. We'll deal with conflicts together, not apart."

I feel the conflict in my chest. The old me–the black and white me–with compartmentalizing walls struggling to breathe as the barriers crumble. The pleasure of the light and warmth war with the need to re-erect my walls.

I surrender to it all. This is what it means to love. To be vulnerable and open. It feeds me at the same time it shakes my world up.

I lean into kiss her, and she pulls back. "Silver." She taps her nose. She took out the diamond I gave her and put the old silver nose ring back in. She really was hurt. "It'll burn."

"Worth it." I stroke my lips across hers in a slow, savoring kiss.

* * *

Aubrey

I bite his lower lip and tug. "Where are you going to bite me?" I make my voice sultry.

Billy's expression turns feral. His eyes change to silver

as he surges to his feet, lifting me. "Somewhere erotic." He carries me to his bedroom.

"Mmm."

"Unfortunately, it's going to hurt, Silver. I have to puncture the skin. So if I'm going to make you scream, I might as well do it in an erogenous zone." He drops me in the center of the bed and whips my shirt off over my head. "That way I can remind you that you belong to me every time I pleasure you."

I reach for his shirt and try to rip it open like we're in a bodice-ripper, but I'm not strong enough.

Billy chuckles and does it for me, sending the buttons spraying around the room.

I give him a tiger-growl and paw at his chest.

He catches my wrists and climbs over me, pinning them beside my head. "So the question is..." --he drops his head to kiss between my breasts– "do I bite you here?" He nips the top of one of my breasts, then abruptly swings his leg off me and rolls me to my belly. "Or am I going to bite this gorgeous ass?" He slips his thumbs in the waistband of my shorts and slides them down with my panties, just below my ass.

I shiver as he runs his large palm lightly around my ass, knowing what's coming. He teases me, keeping the touch a light caress. Then the first spank falls.

I yelp.

He takes my wrists and folds them behind my back, like I'm under arrest, and holds them there. His touch is gentle. Almost reverential, but when he starts spanking, he doesn't hold back.

He delivers a flurry of quick slaps that make me wriggle against his hold.

"Ouch!" I complain, rolling my hips when he stops.

"That's for leaving me, Silver." He resumes the light caressing, stroking his palm around the globes of my ass.

His hand slides up the column of my back until he reaches my bra, which he unhooks. Brushing my braids to the side, he climbs over me once more to nibble and kiss my neck and exposed shoulder.

Then he stops. I wait, but he settles by my side. "It will hurt, Aubrey." His voice is serious.

I roll to face him. His eyes shine completely silver, and I would swear the points of his canine teeth have lengthened.

The room is dark and above the lights of the city the moon shines in, nearly full. It casts a pale glow across his face.

"I don't want to hurt you. I don't want to scare you. I don't want you to ever walk away again."

It strikes me—Billy is scared. He's scared of losing me, and he's sharing his feelings. This moment is more important than any bite, at least to me. This is how we learn to be a real couple. Listening and sharing.

I lay my head on the pillow. "Would it hurt if I were a wolf?"

He shakes his head. "The pain would be pleasurable, and the wound would heal instantly. But for a human, a mating bite could be fatal if I hit the wrong spot. You'll bleed and scar. I heard Madi scream when Brick marked her."

Shock ripples through me. I should've pumped more information from Madi.

"You were there?"

"Yes. We were there to protect Madi. When an alpha wolf doesn't find his fated mate or worse, finds her and doesn't mark her, he can turn feral. We call it moon madness. The wolf takes over, and the human is lost and has to be put down."

My mouth rounds into a silent "O". My eyes probably match the shape.

"Brick went moon mad?"

"Yes. We nearly lost him."

The memory of Ruby coming to get Madi and begging for her help after they broke up returns.

"So he was nearly mad when he bit her."

Something about Billy quiets. He can see where I'm going with this. "Yes."

"But you're perfectly sane right now." I touch his cheek and massage the shell of his ear. "I know you don't like to lose control. Even when we're having sex and you let go at the end, you seem to pull back and try to snap it all together afterwards."

Billy props his head up with one arm and cups my breast with his free hand, thumbing over my nipple. "You saw that?"

I nod. "And you said you didn't like losing control in front of me at the wedding with your dad."

He scrubs a hand over his face. "I hate that you saw me that way."

"*I* don't," I insist. "I'm not afraid of that guy. I know you would never hurt me." I press a kiss to his lips. "I want to see all your parts and pieces. Even the ugly ones. Even the parts you're ashamed of. I love you, Billy. That means all of you. I didn't walk away because I saw something I didn't like. I walked because you weren't willing to share all of you with me."

Vulnerability flashes on Billy's face, and for once, he doesn't shutter his expression.

"So go wild with me. Let yourself off the leash. I love

that you have a powerful animal side, Billy. Mark my body with your teeth and show me what it's like to be claimed."

And just like that, his control snaps.

I find myself pinned on my back. Billy yanks my shorts and panties the rest of the way off.

He unzips his pants, and I reach for his erection.

I've never seen his eyes quite so silver. And his canines are *definitely* long and sharp. He's going to bite me with those. A shiver of excitement jolts through me.

"Condom," I choke when he forgets and starts pushing into me. "Unless you want to start on those pups now."

I don't know what makes me say it, but it feels right. I wasn't lying when I said I was all in. I want this whole thing with Billy–marriage, family, everything.

He freezes on his reach to the bedside table.

"Yes." His voice doesn't sound human. The deep growl from his chest is otherworldly.

He shoves into me, spearing me with his erection, plowing deep on the first thrust.

I gasp and brace my hand against the headboard.

"I'm going to put my pup in you, Aubrey White." He rocks in and out.

"Not taking your name," I interject, but I smile from ear to ear. We're getting married. This is crazy.

"I'm putting my pup in you, Aubrey Cook-White," he amends and continues to thrust into me, holding my shoulder to keep me from flying toward the headboard.

I'm already delirious with pleasure. Steeped in the hormones of love.

He bends his face to flick his tongue over my nipple, then nips it. "I'll do the whole human wedding thing–whatever you want–but tonight, you become mine. Tonight, I embed my scent in your skin, Silver." He says it like it's a

Renee Rose & Lee Savino

warning. Or a punishment. Maybe he's giving me a last chance to back out.

I wouldn't dream of it.

I clasp my ankles behind his back to drag him in deeper, to show him I want more.

"I'm claiming you, and there's no going back. No walking away." His eyes glow in the dark. They make my heart race.

My boyfriend is a wolf. It's thrilling and real and *right* at the same time.

Billy pounds into me, gathering speed, using enough force that I'll be walking funny tomorrow. I want more. I reach for him, scoring his shoulders with my nails, rocking my pelvis to take him even deeper.

"There's no future where we're not together," he growls. "You're my mate, and wolves mate for life."

I laugh, but I'm crying. At least, my face is wet, so I must be.

"Do it," I urge. "Make me yours."

He lets out a wolf-snarl. His jaws open, and his fangs gleam in the moonlight. I experience a flash of fear, but it's instantly eclipsed by pleasure.

He comes inside me, and I orgasm around his pulsing cock. The walls of my channel squeeze to suck his essence in and up. I gasp out my pleasure.

"*Mine*," Billy roars, shoving deep and going still.

"Yes, yours!"

He cups my breast with one hand and lowers his head. "Mine." This time it's quieter.

He closes his jaws. The bite is gentle and shallow, at the outside of my breast, on the pectoral muscle.

I come again, bucking my hips, and squeezing around

his cock as he carefully extracts his teeth from my breast and licks the wounds closed.

"Are you okay, Silver?" He grips my jaw and turns my face to his. His eyes are back to blue, and they search my face with concern.

My lids flutter open, and I smile. I rock my hips to show him how good I am.

"Does it hurt?"

"It's a good hurt."

"Yeah?" He pinches the nipple of the marked breast and holds.

I orgasm again. "Oh," I sob.

He pinches the other one. "Mine." He whispers it this time.

"All yours," I whisper back.

"I love you." He kisses the tears on my face. "I don't know how I got so lucky, but I'm never going to let you go."

"You better not."

Chapter Thirty-One

A*ubrey*

It's a hot day and City College's commencement is outside, so I'm dying in this black gown.

"Congratulations, Class of 2025," the president says into the microphone.

Well, I did it. I'm officially a college grad with a rather useless degree in Women's Studies. I join in the cheering of my fellow classmates and toss my cap in the air.

My parents are in the audience, sitting with my grandma, Caroline, Jan, Madi, and her mom.

I called Jan and Jamie yesterday to let them know that Billy had dismantled Sentience, and they are totally safe now. Jamie still wants vindication, so she's now free to pursue a full expose by sharing everything she has with the *New York Times*.

Madi waves and points up to the sky. I look up. A blimp floats overhead, carrying a banner that reads, "Congratulations, Aubrey!"

I laugh and point at Madi. "You?" I mouth.

She smiles and shakes her head. Billy, then. My mate. Of course.

I scan the crowd.

Where is he? I know he's here somewhere. He moved me back to his apartment the night he marked me, sending some of his pack guys over to get Pepper and pack my stuff.

When I complained that I might want to keep using the apartment because Madi's old room is my studio, he showed me the huge bedroom in his penthouse that he'd already converted into a studio for me.

While we were broken up.

Wow.

When I asked this morning if he wanted to come and meet my parents, he said nothing would keep him away. I warned him that I'd be introducing him as my new boyfriend, not fiancé, because it's way too soon in a human relationship for us to be engaged. He growled, but I learned over the past day that letting him see or smell his mark on me instantly soothes him, so I flashed a boob, and he pulled me onto his lap and kissed between my breasts with enough reverence to start a new religion.

The religion of marked boobs.

I spot the row of wolf shifters standing at the back, behind the white folding chairs on the lawn. Billy, Brick, Nickel, Vance, Jake, and Sully stand against the fence like sentries. All of them are tall, gorgeous and imposing, even without their three-piece suits. Now that I know they're wolves, it makes more sense. They radiate power and charisma.

No wonder they took Wall Street by storm.

I find my way to Billy, and he picks me up and spins me around.

"Ouch. Sore boob," I murmur, and he instantly puts me

down with concern creasing his face. "The blimp was an amazing touch." I stand on my toes and kiss him then turn to Brick. "Thank you so much for coming." I give him a hug.

"Welcome to the pack, Aubrey."

Wow. I'm part of the pack. Crazy!

"Thank you."

"Welcome to the pack." Each of the guys hugs me and issues their welcome. There's a ritualism to it that makes me feel like this is a formal induction. I've been marked, now I don't just belong to Billy, I'm one of them.

I love it.

Madi leads my family over to where we're standing, and I receive all their hugs, balloons, and congratulations.

"Mom, dad, everyone–this is Billy, the guy I've been dating. He was Brick's best man."

My dad shakes Billy's hand. My mom hugs him.

Jan and Caroline decide to play stern dads and give him the stink eye as they shake his hand. Of course, they probably already put together that he's a billionaire bro and are wondering if I lost my mind.

This will all take some adjustment.

I'm not giving up my ideals, but my self-image will have to change. I know I'll figure it all out. Madi did.

Billy clears his throat. "Well, if you'd like, I had some food catered in at our place. We can take everyone over in the limos."

"Your place?" My mom's brows fly up. "Both of yours?" Props to her for not gaping about the limo part.

"Well, it's Billy's place. It's in Brick and Madi's building."

"It's our place," Billy says firmly. "Aubrey's painting murals on my walls."

329

My mom's jaw drops. "Honey! How long has this been going on? Why didn't you tell us?"

I glance at Billy. He's stiff, coming off as aloof, as usual, but I can tell he's trying. "It's recent. Billy hired me to paint the murals and things developed from there." I reach for his hand, and he immediately catches mine.

Madi, who is tucked against Brick's side, smiles. "It's going to be amazing. I can't wait to see. Let's go!"

We walk toward the limos, but Billy pulls me toward his Porsche. He opens the passenger door for me. There's a little jewelry box on my seat tied up with a bow.

"I got you a present," he says. "But if it's not perfect, we'll keep looking."

It's perfect. I know it's going to be perfect. Billy pays attention.

I sit in the car seat and wait until Billy's settled in the driver's seat to pull the end of the ribbon. The ends fall open, and I pry open the lid.

It's three rows of pink diamonds. Simple. Stunning. Totally me.

"I love it." I check his face. "Lab grown?"

"No blood diamonds for my wife."

His wife. Hearing him say those words sends frissons of excitement through me.

"Is this an engagement ring?" I ask, trying it on my ring finger.

He nods. "Marry me?"

He already knows the answer. He already demanded forever.

"Yes."

* * *

Billy

I unlock the door and pick up Aubrey to carry her across the threshold.

She laughs. "I think you're supposed to wait until we're married."

"Am I? I can't get all your human wedding traditions straight." I set her down as the elevator dings announcing the arrival of our guests.

While we were away, the caterers decorated the apartment with silver and black balloons and set up a few high-tops around the room covered in white linen and silver confetti.

"Oh my God! What is this?" Aubrey squeals when Pepper greets us at the door with a graduation cap and tiny cape that represents a gown. "You're so freaking cute!"

She scoops up the puppy and Pepper frantically tries to lick Aubrey's face.

"Who is this cutey?" her mom coos. She sends a curious glance my way, like she's trying to reconcile why or how a man like me would pick a Shi-poo for a pet.

"He's Aubrey's," I say.

"He's *ours*," she insists, the way I insisted the penthouse was ours.

"You two have a *dog*?" Caroline sounds incredulous. She rubs both of Pepper's ears at once, telling the dog how cute he is.

"Yep. Co-parents." Aubrey thinks it's hilarious to say that. I hope she finds it equally entertaining when I put my real pup in her belly.

"Aubrey, this is incredible." Jan surveys the first mural. It's still black and white, but Aubrey wove silver accents through the entire thing which somehow brought it to life.

Just like she brought me to life.

"You like it?" Aubrey takes it in with a critical eye. She hasn't decided if she's finished with it yet.

"I love it," Aubrey's mom exclaims.

"It's a huge departure from your normal style," Jan says. "Your exploration of black and white for flowers is truly inspired."

Aubrey's eyes crinkle, and she sends me a broad smile.

I wink.

I've never winked in my life. I'm not playful. I don't flirt. I can't even imagine what made me wink. But then Aubrey puts her hand on her chest and closes her eyes like she's swooning over the wink, and I feel a million feet tall.

She's the reason for my personality transplant. She breathed life into me. Her chaos disrupted the rules and strict patterns of my life, and I'll never be the same.

I never want to be the same.

"Ooh, I love this one!" Caroline exclaims, catching sight of the second mural that Aubrey spent all day and most of the night yesterday painting.

It is technicolor—painted in bright oranges, blues, yellows, and red. A giant blue wolf faces off to the viewer, hackles raised, teeth bared. Me. To his right, just behind his shoulder sits a tiny red dog, safe under the protection of the wolf. Pepper.

Aubrey left herself out of the mural, which bothers me, but she promised to paint me a self-portrait on canvas next. She claims she loves her new studio that overlooks Central Park, and of course, she can use any of the artist spaces at the Silver Arts Center after we complete the build-out if she prefers.

I nod at the caterers to crack the Dom Perignon as Aubrey tells her family about the Silver Arts Center.

They're all a little stunned at how much has happened that they didn't know about, but no one seems offended.

The caterers carry out the trays of filled champagne glasses, and I lift mine. "I'd like to propose a toast," I say.

Aubrey's face goes soft again. The way she looks at me makes me want to drop to my knees and thank fate and the Moon Goddess for giving me such a female.

"To Aubrey–the woman who turned my life on its head. Who made me change and grow and learn to love. I am so grateful you stomped into my life and kicked me in the head."

Aubrey's mom's eyes widen but everyone laughs.

"To Aubrey," Madi carols.

"To Aubrey," our guests chorus back.

Aubrey clinks her glass with mine, sips, and sets it down. Then her arms twine around my neck, and she's kissing me like it's our last moment on Earth.

Our guests cheer.

I wrap my arms around her, careful not to squeeze too hard this time, and I kiss her breath away, the way I intend to kiss her every day for the rest of her life.

Epilogue

Six months later...

N*oah*

I open the door to the Silver Arts Gallery and step inside.

When the boss invites you to the grand opening of his mate's new art center, you go.

Even if you haven't been invited to join his pack.

There's art everywhere I look. Everything from photography to sculpture to oil paintings. Giant paper flowers cover an entire wall, and the statues carved from ebony wood displayed on slender plinths.

I spy Billy with his human mate holding hands, standing in front of a large floral mural for photographs. A tiny dog stands beside Billy, wearing a tuxedo bib and bow tie. The dog is so completely at odds with Billy's personality that I stare, trying to reconcile it. Then his mate stoops to pick up the little dog, and it becomes clear. Billy, like any good wolf, would do anything for his mate. Including parent a ridiculous little dog if she wanted one.

Cute.

In the center of the space in front of the mural, caterers have turned several tables into one long epic cheese board.

Madi and Blackthroat join Billy. Another surprising match–the alpha of one of the largest packs in the country with a human. She is a remarkable human, though. Brilliant, generous, and friendly. I don't know what happened exactly between them, but I believe Blackthroat nearly went moon mad trying to deny the match.

It had something to do with the Adalwulf pack and a job offer because Blackthroat called me in to lipread a video of Madi talking to Aiden Adalwulf, their alpha.

Madi sees me and waves me over.

I sign "hello" as I approach.

Madi introduces me to Aubrey, her best friend and Billy's mate.

"Aubrey is the artist of this beautiful mural," Madi speaks and signs at the same time, which takes the mastery of not just someone who can sign but an interpreter.

"It's beautiful," I say out loud to Aubrey. "Is the gallery for your work?"

Aubrey laughs and shakes her head. "No. I curated, though. Our next theme will be social justice art–creating change through art, that kind of thing."

I nod.

"The top floors are artist spaces, and the bottom is a gallery."

"Congratulations. It's a bold project," I say.

Aubrey smiles, then her gaze slides to Billy, who tucks her against his side. He's changed drastically in the past few months since he mated. He's no less powerful, but the feral, aggressive edge is gone. He has a more quiet leadership style now.

Blackthroat shakes my hand. "Good to see you here, Noah."

"I'm honored to be included."

He doesn't release my hand for a moment, scrutinizing my face. Maybe he thinks I'm hinting to be let in the pack.

I'm not. I prefer being a lone wolf, but I suspect that's not acceptable to an alpha like Blackthroat.

I approached finding a job on Wall Street like a human would. I graduated from Harvard with an MBA and applied for jobs in Manhattan. I did apply at both companies owned by wolf packs, thinking my scent might give me an in during an interview.

I also knew it could backfire, if the wolves here were like my birth pack and considered me "defective." I didn't approach either pack about membership since I didn't know how they'd treat me or where I'd land with a job. If I didn't get a job with either company, I'd just as soon not be affiliated with any pack.

That was my first mistake.

The HR rep at Moon Co was human, so my scent didn't come into play, but I guess I nailed the interview because I got the job. At the time, I'd loved knowing I was hired based on merit alone.

Then I met the CEO, Brick Blackthroat. He scented me in a meeting and called me to his office afterward. I found myself pinned to a wall by my throat until I swore I wasn't an Adalwulf spy.

Then he demanded to know why I hadn't approached him, as alpha of his territory, to join the pack. There's no lying to an alpha, but telling the truth was my second mistake. He didn't like me admitting I played both sides for a job.

The third mistake was having lunch with Madi before

Renee Rose & Lee Savino

they were mated. She invited me as friends, and she was unmarked, so I had no idea she belonged to him. He told me in no uncertain terms to stay away from her.

So there's been no invitation to join their pack. I don't believe it's because they're bigoted and believe me "defective" like my home pack because after Billy saw Madi signing to me at work, he and the rest of the team promptly learned ASL. In my home pack, only my grandmother bothered to learn it. I learned to lip read and speak and did my best to integrate.

But being without a pack has its downsides. I have nowhere to run in the city. I haven't shifted in months. My wolf grows restless, plaguing me with dream after dream of hunting.

Usually I'm hunting game. Sometimes it's a beautiful girl with moon-pale hair and wide, unfocused eyes.

Like the one I saw step out of a limo with Aiden Adalwulf.

Their pack's seeress, Billy said.

I dreamed about her last night.

She wore an old-fashioned filmy nightgown, and her room—or was it a prison?—was adorned with elegant furnishings from another era.

Her Sight took her beyond the walls of her castle.

Her sight took her to me.

She was sitting on her bed, but looked up at me with a gasp. I was both in my own bed in Soho and in her room at the same time.

"*Noah.*" She spoke my name with wonder. Not with her voice. Not with her hands.

With her mind.

She couldn't be much more than eighteen, not that I'm a

338

judge of she-wolves' ages. She gave me a smile. "I've been waiting to meet you for such a long time."

"Who are you?" I spoke using words in my mind, too.

Her smile was sad and mysterious. "You don't know?"

I did know her, but in the dream, I couldn't remember how.

I wanted to say *yes* because I didn't want to disappoint her. I wanted to say I knew her. That I'd claimed her in a past life. Or was it a future one? There was something achingly familiar about her. Was she a ghost? A spirit guide?

Of course, I couldn't tell her scent. Not in the dream. Maybe if I'd been able to catch her scent, I would know what she meant to me.

I just shook my head. "I want to."

She ducked her head, tucking her hair behind one ear. Was that a blush on her pale skin? Surely a ghost didn't blush. I suddenly became aware of her in a less-than-ephemeral way. I tracked the skin showing above the neckline of her nightdress. The swell of her breasts. Her delicate hands. Those puffy lips. My blood rushed south, below my waist.

"You will," she told me.

I took a step closer to her bed. "Why am I here?"

A line formed between her brows, and her focus went blurry for a moment, then she looked at me thoughtfully and cocked her lovely head.

"The war is coming. You must decide which side you're on. Find me before it's too late."

Want More? Order Alpha's Claim

The werebears from Bad Bear Mountain are back, starting with Darius, the Wall Street Viking who boxes with Brick at the gym. We've included Chapter One below.

Order their story now!

. . .

Chapter One - Alpha's Claim

Paloma

The moment the deadbolt to my bedroom door clicks into place, I dash for the closet.

Black clothes, so I won't be seen against the building at night. Flexible toe socks, so my toes can grip the rough-hewn stone of the mansion.

I quickly strip out of my "work" dress and into my escape gear.

I have an estimated three to eight minutes until they figure out how to get power back up, and in that time, I need to be out to the balcony, down the wall, and into the ocean where the security cameras won't pick me up and thermoscans won't see my heat signature.

"You got this, you got this, you got this," I whisper-chant to myself as my trembling fingers draw the lock-picking tools out of the pouch. I'd stowed them in the pocket of these black yoga pants weeks ago after I caught the gardener's thirteen-year-old son picking a lock to the garage during one of my rare unguarded moments in the garden. He'd told me he hadn't meant any harm and was just practicing his lock-picking skills. He'd shown me the instruction book and tool kit he ordered online. I said I would keep it between us, but I had to confiscate his instruction book and tools.

I drop to my knees in front of the French doors to the balcony.

Slipping the slender tension wrench into the lock, I apply pressure to its plug. Then I slide in the pin. I close my eyes to concentrate. I've practiced this at least a hundred times. I already know how to find and set each pin, one at a time, until the lock fully disengages. With a little more pressure on the tension wrench, I turn the plug.

Click.

This is as far as I've ever gotten. I couldn't open the doors before because the electronic monitor at the top would notify Thom's security team that a door had been breached. Now, with the power cut to the property, I have a moment.

I let out an exhale, stow the tools in my pocket, and use both hands to pull the doors open.

They don't budge.

I scan the door frame. Did I miss something? A second lock? A physical bar or barrier? I don't see anything.

"Come on," I growl in an undertone. I pull harder.

It's not moving.

"*Juepucha*," I mutter. "Come on, you bitch." I yank with all my strength. The doors fly open, and a gust of ocean breeze fills the room, making the curtains flap.

Yes!

My days as the girl in the tower are over. I slip out and silently shut the doors behind me.

You've heard the stories about girls in towers, right? Some of them are supposedly fair maidens. Some princesses. Some have long hair that can be used as a climbing rope to save them.

Me? I guess I'm a mage of sorts. I can see the future of a company, just by looking at its numbers.

Hence, my usefulness as a day trader.

I am also technically a maiden if that means virgin. The jury's out on the fair part. Does that mean good-looking or pale-skinned? I was never sure. Whatever. I'm Latinx, so I identify as BIPOC if you were wondering.

I throw a leg over the carved marble railing that brackets the balcony to straddle it, then the other, balancing my weight on the one-inch ledge that rims the outside.

Don't look down, I whisper.

My particular fairytale lacks the trellis for me to climb down, but metal wires run horizontally along the building to support the ivy. I lean out, wrap my toes around one of them, and test it with my weight. It holds.

Holding my breath, I transfer one hand to another wire. It cuts into my hands but serves. I leave the safety of the ledge and feel with my free foot for a wire below. It's farther than I expect, but I eventually catch it. Then I realize some of the ivy boughs might be thick enough to hold me.

That works better. I scale down, seeking the wires with my feet but sliding my hands along the thicker ivy cords. I'm three floors up, a distance that feels far higher and longer to scale now that I'm doing it. And I've already wasted too much time.

The lights could come back on any second now.

One of the branches I'm holding is too thin, and it breaks. I plunge downward, my fingers grasping for something else to hold and finally catching. My skin is torn, and my fingers burn, but I barely notice. All my focus is on getting down.

I jump before I should, jarring my ankle and smacking my knee on the earth below. But it doesn't matter–I'm out. I take off running for the ocean as fast as I can.

I've been training for this, too. Every day, I race on my treadmill that faces the ocean, whispering to my body that the day will come when we can make a break for it. My illness was a small setback, but the medicine seems to be working.

I wasn't ready for it to be tonight. I wanted to locate Wren and make a plan to get her to safety before I escaped. I also need to figure out how to access the medicine keeping me alive. Last time I tried to escape, I collapsed before I could get far. But I'm feeling stronger now and don't have a choice. I'm out of time.

Thom let me in on his disgusting plan tonight at dinner.

Tomorrow night, he arranged to auction me off to the highest bidder. It's not enough that I make him billions. He must sell me to one of his buddies to cement a merger. His twisted version of an arranged marriage.

Sorry, no.

Not happening.

This time, my escape plan will work. It has to.

The mansion's lights come back on in a sudden blaze.

Dammit.

Run, run, run. I put my head down and sprint as fast as I can. My feet hit sand.

An alarm goes off. It will still take them time to realize I'm gone, hopefully. So long as—

"Hold it right there!" A male voice shouts.

No! I've been spotted.

I could still make it. I'll hide in the water. I reach the water and run in, diving into the cold water before it's deep enough, so it's more of a belly flop. I adjust my hands on the rocks below to propel me into the deeper water.

I don't look behind me. I don't want to see how close they are. Whether they're coming for me. I squeeze my eyes closed and paddle hard, forgetting that I may not survive the ocean even if I'm not caught.

But I am caught.

A strong arm loops around my neck and shoves my head under, holding me down.

I struggle, kicking out, using my elbows, trying to duck out of his grasp. I need to take a breath.

Is this guy trying to kill me?

Clearly he doesn't know that I'm the golden goose.

Everything's muffled by the sound of water around me, but I hear shouts above. Lights blaze in the periphery of my vision. I'm starting to pass out.

And then I'm up. Held by my hair above water.

"What are you doing?" Thom rages from the shore.

"I'm sorry, Mr. Thompson. I thought she was an intruder."

"Get my daughter back to shore."

His *daughter*. Every time he calls me that I want to barf.

Two men grab me by the arms and drag me forward, out of the ocean, onto the beach where Thom slaps me hard across the face.

I figure this is my one chance. If there's any man who works for Thom who has any conscience at all, I need to alert him. If he doesn't disobey now, maybe he'll raise a flag with the authorities.

"Let me go!" I scream. "You can't auction me off. I'm not your property! You can't keep me prisoner here forever!"

A needle jabs into the meaty part of my arm before I even see it coming. I stare into the eyes of the man who delivered it and detect a sadistic gleam of pleasure in them right before my vision goes dark and my legs forget how to hold me.

. . .

#

Darius

Billionaires have a certain sort of smell. Not just clean human skin, but the extra bouquet of expensive skin care products, rare perfumes, richer food.

That's what my bear thinks, anyway. After years living in Manhattan, my poor animal's nose has attuned to all sorts of city smells. It's a relief to helicopter to the Hamptons for the weekend. I step onto the tarmac and breathe my first clean lungful in months. The air tastes sweet with a tang of salt. Across a half-mile of manicured lawn, sunlight flashes on the wind-whipped sea.

The richer you are, the more land you can afford. My host, Thom Thompson, owns a massive estate on the water between wildlife preserves.

Woods, my bear points out. *Let me out!* He wants to strip off my human skin and lumber into the wild. Keeping him caged in has been the hardest part about living in Manhattan. These woods are nothing like the wilderness of Bad Bear Mountain, where I grew up, but it's enough to remind me of what I'm missing now that I've made New York City my home.

Later, I tell him. I can't go romping around in a pine forest. I'm not here to relax. I'm here to network.

I check my collar and shoot my cuffs. I'm in my best off-hours blazer, designed to look casual while still perfectly tailored. My loafers are handmade in a small village outside of Milan. I'm groomed head to toe to fit in with the humans

I'll be rubbing elbows with all weekend, the one percent of the one percent.

My one unruly feature is my thick blond hair. I get it cut every week, but I swear my bear makes it grow faster to spite me. The wind tousles it as I stride from the helicopter.

"This way, sir." An estate staff member in a navy blue uniform takes my suitcase and guides me towards a mansion that would make Great Gatsby turn green. I brace myself, expecting the place to smell old, like oiled wood and ancient horsehair furniture, but the inside is modern.

The owner and the man who invited me is waiting in the foyer to greet all his guests. "Darius, welcome."

"Mr. Thompson," I shake his hand, careful not to use too much pressure. A firm handshake from a bear shifter would crush a human's bones.

"Please, call me Thom," he says in a reedy voice. He's casually dressed in an outfit that costs more than a new car.

"Thanks for inviting me."

"Of course, my boy." Thom and I have met a handful of times, but he's the sort who fancies himself a mentor. He makes a show of taking younger men under his wing, giving himself credit for their success, and discarding them the second they fall from grace. "I'm sure you'll find this weekend instructive." He doesn't let me get a word in, so I settle for murmuring my appreciation as he continues. "Farpoint has several pools and tennis courts. And the golf course. I hope we'll be able to get a few rounds in tomorrow. They tell me it might rain." He frowns as if the weather is an employee who needs a reprimand. Wealth can insulate a person from any inconvenience, but nature is nature.

"I'm just happy to be out of the city."

"Yes, I'm so glad you could come to my humble abode." The *humble abode* he's talking about has almost thirty bedrooms. It's over hundred thousand square feet, not including the guest and pool houses. "Nester will show you to your room, but don't linger. Cocktails will be served here until six, and then we will sit down for dinner."

More guests arrive, so I thank him and move on, following Nester up two flights of stairs and down a long hallway to a room with windows that overlook the ocean.

Let me out.

My bear is still clamoring to get outside, into the woods.

I placate him by opening the windows to clear the smell of billionaire. I throw each of them open and breathe in the ocean air. A breeze ruffles my hair. I swear it grows another centimeter as I stand there. I swipe my hand through it and sigh. I have to go back downstairs.

I'm here to work, and the work takes place over cocktails and dinner.

I head down to the reception room where a waiter takes my drink order, and I carry my whiskey on the rocks over to the fireplace.

There's a massive oil painting of Thom over the mantel. He's in a striking pose, with a younger woman seated by his side. My eyes are immediately drawn to her perfect oval face. Dark hair, dark eyes, plump lips. The woman's skin is a few shades darker than Thom's pasty complexion.

She's the most stunning woman I've ever seen. The painter must have been a little in love with her. She's too beautiful to be real.

I did my research on the host before coming here and didn't find any evidence that Thom was ever married. The woman is probably his partner, but she's young enough to be his daughter. She doesn't look old enough to be out of college, but I've met plenty of men who prefer trophy wives in their twenties.

No, my bear makes his displeasure known. I ignore him. He's been increasingly unhappy with everyone and everything. Living in the city around so many people is hard on him. I work over a hundred hours a week. Now that my business has its legs under it, I need to be better about taking the weekends off to let my bear out.

Next weekend, I promise him. Until then, I'll squash him down.

The grand receiving room fills with people. There are a few older men who look like Thom plus a fresh crop of frat boy-types with weak chins, strong cologne, and expensive watches bought with Daddy's money. The room reeks of entitlement.

These are the people I'm supposed to schmooze with all weekend. For most people, a few days lounging in a mansion with the ultra rich would be a dream come true but not for me. There's nothing relaxing about glad-handing humans all day and convincing them to invest in my company.

But I didn't build Mountain Top Investments from nothing without sacrifice. Thom Thompson owns the most successful hedge fund in the world. I'm here to learn his secrets and see if he was serious about partnering with my investment firm for a real estate deal.

I toss back my drink and prepare to wade into the fray. Before I do, the scent of hothouse flowers catches my attention. It's coming from the nearby hall. I wander that way and stop short at the sight of a woman descending the grand staircase. She's short and curvy with pillowy lips and shining hair.

It's the woman from the painting. I was wrong. The painter didn't exaggerate the flawless balance of her features. She is fifty times as stunning in real life.

She descends slowly, scanning the room. She's dressed in a modest white dress that makes her golden skin glow. Halfway down, she catches me staring, and her lovely dark eyes are narrow with a glare. Her scent blooms for me, orchids and gardenias, with a bitter undertone.

My chest rumbles as my bear tries to voice his opinions. He's as transfixed as I am but unhappy with the rotten edge of her scent. I step back, grunting to cover my bear's growl, and rub my breastbone to settle him.

The woman reaches the bottom step, and two hulking men in black suits and clear earpieces step forward to flank her. Her head bows, and she heads the direction they point. Two more men fall into step behind them.

Something about the way her bodyguards hover upsets my bear.

No.

He's never been so vocal. For a moment he wrestles me for control, and only years of subduing him allow me to keep the upper hand.

What the fuck is happening?

I dart through the doorway, keeping the woman in my sights. This settles my bear. She's standing beside Thompson now, silent and pouting. They had a tiff, perhaps. Her sugar daddy didn't give her the Mercedes she wanted.

When we all head to the dining room for dinner, the bodyguards surround her again. One of them holds the chair out for her, like he's a combination bodyguard / butler, and she sinks into the seat opposite the head of the table.

Something makes me slide into the seat beside her, and she gives me another cold look. She smells wrong—like poison. Is she sick? Up close, I note the dark circles under her eyes. They're not enough to diminish her beauty but could be a sign of poor sleep. Perhaps a headache. That would explain the bad temper.

Thompson stands at the head of the table and clears his throat. "Thank you all for coming." He paces around the table, like he's our school master teaching us a lesson. "This will be a weekend to remember."

Everyone murmurs their assent.

He stops behind the young woman's chair. "And I'm so pleased to present my daughter, Paloma, to you all." He places a hand on her shoulder.

Daughter. My research didn't turn up the fact that Thom had any children. He must have worked hard to keep that information under the radar.

I study Paloma's face for any hint that she might be related to Thom but can't find any. Her mother must have been a rare beauty with dominant genes.

"She's been working hard at her trader position with Thompson Capital, but I was able to convince her to take some time off," Thom continues. "She's done great things at the firm, and I'm so proud of her." There's a smattering of applause.

Paloma doesn't appear moved by his praise. If anything, it seems to deaden her.

Thompson picks up his daughter's hand and kisses it. Her expression never changes. She stares straight ahead as if in silent protest.

If Thompson notices her attitude, he doesn't seem to care. "By the end of the weekend, I might have another announcement regarding a merger of a more personal variety."

More applause, this time louder, with an eager edge. A few of the older businessmen lean in and whisper something to their younger counterparts. "...bidding...tomorrow night..." I hear one say. My shifter hearing is sharp enough to pick up on the words, but they make no sense.

What did Thompson mean by a merger of a more personal variety? Something's going on.

Thompson proposes a toast to his daughter. We all raise our glasses. Paloma doesn't move to take her glass, and one of the bodyguards leans over her and prods her arm.

That's when I notice the purple marks marring her skin between shoulder and elbow. They look like someone grabbed her arm and gripped hard. She lifts her wine glass, and her dress sleeve falls away, revealing more bruises.

My bear rears up. He's going crazy, wanting to burst from my skin. Damn, after all these years living in New York City, I thought I'd learned to suppress that wildness. I blink at my plate, hoping to hide any brightness in my eyes. My fangs sharpen, and I grit my teeth, forcing my bear to retreat. *Stay back*, I tell him.

I force myself to focus on eating, but it's a struggle not to watch Paloma. Three courses in, I dare to look back at her. She's sitting with that hardened look on her beautiful face. If I hadn't seen the bruises, I might think her haughty.

But now I think it's a result of abuse.

Her head bodyguard leans forward again. "Eat," he orders her. She subtly shakes her head, but he reaches over her and cuts her steak like she's a child. He forks a piece of meat and holds it in front of her lips.

A muscle clenches in her jaw. "No," she mutters. "I'm not hungry."

"*Stop*." There's bear in my growl. My outburst attracts the table's attention. Thom and his conversation partners go silent. I half rise out of my chair before I know what's going on. I face off with the bodyguard. "The lady said no."

"It's getting late. Perhaps you're tired," Thom says to his

daughter. He doesn't wait for her to respond. "Take her to her room." He gestures to her bodyguards. They draw back her chair and take her limp arm to guide her away.

My alarm bells are ringing. No one seems to think this is odd, but I am weirded out by the whole interaction between Thom's brooding daughter and her controlling bodyguards.

Something rotten is going on in this mansion, and I intend to figure out what.

Order Alpha's Claim now!

Want FREE books?

Receive a slew of free Renee Rose books: Go to **http://subscribepage.com/alphastemp** to sign up for Renee Rose's newsletter and receive free books. In addition to the free stories and bonus material, you will also get special pricing, exclusive previews and news of new releases.

Download a free Lee Savino book from www. leesavino.com

Other Titles by Renee Rose

Paranormal

Werewolves of Wall Street

Big Bad Boss: Midnight

Big Bad Boss: Moon Mad

Big Bad Boss: Marked

Big Bad Boss: Mated

Big Bad Bully

Wolf Ridge High Series

Alpha Bully

Alpha Knight

Step Alpha

Alpha King

Alpha Varsity

Bad Boy Alphas Series

Alpha's Temptation

Alpha's Danger

Alpha's Prize

Alpha's Challenge

Alpha's Obsession

Alpha's Desire

Alpha's War

Alpha's Mission

Rough

Wild

Feral

Savage

Fierce

Ruthless

Contemporary

Chicago Sin

Den of Sins

Rooted in Sin

Made Men Series

Don't Tease Me

Don't Tempt Me

Don't Make Me

Chicago Bratva

"Prelude" in Black Light: Roulette War

The Director

The Fixer

"Owned" in Black Light: Roulette Rematch

The Enforcer

The Soldier

The Hacker

The Bookie

The Cleaner

The Player

The Gatekeeper

Alpha Mountain

Hero

Rebel

Warrior

Vegas Underground Mafia Romance

King of Diamonds

Mafia Daddy

Jack of Spades

Ace of Hearts

Joker's Wild

His Queen of Clubs

Dead Man's Hand

Wild Card

Daddy Rules Series

Fire Daddy

Hollywood Daddy

Stepbrother Daddy

Master Me Series

Her Royal Master

Her Russian Master

Her Marine Master

Yes, Doctor

Double Doms Series

Also by Lee Savino

Paranormal romance

The Berserker Saga and Berserker Brides (menage werewolves)

These fierce warriors will stop at nothing to claim their mates.

Draekons (Dragons in Exile) with Lili Zander (menage alien dragons)

Crashed spaceship. Prison planet. Two big, hulking, bronzed aliens who turn into dragons. The best part? The dragons insist I'm their mate.

Bad Boy Alphas with Renee Rose (bad boy werewolves)

Never ever date a werewolf.

Tsenturion Masters with Golden Angel

Who knew my e-reader was a portal to another galaxy? Now I'm stuck with a fierce alien commander who wants to claim me as his own.

Contemporary Romance

Royal Bad Boy

I'm not falling in love with my arrogant, annoying, sex god boss. Nope. No way.

Royally Fake Fiancé

The Duke of New Arcadia has an image problem only a fiancé can fix. And I'm the lucky lady he's chosen to play Cinderella.

Beauty & The Lumberjacks

After this logging season, I'm giving up sex. For...reasons.

<u>Her Marine Daddy</u>

My hot Marine hero wants me to call him daddy...

<u>Her Dueling Daddies</u>

Two daddies are better than one.

<u>Innocence: dark mafia romance with Stasia Black</u>

I'm the king of the criminal underworld. I always get what I want. And she is my obsession.

<u>Beauty's Beast: a dark romance with Stasia Black</u>

Years ago, Daphne's father stole from me. Now it's time for her to pay her family's debt...with her body.

About Renee Rose

USA TODAY BESTSELLING AUTHOR RENEE ROSE loves a dominant, dirty-talking alpha hero! She's sold over two million copies of steamy romance with varying levels of kink. Her books have been featured in USA Today's *Happily Ever After* and *Popsugar*. Named Eroticon USA's Next Top Erotic Author in 2013, she has also won *Spunky and Sassy's* Favorite Sci-Fi and Anthology author, *The Romance Reviews* Best Historical Romance, and has hit the *USA Today* list fifteen times with her Bad Boy Alphas, Chicago Bratva, and Wolf Ranch series.

Renee loves to connect with readers!
www.reneeroseromance.com
reneeroseauthor@gmail.com

facebook.com/reneeroseromance
instagram.com/reneeroseromance
bookbub.com/authors/renee-rose
goodreads.com/ReneeRose

About Lee Savino

Lee Savino is a USA today bestselling author, mom and chocoholic.

Warning: Do not read her Berserker series, or you will be addicted to the huge, dominant warriors who will stop at nothing to claim their mates.

I repeat: Do. Not. Read. The Berserker Saga.

Download a free book from www.leesavino.com (don't read that either. Too much hot, sexy lovin').

www.ingramcontent.com/pod-product-compliance
Lightning Source LLC
Chambersburg PA
CBHW050615110726
47899CB00001B/117